Old Crimes and Nursery Rhymes

A White Mountains Romantic Mystery

Jane Firebaugh

First Edition, March, 2016

Cover designed by Jane Firebaugh

ISBN-13: 978-1530630615

ISBN-10: 1530630614

DEDICATION

To all who struggle with addiction—may you never lose hope.

ACKNOWLEDGEMENTS

I would like to thank my Beta Readers and Proof Readers for their generous donation of time and energy, and all my friends (offline and online) who encouraged me, especially my friend and fellow writer Devin O'Branagan who not only encouraged me in my writing, but taught me so much about the aftermath of writing a book, which is the really tough part.

Table of Contents

There was an old woman who lived in a shoe.
She had so many children, she didn't know what to do;
She gave them some broth without any bread;
Then whipped them all soundly and put them to bed.
Origin Unknown

CHAPTER ONE

Raking her fingers through her unruly reddish-brown hair, Olivia McKenna adjusted the visor on her SUV—again. Driving into the morning sun after a rain shower felt a bit like she imagined poking needles into her eyes might feel. No matter how she put the visor, it crept in from some angle or other, with each raindrop on the windshield magnifying the glare a thousandfold. *That's what I get for leaving my sunglasses in Josh's car,* she thought ruefully. Being petite could be a pain sometimes; SUVs seemed to be mostly designed for tall men—definitely not for women who barely touched five-foot-four and one-hundred-ten pounds.

She was running late for a lunch meeting with one of her clients. Her little antique locating business had been steadily growing over the past few years and she now had several clients with rather long lists of items they wanted her to find for them. This particular client, Vicki Rainer was one she especially valued, as she was always looking for things Olivia found interesting too. She was also a good friend.

One of Olivia's favorite perks of her job was getting to search for things that she loved, then keeping them for a little while to enjoy, later selling them to whichever client had asked for them. It kept her antique craving happy, plus it kept her house from overflowing with all of her wonderful finds.

Olivia had quite a few clients from other states who had heard about her from friends or had discovered her from visiting the area in New Hampshire where she lived and finding one of her business cards. She tried to keep a good supply of them available in as many shops as would let her display them. She and her best friend, Abby, who owned an interior decorating business were always on the lookout for places that allowed such self promotion.

She swung her SUV into a parking space right in front of the cozy little family owned breakfast and lunch restaurant in town and locked her doors. Only five minutes late after all—she breathed a sigh of relief. She hated to make people wait for her, as if she didn't value their time.

The delicious aroma of breakfast food wafted out the door causing her stomach to rumble in anticipation. She could see Vicki from behind the checkered half curtains at a table on the right. She looked up from the menu and waved to her as she came in.

"Good morning Olivia, you're looking a bit frazzled this morning—gorgeous as always, but frazzled," the vivacious young woman with a semi discrete magenta stripe in her short dark hair rose to hug her. "What's wrong in your universe today?"

"Hi Vicki, it's just trying to be one of those days, I guess," Olivia sighed. "I desperately need coffee." Olivia flung herself dramatically into her seat, "First thing this morning, I had a call from Mrs. Tanner. Jimmy is scheduled for his cochlear implant surgery later this week, and now the doctor who was supposed to perform the surgery has managed to injure his elbow and won't be able to do the operation for who knows how long."

"Oh, that's a shame. You told me before how excited she was that he was getting it soon enough that he'd be mostly healed and would hopefully be able to hear in time for the Christmas holidays." Vicki poured her a cup of steaming coffee and handed her a menu with a mischievous grin, "Can't that rich and handsome fiancé of yours do anything? I mean after all, what's money for?"

"I haven't even had a chance to tell him yet," Olivia pretended to swat her head. "Like I said, it's been one of those days so far. I'm sure if he can fix it so Jimmy gets his surgery right away, he will. You know Josh."

"Not nearly as well as I'd like to, sweetie," Vicki laughed. "Unfortunately for me, his heart, as well as the rest of his gorgeous self, belongs completely to you."

"You're a shameless fake Vicki; you know full well that you wouldn't trade Andrew for anyone in the world."

"Yeah, I have to admit, he's something pretty special," Vicki's eyes softened. "You and I were lucky enough to find our Mr. Rights."

Olivia patted her hand affectionately. "So what is this secret thing you want me to find for you? It must be a doozey if you're making such a big deal over it, as to buy me breakfast."

Vicki glanced around furtively, "Shush, softly Livvie, it won't be a secret for long if you tell the whole restaurant. This is a small town, remember?"

Olivia grinned, "There's not much forgetting that, is there?" She pulled out the local newspaper to show the headlines: 'Serial Joyride Suspects Caught'. Where else would you hear of 'serial joyriders', much less find their apprehension being the headline in the daily paper?"

Vicki laughed, "That's one of the coolest things about living here; it's often like stepping back in time to a gentler day."

The waitress came and brought more coffee and took their orders.

"So . . . what I want you to look for is . . . ," Vicki lowered her voice to a dramatic whisper, "a cast iron mechanical shoe bank."

Olivia raised her eyebrows, "And this is a secret . . . why? You've had me looking for cast iron banks for Andrew plenty of times; what's so special about this one?"

"I found a letter from 1885 in a secret compartment in an old highboy that I bought at auction recently. It was written to someone named Agatha Baker, in Boston, and signed by a Delia Hill. The letter says that she received the lovely shoe bank for her daughter, Edith, and wanted to thank her for being so thoughtful, and that her daughter loved the nursery rhyme for which it was made. She was glad that the woman in the shoe didn't look like her though, because she looked so mean with that big stick. She explained that she and Martin, (I'm assuming she meant her husband), and little Edith were moving up to Gorham, New Hampshire where Martin was going to work for the railroad. The air in Boston was bad for Edith's health, and although she knew it would be hard for them there, not knowing anyone, Martin was eager to start the new job, as it was a much higher position, from which he should prosper well, and that little Edith should flourish there. She further said that she was especially thankful for the shoe bank, as it would be a wonderful remembrance for Edith from her Aunt Aggie. She hoped Agatha could visit them someday. Well, it went on from there for a bit, but the important parts are about the shoe bank," Vicki whispered excitedly. "If we can find it, and if it is what I think it is, and in good shape, it will be the find of a lifetime for both of us!"

Olivia smiled at Vicki's enthusiasm, "So why do you think we can find it after all this time? Where did you get the highboy, anyway, a local auction?"

"Yes, it was right here in North Conway. It came from Jack Hill's Estate in Birchwood. The name Hill—it's the same as Delia's, and Edith's and I suppose Martin's. Jack Hill must have been a descendant," Vicki grinned her most infectious grin. "Which means girlfriend, that the shoe bank may still be in the family and right there in Birchwood, which is your home sweet home, darling. If it's the bank I am hoping to find, it's worth at least a half million dollars, if it's in great condition maybe up to a million, or even more."

"Wow!" Olivia was properly impressed. "That would definitely be the find of a lifetime, but I can't just go knocking on all the doors in Birchwood, asking if someone has one. Are you sure the bank wasn't sold at the auction too?"

"Livvie, you seriously underestimate me," she laughed. "Yes, I did remember to check that. I know, between you and Andrew, I will never live down the time I didn't. We can't go knocking on doors though, even if we felt like it, because then we would be telling everyone in the valley that there is something very valuable to be found and all the antique dealers from here to Boston would be knocking on the same doors."

"Okay, that makes sense," Olivia grinned. "So . . .."

The waitress came and set a huge plate of eggs, bacon and pancakes down in front of Vicki, and a plate of eggs and toast in front of Olivia, then asked if they needed anything else, before leaving them alone to talk.

"As I was about to say . . ." Olivia spread a tiny bit of jam on her toast and took a healthy bite, "how do you think we are going to go about finding this bank? And what does it look like? Do you have a picture?"

Vicki expertly stacked a bit of bacon and egg onto a bite of syrup covered pancake and speared it with her fork, "I do have a picture. It is a cute little bank shaped like an old fashioned shoe with a woman rising from the top. She's got a stick in her hand and looks like she's about to beat a little boy who is climbing toward her. There are some other children climbing around, coming out of doors in the shoe and stuff. Here is a picture of it," she surreptitiously showed her a picture torn from a magazine.

Olivia eyed it critically, "Hmm, I honestly can't say that I would be fawning over it if you hadn't told me how much it was worth. It's not very attractive, is it?"

Vicki chuckled, "You know how much Andrew loves these old mechanical banks, and even he might not have paid much attention to it otherwise. Well, okay, he would have, just because it is an old mechanical cast iron bank. He loves them all, even the ugly ones."

Olivia ate her food distractedly. "Vicki, are there no other clues at all about where this bank could be? I mean, little Edith must have grown up, and maybe the bank wasn't very attractive to her either then. She could have given it away, sold it or even thrown it out at some point."

"I know, and you're right. I don't have any other clues, and we may never find it, but it's worth keeping our eyes open and discretely asking around—very discretely and you are much better at being discreet than I am," she said theatrically.

"I didn't know Jack Hill, did he have family left in the house? Was the house sold too or just the stuff inside?"

"No, the house he lived in, in Birchwood was left to Hill's son James, I think, along with another even larger one just outside of town. Nobody knows where he is right now though, so they are just sitting there. The stuff that was sold in the auction was inherited by James' sister Jennifer who goes by Jenny. She inherited a much smaller house in Jackson, which her father had been renting out furnished. That is where the stuff in the auction came from. She now has that house up for sale. As far as I know, James will inherit the two big houses, if they ever find him. They're both enormous and still fully furnished with wonderful stuff, especially the huge one up on the hill on Old Candlewick Road. The Hills used to live in that one, but the old man moved to the smaller one, which is still plenty big, that was closer to town once his wife died and just left the other house with all the furnishings unoccupied. As far as I know, that house was never sold."

"James . . . ," Olivia's voice was meditative. "James Hill! Mrs. Tanner said Jimmy's father's name is James Hill," Olivia's face lit up. "Do you think it could be the same one? They could certainly use the extra money from the sale of the houses, or maybe they could move into one of them and sell the other, depending on what is better for them if James will share his inheritance with his son."

"Whoa! Slow down girlfriend," Vicki smiled. "I think you should talk to Josh and maybe check records at the town hall to find out if it's the right Hill, before you get yourself all wound up."

Olivia laughed, "Yes, you're right, I tend to get excited too quickly sometimes, unlike you, who would never get excited over something that might be just 'pie in the sky', right?"

Vicki grinned sheepishly, "Yeah well, I guess we're both a bit excitable, but you know that's a good thing. Life would be really dull if *somebody* wasn't."

Olivia swallowed the last of her eggs and gulped her semi-cold coffee. "I'd better get going. I have a lot of checking up on things to do now. Is it okay if I let Abby in on the secret?" She stood to leave after putting money on the table for the tip.

"Yes, Abby is a definite—she might even bump into it somewhere and not grab it if we haven't told her—and of course, the handsome Josh can be in on the secret." Vicki put more money on the table, stuffed Olivia's money back into her hand and gave her a hug. "I said it was on me, and that includes the tip, sweetie. You can get it next time."

Olivia hugged her back and they walked out into the crisp air together.

"Call me if you have any news," Vicki said as she got into her sports car.

"I will, and you be sure to do the same." Olivia waved. Late autumn leaves whirled through the air as she clicked the unlock button on her remote and sat behind the wheel thinking. Finally, she started the SUV and headed for the Birchwood Town Hall to see if she could get any information on which James Hill was the new absentee owner of Jack Hill's property. In case it wasn't Jimmy's dad, she didn't want to say anything to Mrs. Tanner yet and get her hopes up for nothing. Come to think of it, she didn't even know if it would affect Jimmy at all, if the property did belong to his dad, since James had given sole custody of him to Mrs. Tanner and might not want to share his windfall.

The trip to town hall was a waste. Yes, the property would now belong to James A. Hill, if he was ever found, but Olivia still had no idea if that was Jimmy's father. She drove toward her house debating on her next move. She decided it would be a good time to call Josh and let him know what was going on with Jimmy's surgeon and see if he had any ideas.

He answered on the second ring and said he would check around and see what he could do and asked if they were still on for dinner at his little apartment that night and if she was still up for sneaking Molly, her Golden Retriever, and Sheyna, her long haired Calico cat into his—no pets allowed—apartment. She laughingly assured him that she was ready.

Molly greeted Olivia at the door with a big plush toy in her mouth and a tail that was wagging so hard, she flung Olivia's purse halfway across the room when she accidentally hit it.

"Ouch Molly, didn't that hurt?" Olivia stopped to hug her and play tug-o-war for a moment. Sheyna came and wound herself through Olivia's legs, rubbing against her jeans and giving her head butts. Olivia picked her up and hugged her too.

"Okay girls, let me get in the door and get my stuff put away, then we can go to the park," she retrieved her purse and took her phone, her driver license and a little money out of it and put it in her jacket pockets so she didn't have to deal with her purse at the park.

The dog and cat were both excited and ready to go long before Olivia was. She checked her email, made a couple phone calls, then finally put Sheyna's harness on and clipped a lead onto Molly's collar and loaded both animals into their crates in the SUV.

Olivia had as much fun at the park as Molly and Sheyna. It was a cool, brisk late fall—early winter day, and there were more leaves on the ground than on the trees. Every now and then, a strong breeze would send more leaves skittering from the trees in a swirl of color to land on top of the leafy, mostly deep orange and yellow brown carpet below. Molly was off lead and having a blast chasing all the leaves, trying to catch them before they hit the ground. Sheyna enjoyed batting them around once they were down and Olivia simply soaked in the beauty of the day and the rich earthy smell of the fallen leaves.

When they'd had enough and were ready to get back into the warmth of the SUV, Olivia turned toward the smaller of the two mansions that had been owned by Jack Hill to see what it looked like. She was very curious about the place after listening to Vicki talk about the old letter. There was something really romantic and exciting about it.

She must have passed the house a thousand times, but she never knew who lived there. It was about halfway between her house and Josh's apartment, maybe a little closer to Josh. The house was old, quite large and in beautiful shape. For some reason, she'd expected it to be in sad disrepair, almost falling down. She hoped it would turn out that the house belonged to Jimmy's father and that, maybe, he would offer it to his mother-in-law and his son, or at least allow them to live there, since he obviously wasn't using it. It was on a nice piece of land, closer to town than Mrs. Tanner's place out in Eastman's Grant, so it would certainly be easier and more convenient for them, especially once Jimmy started going to school.

That reminded her, she needed to talk to Josh about possibly getting the five year old into some kind of speech therapy once he had his implant and it was activated. He hadn't been able to hear since he was a year old, due to a virus, so he would need fairly extensive therapy with his communication skills before starting school in order to not be behind from the beginning.

Jimmy was a very bright and sweet boy, and an amazingly good artist who Olivia thought, also, showed a lot of potential for architecture. Olivia had met him and his grandmother, Mrs. Tanner a couple of months ago, after she'd been in the antique shop across from their house when the owner had been murdered. She and Mrs. Tanner had hit it off immediately.

She crossed her fingers for luck and pulled away from the curb by the Hill estate. Stopping at the quaint little gas station / convenience store near her house hadn't crossed her mind until she was almost past it. She quickly decided that other than the beauty salon, this might be the best place to get the scoop on the Hill estate so she could figure out who everyone involved really was.

"Hi Wayne," Olivia smiled at the teenager behind the sandwich counter. "How's life treating you?"

"Pretty good Miss McKenna," the freckled faced, ginger haired boy said, blushing as usual. "It's good to see you."

Olivia headed for the tables on the side of the store where a lot of the old timers frequently sat drinking coffee and reading the paper or chatting with each other and anyone who stopped by to talk. There were three older men at the back table at the moment and she recognized Louise Beck, an older woman, who with her husband, Brady, managed the General Store, sitting by herself at the next table.

"Good afternoon Ed," Olivia walked up to the table. "Bob, Mr. Davis, it's nice weather we're having today."

"Ayuh," Ed replied. "Though I figure it's startin' to breeze up a bit out there."

Mr. Davis nodded his agreement. "Ayuh, it'll be a mite nippy tonight, for sure."

"I was driving by the old Hill place and wondered who owns it now that Jack is gone," Olivia interjected. "It's a pretty house."

"It's his son James who'll get it if they can find him," Bob spoke up. "Last I heard he was in a gaum down in Bahston or somewheyah down theyah."

"Did you hear what kind of trouble he was in down there?" Olivia mentally translated the Maine slang word gaum to trouble, and the old-timers' strong New England accents. "No, ah only heard he was in with a wicked bad crowd and seemed to be getting himself back into the drugs again."

Mr. Davis shook his head, "Linder Harris, whose daughter Sonia, is Jenny Harkins' neighbor, you know, was talkin' the other day about James bein' back up heah in N'Hampshah, over in Laconier, so I guess he must have had enough of Bahston and that mess down theyah."

"Is James the man that was married to Joanie Tanner and had the little boy Jimmy?" Olivia asked.

All three men nodded.

"Do you guys have any idea how I can find James

Hill?"

Ed shrugged, "His sister Jenny lives over in Laconia now, so I guess that's why he was there. She's married to Fred Harkins and they own a hardware store right on Main Street. Maybe she can tell you where he is now. Like Tom said, Linda had been over in Laconia for the last three weeks helping her daughter-in-law with her new granddaughter. She said she'd seen him several times in the last couple of weeks hanging around his sister's house, but then, he stopped coming around a few days ago."

Olivia noticed that Louise Beck was staring fixedly at her and the trio of old men with a sour expression on her thin, heavily made up face. Olivia nodded to her, but she looked away.

"Thank you gentlemen," Olivia smiled. "I'll see if I can find her. "You have a great day."

"Ayuh, you too, and be caheful, if we get any weathah the roads'll be greasy and all the left ovah leafpeepers have no ideer how to drive when the roads are iced up. Tomorrow will probably be even worse if the temperature stays down. I have a strong feelin' we might see some bad wrecks the next couple nights up heah." Mr. Davis said, turning back to his coffee.

Olivia hurried out to her SUV, but detoured before she reached it and walked over to the state liquor store to pick up a bottle of wine for Josh. Since she wasn't sure what he'd planned to cook, she randomly decided on a Chardonnay that they both liked.

Once she got home and had gotten Molly and Sheyna inside, Olivia turned on her laptop and made a cup of tea while she waited for Windows to load. Maybe tomorrow, she would run out to Mrs. Tanner's house and ask her about

James Hill. It's possible she'd heard more news than the guys at the store, since she was related to him by marriage and was raising his son.

When all the icons had popped up, and the hourglass had gone away on her screen, Olivia Googled: 'Fred Harkins, Laconia, NH'. She found a home phone number and she, also, found a listing for Harkins Hardware. She started to call, but decided it might be better to talk to Mrs. Tanner first just in case there were things she didn't know about the situation. She didn't want to cause problems for anyone.

CHAPTER TWO

Just before two PM, Olivia dressed for her Aikido class. She'd started two weeks ago, and she was enjoying it a lot, aside from a few bruises and sore wrists. She thought it was really cool how a woman as petite as she was, could use a much larger male assailant's own momentum against him to protect herself. Josh thought she was doing well given she'd only gone to five classes. Once she'd gotten the hang of the forward rolling fall, she loved it. The rear falls, were not nearly as much fun. She hugged Molly and Sheyna and told them she'd be home soon.

The air was significantly chillier when she came out of her class. She was a little sweated up from all of the exertion, but even so . . . it was just plain cold. She turned the seat heat on as soon as she got in the car, since any other heat would only blow cold air until the engine warmed up. The steering wheel felt like a wheel shaped icicle, and she alternated holding it with each hand while sitting on the other one to warm it between her body and the seat heater.

A light wintry mix was starting to fall when she reached her driveway. She shivered as she unlocked the front door. *Tonight the roads were definitely going to be 'greasy'*, she smiled at the description then quickly sobered, remembering Mr. Davis' grim prediction. The weather site on her computer showed that most of Northern New England was going to be having some kind of precipitation for the next two to three days, along with freezing temperatures, and it recommended staying off the roads as much as possible, especially at night when it was harder to see the icy patches.

Olivia was glad Josh didn't live too far away. They were going to work on their wedding plans tonight after dinner—and he was cooking for her—so she really didn't want to miss it. Josh had told her that he used to love to cook when he was married, but that after his wife Susan died in a car wreck, he hadn't wanted to cook at all until he'd started falling in love with Olivia and she'd cooked for him. They both felt that cooking for someone was a labor of love and sharing meals together was special and important in a relationship.

Olivia started a load of laundry and went to shower and pick out her clothes for tonight. She decided on a pair of dark green wool slacks and a tight but warm, dark forsythia colored sweater. Since the weather was so lousy, her footwear was going to have to be her less than attractive snow boots. Yuck. *Liv, is it really worth wearing sexy heels when you know you are most likely going to slip on black ice and fall on your tuchis right at Josh's feet?* The sexy pumps went back in the closet.

She took extra care with her hair, trying valiantly to smooth it down into a semblance of neatness, but with the humidity, her unruly curls were insisting on doing their own thing. She sighed and gave up on the hair. Josh said he liked her wavy hair, so she could only hope he was telling the truth. A light touch of mascara and clear lip gloss finished her primping. Casting a wistful look at the sexy heels, she headed for the stairs with Molly and Sheyna tagging along behind her.

It was such a chilly raw sort of night that she put Molly's and Sheyna's thick fleece coats on them before she loaded them into their crates in the SUV. They both had warm crate mats, but just in case the car broke down and they were stranded for a while, she felt better knowing they wouldn't be cold. She turned on the car to warm up and went back inside to get her down jacket. She put on a pair of fleece gloves for protection against the cold steering wheel.

Grabbing the bottle of wine, she locked the front door and carefully navigated her way back to the SUV. The driveway was already getting a little slick in spots—so yeah—the heels would definitely not have been good. She turned on her seat heat and pulled out onto the road, feeling much better about her clunky boots.

As she passed the Hill house, she looked over for another glance and saw a light moving around in one of the upstairs windows. She stopped and backed up, then as she pulled into the drive, the light disappeared. She blinked . . . several times, but it was all darkness. Maybe it had been sleet on the windshield playing tricks on her eyes. Perplexed, she backed into the road and continued toward Josh's apartment, glancing in her rear view mirror a couple of times, but not seeing any more lights near the house.

Josh came out as soon as she called him, to help her sneak Molly and Sheyna into the apartment. They were snickering like naughty school children as they quickly led Molly, and carried Sheyna past his landlord's apartment. Not being allowed to have pets was the only thing that really bothered him about living there.

For the past seven years, Josh had worked as a State Trooper, moving up through the ranks to Lieutenant Detective by hard work and extreme dedication. He loved the job and respected and admired most of the men and women he worked with. When he'd been married to Susan, they had a small house in the next town over, but once he was alone, he moved into the tiny bleak little apartment and had thrown himself whole heartedly into his job.

The guys he worked with had no idea that Josh was from a very wealthy family and had no monetary need to work at all, much less as a low paid public servant. It was his way to give back to the community, but he knew a lot of people would resent him and look at him differently if they knew he was wealthy, so he'd kept it a secret. He hadn't even told Olivia until after they were engaged. He secretly donated all his earnings from the job to charity as well. Unfortunately, a co-worker had found out just before he and Olivia had solved the murder that had brought them together, and made sure the whole department knew. So Josh had made the decision to quit his job and open a private investigation agency with Olivia, since they'd discovered that she too, had a real knack for solving mysteries. That way he could still help people, do the kind of work he loved doing and not have to worry about what co-workers thought. He'd given his thirty day's notice a week ago, so he only had three weeks left on the job.

"I know we really shouldn't be doing this," Josh laughed once they were safely inside, "but his reason for making it a no-pet place is because he thinks animals are filthy. Molly and Sheyna are way cleaner than he is! The guy reminds me of Pig Pen from the old Charlie Brown comics. Come on, let's get you guys warm," he hugged her and led the way to the kitchen where there were pots on the stove. It was wonderfully warm, and smelled simply divine.

"Mmm, it smells lovely in here, Honey," Olivia put the wine on the table and melted into Josh's hug. "You're so warm. I could stay like this forever." She stood on tiptoes to kiss him.

"You smell pretty amazing yourself Liv," Josh sniffed, kissing his way from her lips to her neck. "You smell more edible than the food, in fact," he nibbled her neck gently.

Olivia gasped and tickled him, "Whoa cowboy, I came to eat dinner, not be it." She laughed at his pretended consternation.

Josh tickled her back and they chased each other around tickling, kissing and laughing until Olivia was warmed up from the cold. Molly happily joined in the play, while Sheyna hopped up onto a side table out of their way and flicked her tail in annoyance at their silly shenanigans. Olivia collapsed giggling onto a chair to catch her breath, and Josh leaned against the counter, still laughing. Molly barked expectantly, wondering why they'd stopped such a fun game.

"I love you Joshua Abrams," Olivia smiled, pulling him over and hugging him. "So, how about a glass of that wine. Will it go with the dinner?"

We're having vegetable lasagna, mushroom and onion risotto and salad, so it will go perfectly," he kissed her and walked over to the oven to check the lasagna. After making sure it was okay, he poured a glass of wine for each of them, and started the risotto.

"Should I make the salad?"

"That would be great, just don't put the dressing yet,

so it doesn't get soggy while the risotto is cooking. Actually, why don't you feed Molly and Sheyna first, then you can tackle the salad."

"Yum, the lasagna smells so good; my mouth is watering," Olivia sniffed and sighed. "The table is beautiful too Josh," she put their food bowls down for the girls.

The small round kitchen table was covered with a white cloth and had a tall yellow candle and a little blue crystal vase with a yellow rose and white Baby's Breath in it. Josh's blue and brown stoneware dishes complimented the table's décor nicely.

"So, what did Vicki have to tell you?" Josh asked, stirring the risotto. "I have to say that was an intriguing message she left yesterday."

"I know, right?" Olivia laughed. "She is such a hoot. I love it when she gets so excited over things, she's like a little kid."

"Yes, she is," Josh chuckled. "So, what did she want you to look for? As I recall, the Dazey butter churn her husband Andrew wanted was the main reason you were in the antique shop when Jamison was killed a couple of months ago. Hopefully, whatever she is hunting for now won't get you involved with murderers and burglars."

"Well, it wasn't all bad that I happened to be in the shop that day, was it? That is where I met you," Olivia grinned coyly.

"Hah! You got me there."

Olivia laughed, "Vicki found an old letter referring to an extremely rare, and very valuable mechanical bank. It sounds like it was brought to Gorham by some of Hill's ancestors back in the late 1880s from Boston, then possibly ended up in the old Hill place over on Route Sixteen."

"Didn't old man Hill die recently?"

"Yes, the letter Vicki found was in a highboy that came from part of his estate. It seems his daughter Jenny inherited some of the stuff, including one small furnished house and the son got the rest, which is apparently two huge houses, with all the furnishings, and possibly money as well. The daughter evidently sent at least some of her share to auction. The son is James Hill, Jimmy's father."

"Wow!" Josh said in surprise. "So maybe Jimmy will be in line to inherit the houses from his dad someday." He added more liquid to the risotto and kept stirring. "That would be a really nice break for him and his grandmother. They've had precious few."

"It really would. One problem is that no one seems to know where James is right now. I asked around discretely and heard that he might be in Laconia or Boston. His sister is married and lives in Laconia," Olivia finished tearing up lettuce and added some spinach leaves to the salad. "I was thinking about going to see Mrs. Tanner tomorrow, and if she thinks it's a good idea, maybe heading to Laconia to try to speak to James' sister. What do you think?"

Josh turned off the stove and lifted the pot of risotto from the eye, "I think it sounds like a good plan, if Mrs. Tanner agrees. Maybe you'll have better luck than the attorneys at getting her to tell you something. The last thing I had heard about him, when I checked, was that he was living hard and might be in over his head with some bad characters. That was at least two months ago though, so who knows now. I have been trying to keep tabs on James once in a while for Jimmy's and Mrs. Tanner's sake ever since we met them, but he's not always an easy one to locate. Just be really careful driving, and please rethink it if the roads are too bad."

"I will. I hope for Jimmy's sake that his father is okay and not into anything really bad," Olivia said with a sigh, cutting a couple of tomatoes into the salad.

"Dinner is served, M'Lady," Josh said, gesturing to the table with a flair and a crooked grin. Please, have a seat."

Olivia laughed, brought the salad bowl to the table and sat in the chair on the far side so Josh could be closer to the counter to bring the food over. She loved watching him in the kitchen. She loved watching him period. *What a hunk he is,* she thought. *His wavy dark hair and sexy green eyes that seemed to change to blue once in a while were enough all by themselves, but he was in wicked good shape too, with a broad chest, trim waist and lots of lovely muscles.* She sighed.

Josh served the lasagna, salad and risotto, refilled their wine glasses and sat across from Olivia.

"It looks delicious Josh. Thank you for cooking for me."

"You've cooked for me so many times since we met, I've been wanting to fix you something special for ages, but something always came up to keep it from happening."

Olivia took a bite of lasagna, "Oh my stars, Josh! This is incredible! What spices do you use? I have angels dancing on my tongue."

Josh laughed, "Are you sure it isn't the secret spice that's tickling your tongue?"

"Oh no, it's definitely angels," Olivia grinned. "My taste buds are in heaven."

Their talk was centered around the food for a while, then Josh decided it was time to discuss the wedding and future business, and Olivia happily agreed.

"Have you had any more thoughts about where you want to have the wedding?"

"Oh Josh, sometimes I wish we could just run off and elope, but then the rest of the time I really want to have a nice, sweet old fashioned kind of outdoor wedding. Finding the right place is what's driving me crazy," she chuckled ruefully. "If Tiny's place or Mrs. Tanner's were a little bigger, I'd love to be married in either one of their yards. We could do all of the decorating together and make it beautiful, but simple. There just isn't enough room in either one . . . ," she stopped short. "Josh, if Jimmy's father owns the Hill house here in town, and we can find him, maybe he would let us use the yard for the wedding. It would be better than any place I've been able to think of so far."

"Hmm, Liv, it may be a good idea not to get your hopes up too high on that one, since we don't know where he is, or if he would have the slightest desire to let us use the yard of a house he might possibly inherit," Josh said wryly. "It seems a bit on the 'iffy' side to me."

Olivia sighed, "I know, and I'm not really getting my hopes up. It's just that when I sat in front of the house I could almost see Jimmy and Mrs. Tanner living there. It would be so much better for them. Oh, Josh! When I was on the way here, for a second, I thought I saw a light moving around in the upstairs of that house, but when I pulled in, it vanished."

"Do you still think you saw it or was it just weird lighting from the weather and such?"

"I'm not sure," Olivia said slowly. "I thought maybe it was just a reflection off the ice on the windshield, but I just don't know, the way it was moving seemed too random, as if someone were wearing a headlamp and looking around the room. Since you are still a police officer, can you take a closer look next time you go by just to see if anything looks odd?"

"Definitely," Josh smiled. "There could be kids hanging around up to mischief, or vagrants breaking in for a place to sleep out of the inclement weather. It happens sometimes even in our small town. As you know, there's been a lot more drug activity up here lately than there ever used to be. I'll drive up there tomorrow and nose around a little to make sure there are no broken windows or doors."

"Thanks sweetheart. It may be nothing, but it really seemed like someone was in there. Oh, I need to go back to the Town Hall too; I forgot to check on the other house Jack Hill supposedly left James." She smiled and shook her head to clear it of mysteries. "Anyway, about the wedding . . . I still haven't met your father. Don't you think maybe we should meet before we become relatives?"

Josh laughed, "Ya think? I keep meaning to figure out the logistics of getting us all together, but with the excitement of the past couple months, murders, engagement and now the job thing, I just haven't gotten around to it. He still lives on the South Side of Lantern Knoll, so it isn't that far, we just have to all be able to arrange our schedules to fit it in."

"I'm looking forward to meeting him, but I'm a little nervous about it too. I mean, he's rich, and 'old money'; what if he thinks I'm just after you for your wealth?"

Josh laughed and squeezed her hand, "First off, your face is such an open book, it would be impossible for him to think that, and secondly, you didn't even know I had money when I asked you to marry me. You probably even thought I had less money than you did. After all, you own a house and I have a tiny apartment." He smiled, "Don't worry, Dad isn't like that. He's a pretty great guy actually, and I know you're going to adore each other."

"Oh, I hope so," Olivia said wistfully. "I so want it all to be perfect. Family is incredibly important."

"It will be, don't you worry about it," Josh said, getting up and kissing the top of her head on his way to put some dishes in the sink. "Wait until you meet him, you'll see."

"I wish we could go to visit my parents, but I guess we'll have to wait until your time is up at work to take such a long trip," Olivia sighed. "I haven't seen them or Nana and Pop in over a year."

"I've never been to Ireland, so I'm looking forward to it for a lot of reasons," Josh hugged her. "Your folks sound wonderful and I think it's great that your parents were willing to pick up and move to Ireland to take care of your mother's parents. So many people nowadays don't bother to take care of their parents when they get old. They just stick them in a home and forget about them." Josh picked up the dish rag. "Your dad was born here, right?"

"Yes, he was born in New Hampshire, right in North Conway. Mam was born in Ireland and met my da when she came here for a year of college. The rest is history."

They quickly washed and dried the dishes together, talking lightly about wedding plans, but not really getting much decided, as the biggest issue was still the location. They'd originally thought of getting married on a mountain top, but realistically, it made no sense, as most of their friends and family wouldn't be able to get up there. They'd thought of the beach, but it was too far and they really weren't beach goers as much as they were river rats. The river might have been a good choice, but the rocks all along the riverbanks would make things way too difficult and thoughts of guests with sprained ankles quickly pushed that idea out of the running. Either they were going to have to find some wonderful outdoor venue, someone's very large lawn, or end up having it indoors after all.

They retired to the living room with their wine after giving Molly and Sheyna some treats. Josh put on some soft music and asked Olivia to dance. It was very romantic and there was a lot of steamy kissing until they realized that Molly was dancing with them. Josh was leading Olivia and Molly was following too, in almost perfect step.

They stood in stunned amazement and Molly looked up at them, seeming puzzled. She didn't understand why they were laughing instead of dancing. Olivia stooped and hugged her.

"Molly, you've been keeping that talent a secret. You're a better dancer than I am, wow!"

Josh laughed, "She's not better than you; you're both wonderful! Now we need to teach Sheyna to dance and we can have our own TV show."

"Who ever had Molly before she ended up in the shelter was a fabulous trainer, and obviously loved her, because she enjoys doing all the cool tricks she knows. I can't imagine how she wound up at the pound."

"I know. I was floored when you yelled 'tackle' and she actually tackled one of the murder suspects. She is pretty awesome, a football player, a dancer, what will she surprise us with next?" Josh chuckled. "How did you discover the tackle trick?"

Olivia laughed, "Painfully. I was standing in the living room talking to a hard of hearing client on the phone who wanted me to find antique fishing tackle for him. I asked him rather loudly what kind of tackle, and Molly tackled me."

"She's a wicked cool dog," Josh scratched Molly's ears. "Smart as a whip."

"She is definitely a dog of many talents," Olivia grinned kissing Molly's nose. "We will have to play with the dancing more; that is way too cool! Ooh, she can dance at our wedding!"

"That's a terrific idea. Oh, speaking of dancing, you'd mentioned having Tiny and Abby over for dinner at your place or inviting them out to a restaurant. Why don't we see if we can set it up for Saturday night at the Christmas Tree Inn? We can make a reservation and try the double date thing to see if they hit it off. I think that if they don't, it will be easier to deal with extricating them from each others' company in a restaurant setting than at your place."

"Excellent thought." Olivia smiled. "I am hoping they'll like each other, but just because we like them both and they both have a few tattoos . . . okay Tiny has more than a few and Abby has a couple piercings . . . doesn't mean they will get along or be attracted to each other, but we can hope. I'll give them both a call tomorrow and see if we can plan it for Saturday."

"It will be an interesting dinner either way," Josh laughed.

"So what do we still need to do to get the detective agency going? I know we can't officially open until you're off the Police payroll, but did you get all the licensing sorted out?" Olivia sank onto the couch and cradled Sheyna in her arms. Molly hopped up and put her head on Olivia's knees next to Sheyna.

"I think I've got it all ready, and once we get

everything signed and notarized it should go through okay, hopefully. You can work as a full time investigator for the agency, but you still can't apply for your very own license until you have four years' experience," Josh put his arms around her and Sheyna and patted Molly's head. "You won't be allowed to carry a gun while you're working either, until you have the license." he hugged her. "I do want you to become proficient with a gun, just in case, though you're doing so well with your Aikido, you won't even need a gun." He paused with a grimace, "Actually I'm hoping the cases we get won't be dangerous, and neither of us will need a gun."

Olivia sighed happily, "It's going to be interesting and fun and I am so excited about it. I loved working with you on the murder case."

Josh hugged her tight, "We work well together. You know, I was thinking, what if we got married in December? A winter wedding. I know we'd talked about June and outdoors, but we could plan the whole thing and end up with a freak rain storm that would ruin it. What do you think? I want to be married to you already," he laughed.

"Wow Josh! I'd love to have a winter wedding, and I'm dying to be married to you, but it's such short notice, can we pull it off?"

"I don't know, but if you really would like to do it, we can try. I think we can manage."

"Okay, now I am seriously starting to freak out. It's already November seventh and we are going to have so much work to do! Do you want to try to do it for the holidays? I had talked to Pam about bringing the girls for what she is calling a 'Chrisnukkah' celebration at the retirement home, since they are falling around the same time, so that is yet another thing on my agenda."

Josh laughed, "Chrisnukkah? That ought to be interesting. It's a nice idea actually."

"Yes, I think it works pretty well for everyone," Olivia smiled. "Josh, let's do it! Let's get married around the holidays. There's always so much excitement in the air with all the lights everywhere that it will make it even more magical."

"I agree. We're really going to have to find a place to have it quickly now and get everything else chosen and lined up."

Olivia snuggled up against Josh, shifting Sheyna on her lap. Molly moved closer and inched her head further into Olivia's lap earning a light velveted smack from Sheyna.

After a few minutes of cuddling, Olivia got up to peek out the window.

"It's snowing now," she said. "I think we'd better get going before it gets worse."

"Are you sure it's not too slick out there? How much snow is there?" Josh joined her at the window. "Oh, it's just started, so you should be okay, though you know you're welcome to stay overnight. Walking Molly might be on the difficult side, but we could manage," he grinned.

"We'll have to sneak them out already for us to leave, so we'd better not press our luck trying to do it too many times," Olivia laughed. "I want to get home in time to get a good night's sleep so I am refreshed to try to get information out of James' sister tomorrow. If I'm half asleep, I won't have a very good chance of it. I'm still planning to go to Mrs. Tanner's house first, so it will be a pretty full day if she okays my visiting Jenny Harkins."

Josh helped Olivia get the coats on the girls, and held her down jacket for her, then went to see if the coast was clear. He took Molly's lead and motioned quietly for Olivia to bring Sheyna. They hurried soundlessly out of the building and he helped her load Molly and Sheyna into their crates and they closed the hatch.

"I had such a good time tonight Josh, and the food was magnificent," Olivia said into Josh's chest as he held her tightly.

"I'm glad. I love you Livvie," he bent and kissed her. "Do you want me to follow you home to make sure you get there safely?"

Olivia laughed, "Then I'd have to follow you back to make sure you did. We'll be fine sweetie. I'll drive slowly and carefully." She kissed him again, "I love you too."

Olivia drove very carefully on the slick roads. Luckily there weren't many cars out and they made it home safely. Once everyone was inside and Molly had gone out and back in again, they all headed up to Olivia's bedroom and snuggled up on the bed, falling asleep quickly.

CHAPTER THREE

It was grey and cold in the morning when Olivia awoke, but at least it wasn't snowing or raining anymore. She yawned and brushed her teeth, then took a quick hot shower and dressed in warm clothes. Her hair was being its typical wavy curly mess, so she grabbed a cute knitted wool beret that she could pop on top of her head to cover it up and went downstairs to feed Molly and Sheyna and fix a quick breakfast for herself.

She decided to leave Molly and Sheyna at home, since she didn't know how long she would be talking to Jenny Harkins, or if she would need to stop a few places to ask about her if she didn't find her at home. She made sure they both had enough water and that Molly had gone out to do her business then said goodbye and locked them in the house.

She looked at the old Hill house as she passed by, but it looked normal in the daylight. *It was probably just the light Liv,* she told herself. *Wet windshields can play tricks on your eyes.* It was a pretty old house, large and spacious, and she could easily picture Mrs. Tanner and Jimmy being happy there. Maybe James would want to do the right thing for his son, especially if he was inheriting the other house too and could probably sell it for enough money to live wherever he wanted.

She stopped off at the Town Hall on the way to get the address for Jack Hill's other house that James was supposed to be inheriting just to see what it was like. It was not far from her house so she decided she would drive by later to see it after all of her other errands.

It was around ten AM when she arrived at Mrs. Tanner's house. She had good news to give her. One of the things she and Josh had discussed last night was Jimmy's surgery, and Josh said he was arranging for another specialist to come in from Boston to do the implant on schedule, so Jimmy would still be able to have his implant and be activated before the holidays. The insurance was covering everything, except the new doctor's transportation and hotel stay for the trip. Josh was paying for that, though he didn't want her to tell Mrs. Tanner about that part.

Mrs. Tanner opened the door and quickly ushered Olivia into the warmth of the house, giving her a floury hug, then laughingly brushing the flour off both of them.

"I've been baking gingerbread cookies. They are Jimmy's favorite, especially if I ice them. He can eat them almost as fast as I can bake them."

"I've tasted those cookies and I can completely understand why he eats them so fast. They are scrumptious!" Olivia laughed, following her into the warm kitchen, redolent with the aroma of spiced gingerbread.

"You just sit right down here and I'll get you some fresh from the oven. These don't have the icing on them yet, but if you're like me, you might even like them better plain." Mrs. Tanner took the pan, set it on a cooling rack on the table and got a little plate and napkin for Olivia. "I'm going to take some of the ones I already iced in to Jimmy.

You just help yourself to these," she handed her a spatula. "I'll be making more as soon as the pan is empty."

Olivia grinned at Mrs. Tanner's usual garrulous manner, and holding the pan with a glove Mrs. Tanner had left on the table, she quickly popped two cookies from the pan and put one on her plate and bit into the other one with a groan of pleasure. There was not much to compare to the rich, spicy sweet taste of fresh gingerbread. She popped another cookie onto her plate and chewed happily.

"Jimmy said to say hi to you, and I'm sure he'll be in in a few minutes, but he's busy eating cookies and working on a new drawing. I think his drawings are getting better all the time, his building too," she stopped for breath and took a cookie. "How have you been doing? It's been too long since you came over."

"I'm doing fine, and Josh and I are hoping to get married sometime over the winter holidays, though it's not a sure thing yet, by any means. We are hoping you and Jimmy can be there whenever it ends up happening."

"You just tell me when and where and you can be sure we'll be there. I wouldn't miss it for the world."

"Josh wanted me to ask if Jimmy would be his ring bearer."

"Oh my! I'm sure he would love to do that. What would he need to do? He doesn't have a fancy suit though, would that be a problem?"

"Not at all, Josh has insisted that he is buying the wedding clothes for all of our friends in the wedding party, so it isn't a burden to anyone."

"He is such a thoughtful and generous man. You found yourself a good one child. My Albert was like that too, bless his soul. He didn't have money like your man does, but he'd give you the shirt off his back if you were cold. Your young man reminds me of him a lot." Mrs. Tanner dabbed her eyes with her apron.

"I'm so glad you had a wonderful man like him, and I'm sorry for your loss," Olivia hugged her.

"Thank you child. It's nearing the anniversary of his death, so I'm finding myself a bit more weepy than usual," she stood and shook herself slightly as if to shake out the sorrow. "I'm so happy that you came out today, but it couldn't have just been to have me cryin' all over you. What brought you out here?" she smiled trying to get back to her normally cheerful self.

"Well, a couple of things actually, Josh has arranged for another surgeon to fly up from Boston to do Jimmy's surgery next week, so everything is still on schedule."

"Oh Olivia, thank him for me! The insurance is still covering it all?"

"Yes, it's still covering the whole surgery," Olivia said, deciding that what she said was true as Josh was only covering the flight and hotel, nothing to do with the actual surgery.

"I am so happy, child! It was a dream come true for me that he was going to be able to hear by Christmas time. I didn't want to let you know how disappointed I was because I didn't want you to think I was ungrateful for all you did for us, finding that foundation to help him get the implant, but it means the world to me that he'll have this for a Christmas present," she dabbed her eyes again, this time to wipe away tears of joy.

Olivia smiled and patted her hand, "I'm so glad it's going to happen. Jimmy is such a great little guy." She took a deep breath, "The other thing I wanted to talk to you about is Jimmy's father, James. Did you know that James' father Jack had died recently?"

"Yes, I read about it in the paper, but I didn't really know him very well, so I haven't mentioned it to Jimmy. He hadn't even met him."

"Apparently Jack left two large houses to James, along with everything in them, and maybe even some money as well, but no one seems to know where James is now. Have you heard from him recently?"

"No, not for a couple years now. After he signed his rights to Jimmy over to me, he only called once to ask how I was, but didn't even ask about Jimmy, though he listened when I told him all about him anyway. I'd like to think it was his way of asking, just to call, because he knew I'd tell him whether he asked or not."

"Do you know his sister Jenny at all? She supposedly lives in the Laconia area with her husband who owns a hardware store. She inherited another house with all the furnishings."

"I knew he had a sister, and I met her once very briefly at his and Joanie's wedding, but she was such a mousy, timid little thing and didn't talk at all. Just stayed for the wedding and took off really fast as soon as it was over," Mrs. Tanner reminisced. "Joanie said she was unusually shy and insecure, though when they were children, she used to be a very happy, outgoing girl."

"I was thinking about going to Laconia to see if she knows where James is, if you approve. He may not even know about his father's death, or about his inheritance. You know him a lot better than I do, but I was wondering if you thought if might be possible that he would give one of the houses to Jimmy and you, or at least let you live there.

They are both much closer to town and would be so much more convenient for you when Jimmy starts school," Olivia said.

"Oh my, I hadn't even thought about how Jack's death might affect Jimmy. James isn't a bad person, just a little weak sometimes and unsure of himself. He always seemed to feel so much guilt over his mother's death that it was like he was carrying the weight of the world on his shoulders. If he inherited two big houses, I'm almost sure he'd be willing to give one to his son, seeing as he never gave him anything else. Once I got over my anger at him for leaving Joanie and Jimmy, I always thought he felt really bad about it."

"So, you approve of me trying to find him?" Olivia asked smiling.

"Yes, I sure do. It would be wonderful if he would that for Jimmy. I think it would be better for Jimmy if we didn't live so far out in the country some times, especially now that he's going to be able to hear and go to school with the other kids. You are so wonderful to us Olivia! How can I ever thank you?"

"There's no need for thanks. That's what friends are for," Olivia squeezed her hand. "The third thing I wanted to talk to you about is that there is apparently a valuable antique that may possibly be in one of those three houses, either one of the two that James inherited or the small one his sister did. It may not even exist anymore, but from an old letter than a friend of mine found, it is quite possible that it does. If so, and we can find it, James would be a very wealthy man, or Jenny would be the wealthy one if it was in her house."

"How fun! A mystery to solve as well. I've always

loved mysteries. You know, that story sounds familiar . . . But for the life of me, I can't remember why. I hope you can find James and the antique too. Let me know if I can help in any way."

"I will Mrs. Tanner. Thanks for giving me the go ahead, I love mysteries too and I'd, also, love to see you and Jimmy living closer to town, not that your house here isn't lovely, but I know it won't be easy when he starts school. Oh! Josh and I were talking about it and he wants to put Jimmy into a speech therapy program with a woman in North Conway who has an excellent reputation for working with deaf kids, so he will be better prepared for school. Would you be okay with that?"

"You are marrying a saint, Olivia! Though you're one too, so it's perfect. I am more than okay with it; I am thrilled! Please thank him for me and give him a big hug."

"We're definitely not saints," Olivia laughed. "Josh is just lucky to have money from his family and he loves helping people who have been dealt a tougher hand. You're the one I find amazing. You've been through so much, losing your daughter, raising your deaf grandson with no help from his father, and you are so cheerful and sweet and giving. You're a lot more saint-like than either of us."

Olivia stood up, snagging one last cookie, "I'd better be going, since I am heading to Laconia. It's a bit of a drive and I don't want to be late getting back. It's no fun driving on these roads in the dark even when it's not icy, but I think tonight it'll be pretty awful."

"You're right about that for sure," Mrs. Tanner walked her to the door. "You make sure to be back home before dark, okay?"

"I will, I promise." Olivia waved to Jimmy from the

living room doorway. He jumped up from his drawing and ran over to hug her. She hugged him back and reached into her purse and pulled out a small box of colored pencils and handed it to him. He beamed from ear to ear, hugged her again and ran back to try them out. As he sat back down on the floor, he looked up and waved to her with a bright happy smile.

Olivia drove off smiling to herself. *Jimmy was such a cutie and a sweetheart too. Thank goodness he would get his implant and hopefully it would work well for him.* She drove carefully on the slightly slick roads. They were better than they'd been last night, since the precipitation had stopped, but it was supposed to start up again later. All the more reason to get there and back as soon as possible. She really couldn't chance driving the icy winding roads in the dark. Even if she wasn't heading into the mountains right now—she would be on the way back.

Olivia admired the huge lake on the way. It was always so beautiful, even on dreary grey days like this one. She decided to stop for gas in Meredith, as the gas was always way cheaper there than anywhere else in the area.

It was noon when she arrived in Laconia, and by the time she'd found the address where Jenny Harkins lived, it was twenty past. Olivia smoothed her clothes and made sure her beret was secure before she walked up the steps to the front porch. It was a nice, though a rather nondescript, medium sized, wood sided, beige house. Just the sort of place she'd imagined it might be from the description Mrs. Tanner had given of Jenny Harkins.

She knocked on the door and waited a little bit, then knocked again. After a few more seconds, she heard the lock rattling on the other side and the door finally opened just a crack at first, then wider to reveal a short, thin thirtyish woman with unkempt pale blond hair and scared looking, red rimmed eyes.

"Hi, Mrs. Harkins?" Olivia asked.

"Yes, I'm Jenny Harkins," the woman said warily. "How can I help you?" she held the door half closed.

"I'm Olivia McKenna from Birchwood and I'm trying to find your brother James. I'm a friend of his little son, Jimmy, and Jimmy's grandmother. Could I come in and talk with you about him?" Olivia asked, trying to be as non-threatening as possible, since the woman looked terrified and very upset.

"I don't have any idea where he is," she said a little too quickly. "Haven't seen him in ages."

"Are you sure? I heard he'd been seen here in town recently, and I can't imagine him being here without visiting his sister," Olivia said softly. "Are you okay? Can I help you somehow?" Olivia pressed one of her business cards into her hand.

The woman took a shuddering breath and looked around wildly, "No, I'm fine, everything is fine and I don't know where James is. I have to go now, sorry." She closed the door.

Olivia stood for a moment in indecision then knocked again, but Mrs. Harkins didn't come back to the door and Olivia finally gave up and went back to her car. She looked at the house for a minute and thought she could see the curtains fluttering slightly in the front window. Something was seriously not right there. She drove a few streets away and parked on the side of the road to think, where she wasn't visible from the house.

She decided to call Josh and ask him what she should

do. He was a cop, and had a lot more experience with dealing with strange things like this. Olivia wondered whether there was someone in the house threatening the woman, or if she was maybe a bit off, and just came across as freaked out a lot of the time. She could be paranoid or something and just be like that all the time. Mrs. Tanner *had* said that she seemed to be a nervous sort or woman.

Josh told her not to go back to the house in case either of those scenarios were true, as either one could be dangerous. He offered to place a call to the local PD and ask if they knew anything about Mrs. Harkins and whether they'd had any calls about her being weird or acting crazy in the past.

As Olivia waited for him to call her back, she took stock of the neighborhood around her. It was a pretty typical working class neighborhood, looking as though most people were out at work right now. She saw only a couple of cars in the driveways and there weren't many houses with garages. Jenny Harkins' street had been much the same.

Josh called back to say that the local cops hadn't ever received any complaints about her or her husband and doubted that anything was wrong at the house. They suggested that maybe she and her husband probably had a tiff and that's why she was upset. Josh said he trusted Olivia's instincts, but there wasn't anything he or she could do if the woman refused Olivia's offer of help and the cops weren't interested in checking it out. They would just have to hope everything was okay, as anything else Olivia might try to do would be both illegal and possibly dangerous.

Olivia drove slowly past the house again on her way out of town, but it looked quite ordinary with only an old vintage 1970's Chevy Impala in the driveway. She had a sick feeling in her stomach as she drove away. The woman had looked so scared. Hopefully she was just a paranoid sort and nothing was really wrong. She would try calling her later, since she had the phone number. She'd wanted to talk to her in person first, hoping to be able to get her to talk easier, but that obviously didn't go according to plan. Now she just wanted to make sure she was all right.

The trip back started well enough, but after a few minutes, it started raining, then the rain turned to a wintry mix, then finally to snow. The temperature dropped steadily and Olivia drove slower and more carefully each mile she went. She reached Birchwood safely and decided to check out the other house Jack Hill had owned, that James was supposed to be inheriting, before she went home, as it wasn't far. It was already three-thirty PM but she knew she should have at least a half hour or more before it got too dark to safely drive on the 'greasy' roads.

It didn't take her long to find the house. It was set back off Old Candlewick Road up a long, slightly winding driveway. Olivia drove up the driveway and stopped halfway up to take in the whole place. It wasn't a house, Olivia thought, it was a mansion. A huge sprawling 'L' shaped Cape Cod style house, complete with gables, gambrels, columns, round multi windowed turrets and sweeping verandas on an enormous lot, that looked like it had once been beautifully landscaped. It had to be several acres, not including the woods behind and around it. Each of the two sections of the 'L' shape was large enough to call a mansion in itself; joined together, she was awestruck.

It was badly neglected, but beneath it all, it was still beautiful, elegant and more than a little mysterious, and she wanted to move in tomorrow. Well, she wanted to start cleaning it up tomorrow and fixing whatever was broken and turning it into a beautiful home again. She could be married here, she thought suddenly. There was no place in the world as perfect for their wedding as this place, but that would mean postponing the wedding until the place could be put in order. If she could find James and talk him into renting it to them for the wedding or maybe even selling it to them, if Josh loved it as much as she did. Her thoughts were running wild. She drove up to the top of the drive, while she dialed Josh on her cell phone, staring at the lovely bedraggled house, entranced, while waiting for him to answer. He agreed to meet her there, as he was actually close by on his way back to Headquarters from partnering a rookie Trooper on a call to a bad three car wreck on one of the busier roads in Birchwood. Luckily Josh had driven his own patrol car, and met the other Trooper there, so he didn't have to take the rookie back to the HQ.

Olivia put her beret back on her head and shrugged into her down jacket. Stepping out into the cold, snowy air only made it more beautiful. She stood breathing it all in and falling totally in love with the place. Yes, she could definitely live here; she might never want to leave. She felt like a fairy princess just being on the property. There was a beautiful little pond, or it would be once it was cleaned out and the weeds gone, and even though there weren't any ducks swimming in it, Olivia could picture them there—stunning green headed daddy ducks, plain but pretty mama ducks with fluffy little yellow babies following them around.

This could be her and Josh's little corner of paradise if he liked it too; if it was structurally sound, and if they could find James, and if he would sell it to them. Her face fell slightly—so many ifs. Olivia had never lived in a large house like this, had never even thought of it really since she was a very little girl, but this place touched something inside her that was purely magical. She felt like it was meant to belong to her and Josh. There were no cars in sight, but there could easily be one or even three in the huge garage that was detached except for a small enclosed walkway from one end of the house.

Olivia walked hesitantly to the front door and knocked just in case. After a couple minutes, she peeked into the side window, and saw that though there was furniture, it had all been covered and it was obvious that no one had lived there in a very long time. She looked in the next window and was taking in the formal dining room inside it when she heard Josh drive up and park beside her car.

He came up on the porch to join her in window peeking.

"Wow! This is some place!" he whistled, "I thought I'd been all over the whole town, but I've never seen this house before."

"Isn't it beautiful Josh?" Olivia said in wonder. "It's like a fairyland right here in our own little town."

Josh was still looking around, "It's magnificent, at least it could be if it was fixed up," he noticed Olivia's rapturous face, "I wonder if James would sell it to us if we find him? Would you like to live here sweetheart? You look like you are already in love with it."

"Oh Josh, it's the most magical, beautiful place I've ever seen. I would love for us to live here," she hugged him. "I've seen huge mansions before, as well as a million other styles and sizes of homes, but I've never seen a place that instantly felt like I needed to live in it. This one does."

"I agree," Josh said. "It is an incredible find. I can't believe I've never seen this house. I'm going to let the estate lawyers know we are interested in buying it, so that whenever James is found, we will hopefully be first in line if he decides to sell it, which I think he probably will."

Olivia jumped up and down in excitement, hugging Josh. "Josh, I want us to be married here. We have to find him!"

Josh, catching her excitement, spun her around, "I agree again. It's perfect." He set her down, "We will find him. I'm going to ask all the guys at work to keep an eye out for him unofficially too," he thought for a moment, "You know another place we could consider getting married is at my family's vacation home on Mary's Orchard. Just in case this doesn't work out; I don't want you to be too disappointed. I know we said we didn't want a beach type wedding, but it is a beautiful place. We would probably have to move the wedding back until spring or even summer if we get married here."

They wandered around the outside of the front, not getting too close to the house in case there were alarms that might go off. They didn't want to end up being mistaken for burglars.

"I'm going to call the lawyers as soon as I get to Headquarters. Are you going straight home? The weather is getting worse by the minute and it will be dark soon."

"Yes I am. I don't want to be out on the roads after dark on a night like this. I wish you didn't have to be either. It's a nasty drive back here for you after dark. Please be careful," Olivia hugged him.

"I will. I'll call you when I leave the HQ and again

when I am home."

Josh waited for Olivia to go first around the circle and down the driveway, then he followed until she went toward her house and he headed the other way toward Headquarters, or the barracks, as the New Hampshire state trooper stations were called.

CHAPTER FOUR

Olivia was filled with excitement the whole way home. As usual, Molly and Sheyna were very excited to see her, so there was a lot of barking, meowing and laughing once she got inside her house.

"Okay girls, let me get changed really quickly and I'll feed you and then we can play," she laughed, extricating herself from both of them and jogging up the stairs to her room.

She changed into sweat pants and a soft fleece top and put on her wooly house slippers. She was about to head downstairs when she remembered that she'd meant to call Jenny Harkins again to try to see if she was okay. She dialed her number from her cell phone as she descended the stairs. She'd made it to the kitchen by the time the voicemail picked up. Olivia sighed. She would have felt much better if Jenny had answered. Now she was back to being worried.

She mixed food for Molly and Sheyna and put it in their usual dining spots, and heated some water for tea to drink while checking her email and home phone messages. Nothing exciting in the email, though there was a new item to add to her list for one client. When she played the phone messages, there was a very strange one. No one said anything, but she heard a sort of gasping sound, then a short sigh and the click of the receiver hanging up. It sounded to her like someone had wanted to say something, but changed their mind. Olivia had a strong feeling it had been Jenny Harkins, but unfortunately she didn't have caller ID on her land line, so she couldn't be sure. She tried calling her again, but still ended up with voice mail.

Feeling considerably less happy, she fixed herself a big salad, warmed up some leftover spicy black bean chili and sat in front of her computer to eat. She chatted with a couple friends on Facebook, replied to the email from the client, then googled Mary's Orchard. She had of course heard of it, but she really had no idea what it was like and hated to look so 'country' as to have to ask Josh.

She was stunned at the pictures of the houses she saw online. Some of them made the huge house she'd just fallen in love with look like a tiny cottage. She'd heard some of the wealthy people visiting the area to ski, talk about vacationing in their cottages on Mary's Orchard in the summer and had assumed they really were cottages. *Wow! This is how Josh had grown up—with a vacation home the size of a small hotel?* She scrolled through the pictures in amazement. It said a lot about how wonderful his parents were that he had turned out to be the hard working, giving kind of man he was. Suddenly she wasn't afraid to meet his dad anymore. She knew he would be everything Josh had said he was.

Olivia finished her early dinner and glancing at the time on the computer, realized that Josh should have called her to say he was leaving work over a half hour ago. She dialed his cell phone, hoping he hadn't gotten stuck at work late.

"Liv, I'll have to ring you back later, I'm out on a call right now and can't talk," Josh said quietly and quickly into the phone. "Sorry sweetheart, I'll call you soon as I can. Don't worry, I'm fine."

Olivia hung up feeling curious but relieved that he was okay. *What could have happened to take him out on this kind of night just at quitting time?* She sighed, hopefully it wasn't anything too bad or time consuming and he could get home before the roads got even worse. It was a long dangerous drive from Headquarters on a night like this.

She curled up on the couch with Molly and Sheyna and popped a DVD into the player. She'd just distract herself with old Supernatural episodes until he called her back. She was just about to play the fourth episode when her cell phone finally rang. Josh asked if he could come over even though it was late.

She ran upstairs to change into jeans and a nicer top, and real shoes instead of her wooly slippers. She brushed her teeth and her hair and ran back downstairs.

Molly announced Josh's arrival before he could even park his car. Olivia opened the front door and took his raincoat as he stepped inside. She led him into the warm kitchen and took his parka too so he could sit comfortably at the table. One look at his face in the light and she knew he didn't have good news.

"Josh, what happened? What were you called out on?"

"There was a bad wreck in the notch, a car apparently missed the curve coming down on the Headquarters side of the notch and went off into the woods, hitting a tree. I was called out because the officers on the scene said it looked like the brake lines had been slit in a way that would have caused a slow leak," Josh sighed. "The driver was Jenny

Harkins. She's in a coma at the hospital and they don't think she's going to make it."

"Oh no! Josh, no!" Olivia cried, sinking into a chair with one hand over her mouth and the other at her throat. "I should have done something when I was there. I knew something was wrong and I just left her there." Tears welled in her eyes.

Josh put his arms around her, kneeling beside her chair, "I wanted to be here when you heard about it because I knew it would hit you hard. It isn't your fault. There was nothing you could safely do once she refused your help." He kissed her forehead, holding her and rocking her. "But I know you, and I know that doesn't make it feel any better."

"I should have dragged her out of there and run or something. There was probably someone in there with a gun or knife or something, and I just left her there alone."

Josh picked her up and carried her to the couch, sitting down with her in his lap, holding her while she cried, like a child that needed comforting.

"If you had done that, Molly and Sheyna and I might be grieving for you now, and Mrs. Harkins might be dead instead of in a coma. It may be a cliché but it's true, where there's life, there's hope. She may yet come out of it and be okay. If you'd grabbed her and run, and someone really was in that house with a gun, they could have shot and killed both of you, right then and there," Josh spoke quietly and convincingly. "I'm shaking, just thinking about that scenario, Olivia."

Olivia was calming down slowly, though the tears were still falling. "I'm sorry Josh, I just feel so guilty. I knew she was in trouble, deep down, no matter how much I tried to convince myself that she was always like that. She just looked too terrified."

"I'm sorry you couldn't do something to save her from this, and I'm sorry I couldn't step in as a cop and do something, but without her cooperation, and that of the local PD and my department, I could have been in major legal trouble if I had forced her out of her house and it turned out that she was only upset about an argument with her husband." Josh smoothed her hair back from her wet face and kissed her tears away. "I should have known that your instincts were spot on though. They always are."

"Thanks Josh," Olivia said quietly. "You know, I'd sort of forgotten about her for a while in the excitement of seeing the house, and I think that made me feel even more guilty. Oh! I think she tried to call me earlier before I got home," Olivia sat up. "There was a weird message on the voicemail of my home phone, but I don't have caller ID, so I couldn't see if it really was her. I didn't erase it, so maybe you can check it somehow?" she ended the sentence with a questioning tone. "Do you have a way to check things like that? I made her take my card when I was at her house, so she had my number."

"Yes, it can be checked, though it may require a court order. At this point, aside from possibly causing you to blame yourself even more, I don't think it would help us any," he said pulling her back against his chest and hugging her.

Olivia sighed. "Thanks for saving me from myself. Logically, now that I've calmed down, I know that I couldn't have done anything, because I would have at the time if it felt like I could have. I badly wanted to. I just didn't know enough about her to be sure if something was really wrong or not. I was afraid to go completely on instinct."

"I'm sorry for what happened to her, but I'm glad you didn't try to do anything. Seriously, Liv, you could be dead right now," Josh brushed her hair from her tearstained face. "Okay, now we just need to figure out who did this to her and why. Was it something to do with her brother James or something unrelated," Josh pondered.

"I'm betting it's related to James. Old Mr. Davis said he'd been seen there recently, and Bob Pulser said he'd been in trouble in Boston just before that, so maybe he brought his trouble with him up to his sister's house," Olivia said sadly, "and if that's the case, where is he now?"

Olivia's cell phone rang, startling them both. She answered and listened intently for a moment.

"Oh Vicki, that's awful. Listen, Josh is here and we'll be right over. Give us twenty minutes."

"Someone broke into Vicki's and Andrew's house today while they were at work and stole the highboy that had the letter in it. Thankfully, the letter wasn't in it anymore. I told her we would come now."

"Yes, we should go. Let me drive and we'll take my car because my investigative gear is in there already," Josh helped Olivia off his lap and stood up. "I think Molly and Sheyna should come with us."

"Oh no! The bad guys, whoever they are, might have my business card with my phone number and be able to trace it to my address," Olivia grabbed her curls and tugged in frustration. "Here we go again. I thought I was all done with stalkers after we solved Jamison's murder."

"If there are any strange things happening at all, I will come stay in your guestroom again or we'll move you and the girls somewhere safe until this person or these people are caught," Josh assured her. "Let's see what we find at Vicki's."

They loaded the girls into the backseat of Josh's patrol car and drove carefully to Vicki's and Andrew's house in North Conway. Every light in the house and on the grounds was on when they pulled into the driveway. Vicki met them at the door looking decidedly less cheerful than usual.

"Please bring Molly and Sheyna inside where it's warm," she reached in and took Sheyna from the back seat and helped Olivia get Molly out and on the lead.

"Not only did they break the window in the French doors in the back, but they tracked mud all over the carpet, knocked over our indoor Ficus tree, spilling the soil all over, and then stole the highboy, along with Andrew's spare laptop which was sitting on top of it. Fortunately, we both had our good laptops with us at work."

"Did they steal anything else?" Josh asked. "Have you touched the French doors?"

"No they didn't. Thank goodness they didn't take any of Andrew's banks or other collectibles," Vicki exhaled sharply in frustration. "I'm just so ticked off that they did this. How did they find out about the letter? That has to be what they were after, since beside the computer, the highboy was the only thing taken. And, to answer your other question, no, I know better, thanks to Olivia, and I wouldn't let Andrew touch anything either."

"Good woman!" Josh hugged her. "Let me see what I can find out from the mud and possible fingerprints," he headed toward the back of the house with his kit.

Vicki sank down onto a chair in the living room looking depressed. Andrew came downstairs and hugged Olivia, then sat on the couch.

"Olivia, it's good to see you. I wish you were just here for dinner though; this is not the way I like to entertain friends," Andrew looked almost as depressed as his wife.

"Was there anything on your laptop that was sensitive, like financial records, or bank passwords?" Olivia asked hesitantly, not wanting to make them feel even worse.

"Oh no!" Vicki looked ill. "Andrew, was there?"

"No, thank goodness! Calm down Vic, it only had lists of antiques I want to find, pictures and whimsical stuff. There was nothing critical on that one," Andrew assured them. "All of my important files are on the one I carry with me, and the backups are locked in the safe room."

"Whew!" Vicki sighed in relief, leaning her head against the back of the chair with the back of her hand over her forehead and closing her eyes. "I just died a thousand deaths."

"Okay, Vicki you can come back to life now," Olivia smiled. "I'm sorry they took your computer Andrew, but boy am I glad it wasn't worse."

She told them what had happened so far with her investigation, and then about the incident with Mrs. Harkins in the afternoon, and the wreck that evening. They were both shocked by the news.

"I'm starting to wish I'd never found that letter," Vicki said sadly. "That poor woman."

"Vicki, whether you had found it or not didn't change anything. I think everything would have still happened the same way, except that we would never have known anything about it," Olivia said earnestly. "In fact, if you hadn't found it, and we didn't know, there would have been absolutely no clues as to why someone cut her brakes. At least now we are pretty sure we know at part, if not all of the reason. That should help us to solve it."

"She's right Vicki," Josh walked in from the back carrying his gear and looking slightly satisfied. "We are much better off, knowing what we do, than we would have been without you finding that letter, so don't beat yourself up. The letter about the shoe bank, James' recent appearance and subsequent disappearance, and Jenny's slit brakes all have to be connected, since the highboy was stolen at the same time. There's no way I'm buying that many coincidences.

"Andrew, it's good to see you," he hugged Andrew, then Vicki, picked up Sheyna and headed toward the door. "Sorry to run, but we need to get going. I want to get these prints back to the HQ and start the process going on them so we can get results as soon as possible. Take extra care for the next few days, or until we catch these people. If anything strange happens, or you need anything, call me."

Olivia got up and hugged Vicki and Andrew goodbye and Vicki and Andrew patted Molly and Sheyna goodbye too. The couple waved from the door as they drove away.

"Josh, do you think Vicki and Andrew are safe? They won't try to break in again to look for the letter will they?" Olivia worried. "I don't want them to get hurt."

"I think they will be okay sweetie," Josh consoled her. "They know to be careful now and I told them to call if anything happened. I'm going to take you home and then go back to Headquarters to start things rolling on these prints. We might get lucky and get a hit on them," he smiled.

"Yay! I thought you looked happy with yourself when you came in the room. Did you get more than one print?"

"There are two decent looking prints, completely

different from each other, so I am really hoping we'll have something to go on."

"I'm so glad you got a lead, but I wish you didn't have to go back all the way over there again tonight. Are you sure it can't wait until morning?" Olivia asked. "I was hoping you'd be able to stay home, since the roads are so awful."

"If I wasn't worried that they might be even worse in the morning, I would love to stay home," Josh squeezed her hand. "The weather isn't getting any better though and if I don't get the prints in there soon, we'll waste too much time."

Olivia made a rueful face, "I know you're right, and we really do need every minute to try to find James before something bad happens to him, if it hasn't already. Hopefully he wasn't the one threatening her. Actually, I doubt that he was. Mrs. Tanner says he is not a bad person, just a bit unsure of himself and plagued by guilt. Which means he may be weak enough to bring trouble to his sister, but he probably wouldn't hurt her himself."

It was sleeting a little when they got back to Olivia's house and she made Josh come inside for a few minutes so she could fix him a thermos of coffee for the drive over the notch. It wasn't hard to get him to cooperate. Josh almost never turned down hot coffee, especially good coffee which was a rare thing at Headquarters.

After Josh left, Olivia walked out back with Molly for a few minutes, then made a cup of decaf tea and headed upstairs to read until Josh called to say he had arrived safely. Sheyna curled up beside her ear and purred loudly until Olivia laughed and scratched her head. Molly sprawled across the bottom of the bed diagonally, and after a few minutes was sleeping soundly.

After another half hour Josh called and Olivia was finally able to relax. He was going to catch some sleep at the HQ once he'd gotten the fingerprints in to AFIS. She hung up after a few minutes and turned out the light. She fell asleep quickly, but her dreams were filled with guns, exploding cars and the sad, reproachful face of Jenny Harkins.

CHAPTER FIVE

Olivia woke up feeling like she had a hangover. Obviously it wasn't from the one glass of wine she'd had with dinner, so she figured it must be from the evil haunted dreams that had plagued most of her night. She fed Molly and Sheyna, went into the backyard and played ball with Molly for a few minutes, while the coffee brewed, then sat at the table drinking her coffee slowly. She was having a very hard time not feeling guilty over Jenny Harkins and realized she was postponing the call to find out if she had awakened, was still in a coma, or if she had died.

Once she poured her second cup of coffee, Olivia felt better able to deal with hearing the answer. She decided to call Josh first, as he might know the scoop and because hearing his voice would make her feel better, especially if the news were bad.

Josh answered on the first ring, "Abrams."

"Hi Josh, Did you get any sleep?"

"Hi Babes, I got a little. Waiting to hear back from AFIS now, hopefully soon. How about you? Did you sleep okay? I missed you and was worried that you'd be up feeling guilty all night."

"I missed you too Josh. I slept, but I had awful dreams. Have you heard anything about Jenny Harkins' condition?"

Josh sighed heavily, "She didn't make it sweetheart; I'm sorry."

Olivia gasped and sighed sadly. "Oh Josh, I was so hoping she would be okay, but I didn't have a good feeling about it, especially after the dreams I had last night. Her poor husband."

"Yes, and I'm even more concerned about James now that these people are murderers. They don't have much more to lose by killing a second time, and they will be more desperate not to get caught, so if he becomes a liability, he'll be in extreme danger."

Olivia gasped again, "Josh, if they were there when I went to talk to Jenny, they might have heard me mention Jimmy to her. We have to make sure he and Mrs. Tanner are okay. If James would sacrifice his sister's safety for his own, he may do the same thing to them."

"I'm on my way. I'll call you as soon as I get there," Josh said quickly.

"I'll call Mrs. Tanner now and tell her to make sure everything is locked up tight. I'm going to meet you there Josh. We can all figure out what to do once we're there."

"That's a good idea. Bring the girls with you just in case. Remember they may have your business card."

"Yikes, I'd forgotten that," Olivia moaned. "The girls are definitely coming too. I'll call you after I talk to her."

Olivia hung up with Josh and quickly dialed Mrs. Tanner's number. Luckily she reached her and was able to pass on the warning to lock up and wait until she and Josh arrived. Mrs. Tanner was worried, but calm in spite of it.

Olivia ran upstairs and changed into a pair of lined jeans, a just-tight-enough-to-be-mildly-sexy cowl neck sweater and her winter boots. She put the girls' coats on them, donned her own coat and loaded them into the SUV. Grabbing her cell phone, wallet and keys, she jumped into the car and backed out of the driveway heading for Eastman's Grant.

The roads were better this morning, but Olivia still saw a few slick spots, so she drove very carefully. She looked over as she slowly passed the antique shop where she'd been present during a murder a couple months ago, then slowed even more as she passed the next house on the other side of the street. She'd made friends with the owner, Tiny Dawson during the murder investigation. She didn't see Tiny, but in case he was looking out the window, she waved.

Mrs. Tanner and her grandson Jimmy Hill, lived next door to Tiny. Olivia pulled in behind Josh's police car and hurried up to the porch. Before she could knock, Josh opened the door with a smile to let her know things were okay.

"Oh thank goodness! I was worried that I should have kept Mrs. Tanner on the phone until you got here, but then she couldn't have locked up," Olivia said, hugging Josh and managing a quick kiss before they went inside.

Jimmy ran up and hugged Olivia, and handed her a drawing he'd done of a huge castle surrounded by a moat with a forest behind it. Olivia was stunned at how good his artwork was. Every drawing she saw was better than the last.

She beamed her delight at him and put her hand over her heart to show him that she loved it. She tried to give it back to him, but he motioned for her to keep it. She hugged him tight and he hugged her back then squirmed and ran back to his Lincoln logs to work on building the castle he'd drawn.

Olivia could hear Josh and Mrs. Tanner talking in the kitchen, so she went in to join them. Mrs. Tanner was putting a plate of cookies on the table.

Olivia laughed, "Mrs. Tanner, I've never come here and not found you with a fresh batch of cookies. You seem to always be ready for company."

Mrs. Tanner smiled, "I love to bake, and it seems like whenever I indulge myself in my favorite pastime, someone I love comes to visit, so I bake whenever I get a chance."

Olivia joined Josh at the table and snagged a cookie to go with the hot spicy smelling tea Mrs. Tanner poured for them. Josh winked at her and grinned.

"So what is going on that makes you think someone may come here and try to harm us?" Mrs. Tanner asked. "Is it something to do with the antique bank you were telling me about or James and the inheritance?"

Josh and Olivia filled her in on what had happened since Olivia was there the day before. She was shocked at Jenny Harkins' death and worried about Olivia as well as Jimmy.

"What should we do? I can't let anything happen to Jimmy. We don't have anyone close we could stay with until they are caught, except maybe Tiny, but I would feel really awkward doing that."

"Jimmy and you should come and stay at my house until it's safe," Olivia spoke up. "Josh, don't you think so?"

"Actually, that's a perfect idea," Josh smiled. "All three of you could possibly be in danger and it will be a lot easier making sure you're safe if you're all together. I may invite myself to stay on your couch as well, if that's okay with you."

"Olivia smiled, "Of course it's okay. Mrs. Tanner, would you mind staying with me for a little while? It isn't a big house and we may be a little cramped, but there is definitely safety in numbers and I'd love to have you both. It will also be much easier for you since Jimmy's surgery is scheduled for next week. You'll be a lot closer to the hospital."

"Are you sure we won't be putting you out too much?"

"Not at all, in fact, I'll feel safer, and I'll feel much better not having to worry about you guys out here all alone, plus the company will be a fun change," Olivia hugged her. "Why don't you go ahead and pack some things for a few days at least. We can always come and pick up more stuff if you need to stay longer."

Mrs. Tanner turned to Josh, "Do you think our stuff will be safe here?"

"I think I would like to have someone stay here for now to keep an eye on things and make sure no one breaks in. Would you be all right with a cop staying here and sleeping on the couch, at least for a couple days, while you're gone?" Josh asked. "I'll make sure it is someone trustworthy."

"I wouldn't have any problem at all with that. I don't really have much that's worth stealing, just a lot of sentimentally valuable things that I'd hate to lose."

Josh smiled, "Okay, I'll set it up. Meanwhile take your most treasured things and enough clothes for a few days for both of you."

Olivia cast a sideways look at him, with the corner of her mouth twitching up.

Mrs. Tanner hurried from the room to start packing,

leaving Olivia and Josh alone in the kitchen.

"You're such a sweetheart Josh, letting her think she has regular police protection for the house, when I know you will be paying someone out of your pocket to stay here," Olivia came around and hugged him from behind, leaning over his shoulders to kiss his cheek.

Josh pulled her around and sat her in his lap to give her a deep slow kiss on the lips. She melted in his arms and the electricity flew between them like sparklers on the fourth of July.

"Whoa Cowboy," Olivia laughed, standing up and looking around guiltily. "There's a five year old around here somewhere, and he may be deaf, but he isn't blind."

Josh laughed, "You're right, and there's going to be a five year old around a lot for a while too, as well as his grandma. I hadn't thought about that part yet."

Olivia smiled, "We'll figure out a safe way to have some alone time, don't worry—where there's a will . . .."

"Oh there's definitely a will," Josh said in his deep sexy voice, kissing her palm.

Olivia's stomach fluttered, "There sure is."

~~~

They loaded everything into Olivia's SUV and Josh took Molly and Sheyna in his car while Mrs. Tanner and Jimmy climbed into their car. Olivia led the way. They stopped at Tiny's house and Mrs. Tanner asked him if he could help keep an eye on the place and feed the chickens while they were gone. He cheerfully agreed, though he expressed concern over the danger to Mrs. Tanner and Jimmy.

Josh helped unload the heavier things from Olivia's SUV, then he had to go back to work for the rest of the day,
~~~

but promised to bring some clothes to stay with them until the criminals who might be a threat to them were caught.

Olivia put new linens on the two twin beds in her second guest room for Mrs. Tanner and Jimmy, then did the same for Josh in the other guest room. She handed fresh towels and washcloths to Mrs. Tanner for her bathroom, and put another set for Josh in his bathroom.

Olivia tried to organize her storage room a bit better, to accommodate the few treasures Mrs. Tanner couldn't leave behind that wouldn't fit in the guestroom such as her antique cedar chest that had belonged to her grandmother and was filled with quilts that her mother and grandmother had made as well as some that she herself had made.

Mrs. Tanner had put Jimmy's Lincoln logs and art supplies in the guestroom, along with photo albums and a few framed pictures of her late husband Albert, her late daughter Joanie, (Jimmy's mother), and a picture showing James with his arm around Joanie, who was holding baby Jimmy.

"Mrs. Tanner, why don't we put Jimmy's logs and pencils and stuff in the living room so he will have more room; it's too cramped in here with all that," Olivia smiled. "You guys will be tripping all over each other."

"I don't want to take over your whole house Olivia."

"You're not even close. Please don't worry about that. You have no idea how much stuff I've had sitting all over everywhere for days and days after a good house sale," Olivia laughed. "A few Lincoln logs and pencils are nothing, trust me."

Mrs. Tanner laughed, "I can imagine. I've had a couple other friends who loved collecting various things and it could easily get out of hand for a while. If you're sure you don't mind, it will definitely make it easier to get around in here and less likely for me to trample Jimmy's castles or slide on his pencils and break my neck."

"I'm absolutely sure. There is still a little room in my storage room too, if you want to put your albums and pictures in there."

"I think I'll put the albums there then, but I want to keep the framed pictures here where we can look at them. It may be a little hard on Jimmy being in a new place, since he's never really been away from home before, so I'd like him to have the pictures he's used to seeing."

"That's a great idea. Molly or Sheyna could sleep with him too if he would like that. They both adore him."

"Oh, I'm sure he will love that. He has his Teddy Bear, but a real live snuggly animal is always better."

They gathered up the Lincoln logs, art supplies and the photo albums and after dropping the albums off in the storage room, they set up an area in the living room for Jimmy's stuff where he would have room to play and not be in the middle of foot traffic.

"Hopefully Sheyna won't hide any of his logs," Olivia said. "She has been known to grab things she likes and run under furniture with them."

"Well, Jimmy's small enough to crawl under there and get it back if she does," laughed Mrs. Tanner. "If it's too low, he can lie down and reach until he finds it."

Jimmy came in from the guestroom with Sheyna trailing him and saw the play area they'd created for him. He grinned from ear to ear. Molly bounded in from the other room and sat in front of him with a toy in her mouth, hoping for ear scratches. He patted her head and held his hand up for her to sit. When she did, he scratched her ears and she thumped her tail happily.

The two women left Jimmy and the girls playing and headed to the kitchen. Olivia showed Mrs. Tanner where everything was kept in case she wanted to fix herself something or indulge her passion for baking.

"Oh my, look at all those pretty little sugar shakers you have on that shelf. I have a fancy silver one that I've never even used that Albert's aunt gave me. It came from England. If you collect them, you are more than welcome to it. It's been sitting in the cabinet since we were married. She said it was an antique, so I figured it was better not to use it and I like my plain glass one so I can see how much sugar is inside."

"I'd love to see it, but if it is valuable, I couldn't take it from you," Olivia smiled. "I can help you figure out what it's worth though if I see it, and if it is valuable I can help you sell it if you'd like to."

"Thanks Olivia. I just want to do something special for you after all you've done for us, and now letting us stay here too. You and Josh are like Jimmy's guardian angels."

"That's what friends are for," Olivia smiled.

"If we're staying in the same house together, you have simply got to start calling me by my first name. It's Sally, remember? I know I'm an old lady, but I still catch myself looking for my mother-in-law when people call me Mrs. Tanner," she laughed. "Not only that, but there's precious few left to call me Sally anymore."

"Okay, I'll be happy to, Sally," Olivia hugged her. "It's how I was raised—you call people in the generation above you Mr., Mrs., Miss, or Aunt, Uncle, etcetera,."

"Yes, I was raised that way too, but we've become almost family lately," she laughed, "and I refuse to be

'Aunt Sally'."

Once things were all set up and everyone settled in, Olivia called Josh to report that things were under control and to see if he'd found out anything more about James.

He said he hadn't, but that he had gotten the results from AFIS and found out that one of the prints found at Vicki's and Andrew's house belonged to Frank Cordell Salger, Jr., a career criminal that grew up in Birchwood and later moved to Boston, where he got involved in drugs and became a medium to low level dealer. He apparently goes by his middle name, Cordell. The other print wasn't in the data base, so they didn't know who it belonged to.

"What time will you be here; do you know yet?" Olivia asked. Sally, Mrs. Tanner, and I are cooking dinner together tonight, and I think it will be scrumptious, if it's anything like her cookies."

Josh laughed, "With that as an incentive, I'll be there as fast as I can. It'll probably be around 5:30. Can I pick up anything from the store on the way?"

"Actually, yes. I'm almost out of milk and we could use some oatmeal for breakfast. It's Jimmy's favorite. Oh, also more coffee, since we will now have three of us drinking it," Olivia laughed. "Sally and I will have to go to the store tomorrow to buy whatever else we come up with, but those are all fairly urgent. Thanks Josh."

"You're welcome, Babes. See you soon."

Dinner was a lively event and the food was delicious. They had made spinach and feta cheese pizza, a huge salad and crispy garlic bread with parmesan on top. Josh had brought a carrot cake from the bakery as well as the groceries Olivia had asked for.

The four played dominoes after dinner until it was

Jimmy's bedtime. Sally made herself a cup of Chamomile tea and announced that she was going to bed early, as it had been a long day.

Once the house was quiet, Josh and Olivia sat on the couch to discuss what was going on with Jenny Harkins murder and James' apparent disappearance.

"I'm going tomorrow to talk to Mr. Harkins and see if he can tell me anything new. I had O'Brian and Hendricks over there, but he said he didn't know anything at all. I'm not sure if that's true, or if he's just scared to talk."

"Josh, how about if I talk to him? If he's scared, maybe he would open up to me better than to the police. What do you think? Does it make sense?" Olivia asked.

"Yes, it does. Just be very alert and very careful in case there is something else going on that we don't know about. I honestly don't think the husband has anything to do with it, but it's better safe than sorry."

"I want to find out if he's seen James around recently, for one thing, and, of course, if he knows anything at all about what happened to Jenny," Olivia said. "Any tiny bit of information we can get will help, right?"

"That's for sure. We don't have much to go on right now. I put out an APB on Salger, but we have no idea where he is. They have to be holed up somewhere fairly close by if they're looking for that antique shoe bank, which is what they must be after, since they stole the highboy from Vicki and Andrew."

"Oh Josh, have you talked to either of them today?"

"Yes, I told Vicki we'd gotten a hit on one of the prints and told her to be vigilant until we'd caught this guy or these guys, whichever it turns out to be," Josh answered. "She was relieved to hear that and promised they would be alert."

"That's good, I was worried about them. I know firsthand how unnerving it is to have your home broken into."

Josh hugged her, "Oh, by the way, I talked to the estate lawyer about the houses that were left to James Hill by his father and let him know we were interested. Actually, I told him we were interested in both, because we are interested in the other one for Sally Tanner and Jimmy at least, and want to know if anything is happening with it."

"Thanks Josh." Olivia hugged him back. "I wish I knew if we were going to be able to buy the one we want. We could start cleaning it up and repairing things and it would be such fun."

"Yes it would, and I think eventually it will work out, but we have got to find James. You know the people who are holding him might be trying to get him to sign over his inheritance to them, or make a will leaving everything to him."

"That's a truly scary thought, because for sure, they would just kill him as soon as he did that. I don't think he's that dumb." Olivia said. "He may be weak because of his addiction and whatever other personal demons plague him, but I don't think he's stupid. You said Salger is a drug dealer. We know James had been into drugs at one point before he married Joanie. Sally told me. I wonder if he owed Salger money for drugs, and couldn't pay him, so he told him about the bank, hoping they'd just find it and accept that as payment.

"You're probably right. Getting himself in trouble doesn't mean he's dumb, just weak and addicted. It was actually clever of him to think of telling them about the antique bank, as it at least bought him time, even though it may have ultimately killed his sister, if we're guessing right about what happened."

"Josh, after I talk to Mr. Harkins tomorrow, I'm going to go look at the house on Old Candlewick. Do you want to meet me there?"

"I'm not sure sweetheart. If I can get there, I would love to, but I don't know where I'll be yet."

"I know, I'm just putting the thought in your head in case you can," Olivia smiled, kissing him.

"You are never out of my thoughts Liv, not for a minute," he ran his fingers down her throat trailing his lips behind them.

Olivia's pulse raced and just as she thought her knees would fail her, she felt something tugging at her shirt in the back. She released Josh and looked behind her to find Jimmy holding an empty glass and motioning imploringly that he was thirsty. She looked back at Josh and saw that he was grinning. That made her love him even more.

CHAPTER SIX

Breakfast was a two part affair, since Josh had to leave early for work. Olivia made him an early meal of toast and eggs with lots of hot coffee, so he could take some for his drive to work, then later she and Sally Tanner had their own eggs and toast while Jimmy ate oatmeal and one piece of toast with lots of jam.

Once they'd cleaned up the kitchen, Olivia asked Sally if she would mind if she left the girls with her and Jimmy while she went to Laconia to talk to Mr. Harkins. Josh had hired a security guard friend of his to watch Olivia's house when he wasn't there as well as a retired cop to stay at Mrs. Tanner's place. Dave Johnson, the security guard was parked outside on the street in his unobtrusive sedan.

Before she left, Olivia invited him to watch from inside, as Josh had said he was completely trustworthy. Sally felt better about it too for the guard's sake and for hers and Jimmy's. Sally promptly started cooking more eggs and soon had the delighted guard sitting at the table drinking orange juice and hot coffee while he waited on his breakfast.

Olivia dressed in casual but nice clothes so she would look presentable to meet with someone who was in mourning, but still be able to walk around the property of her 'dream house' later. She decided to take Josh's SUV as it was smaller than hers and easier to park in town, since she intended to stop off for a couple of errands on the way back. She donned her down parka and warm driving gloves and started the car.

As she was driving, she called Mr. Harkins' hardware store to see if he'd gone to work. A machine answered, as she had expected, so she would try his house.

It felt sad and not a little creepy pulling into that driveway again. Olivia's mouth went dry and she had to force herself to go up to the front door. *What if the people who'd killed Jenny had come back and were inside that house again.*

Livvie, stop scaring yourself like this. You know they aren't going to be there, now that the police are involved. She scolded herself mentally. *Just calm down and knock.*

It was only a moment before she heard someone unlocking the door from the other side. It opened and she faced a sad looking man in his mid to late thirties who looked at her inquiringly.

"Hi Mr. Harkins, I am so sorry for your loss. My name is Olivia McKenna and I really need to talk to you about Jenny and James and what is going on," Olivia said quietly, looking him in the eyes sympathetically. "It's really important."

He sighed resignedly and stepped back to allow her to enter the house.

Her heart was in her throat as she walked in and he closed the door behind her, and she looked around to make sure no one was holding a gun on them, but he merely led her to the living room and offered her a seat. He sat across from her and waited for her to open the conversation.

"I met Jenny earlier the day of the crash," Olivia began, swallowing hard. "I am a friend of Sally Tanner and her grandson Jimmy, Jenny's nephew."

Olivia explained some of the circumstances surrounding her visit to Jenny, including James' inheritance and what she'd heard about James being in Laconia and possibly being in trouble.

"I need to know if you've seen James recently." Olivia said. "I also need to know if there is anything at all that you know about what happened to Jenny. Right now, Jimmy and his grandmother, and even I may be in danger from the same people because I mentioned Jimmy to Jenny and gave her my business card that day. I think that whoever did this to Jenny may have been in the house at the time and heard me and may have even taken my card."

"They didn't take the card. They might have looked at it and written the information down, but I doubt it because I found the card on the floor, crumpled up near the door behind the flower pot. Jenny probably hid it so they wouldn't be able to find you," Mr. Harkins said sadly. "She wouldn't ever have let anything happen to James' little boy."

"I am so sorry I couldn't save her!" Olivia cried, tears springing to her eyes. "She looked so scared, but she said everything was fine and she wouldn't let me in. The police said she was probably upset from an argument with her husband and refused to get involved unless she asked for help. I wanted to do something, but I just couldn't figure out if something was really wrong or if I was imagining it." Olivia took a tissue from her pocket and wiped her streaming eyes.

"Don't blame yourself," he said. "What could you

have done? They probably had a gun. I don't blame you, and Jenny wouldn't either. You asked if I'd seen James. The answer is yes. He's come around several times lately, asking Jenny if he could borrow money. He looked bad, like he was on drugs," he paused. "Jenny didn't tell him about his inheritance or hers either, because she knew if he was doing drugs, he'd just throw it all away. She gave him a few dollars and paid for a motel room for him for a couple of weeks, but that was it. The last time I know about him being here was four days before she died," his eyes grew moist. "I hope her own brother didn't kill her. I never thought he was capable of something like that."

"I don't think he did, Mr. Harkins," Olivia said. "I think he was being held at gunpoint too. From what I've heard about him, he is troubled, and heavily addicted to drugs, but not a bad person. It's more likely that he owed money to the killers and they followed him here," She paused and sighed. "Did Jenny ever show you an old letter about an antique shoe bank that is supposed to be worth a huge amount of money nowadays?"

He thought for a minute, "I vaguely remember something like that, but that was years ago, and she never had the bank, just the letter. Is that what this is all about?"

"I think so, yes. I'm guessing that James owed money to drug dealers and when they threatened him, he told them about the letter and probably tried to convince them that the bank was here in Birchwood somewhere, and that he'd find it and bring it to them, then when he didn't bring it, they came looking for him. He must have been hiding from them, and came here, hoping his sister would fix things somehow."

"She always tried to fix things for him. I think that

may have been part of the problem all along. He knew she'd be there for him and help him out of whatever jam he got himself into, so he never had to be responsible," Mr. Harkins shook his head and sighed. "Maybe if she'd let him suffer through his own messes, he'd have stopped making them."

"I don't know, but she must have loved him a lot and he probably loved her in his own way. They say tough love is better, but who knows really? I think it depends on the people involved and how they respond."

"Well, there's no way of knowing now. Jenny's gone and James may be too," Mr. Harkins wiped his eyes. "If he's still alive, he's in way over his head for sure."

Olivia nodded, "Yes he is. Mr. Harkins, do you know anything about your wife's death, or what James is into? Anything at all that could help us find him and help catch Jenny's killers?"

He shook his head slowly, "I don't think so, no. I found your card behind the flower pot and some cigarette butts on the back porch in a saucer when I came home the day she died . . . ashes on the floor. The police came and went through everything, but I forgot to tell them about the cigarettes and the card. I think I was still in shock."

"Did you save the butts or throw them out?"

"I threw them out, but the trash hasn't been taken yet. The police didn't go through the trash outside, because I told them it was all old. I'd forgotten about the cigarette butts until now."

"Is it okay if I take them? Do you happen to have a pair of rubber gloves I could use to find them and a couple plastic baggies to put them in?"

"Sure, I'll get them and I'll find the butts for you. I'm

not letting you go through my nasty garbage bags," he smiled sadly as he went to find the gloves and baggies.

Olivia felt bad having to ask him to relive anything from that awful day, but they needed every scrap of information they could get, and cigarette butts with possible DNA could not only help them track down the killer or killers, but it could even make the case later in court once they did.

Mr. Harkins returned wearing a pair of latex gloves that looked like they came from a box of his wife's hair color. He had three zipper baggies and a small indoor garbage can.

Olivia followed him outside to the big trash can. She used her cell phone to take a video of the whole procedure. He pulled out a bag and methodically emptied it piece by piece into the small garbage can until it was empty. The butts weren't there. He dumped all the trash back into the bag and opened the second one. At the bottom, he found several cigarette butts. They appeared to be all the same brand. He scooped them out and put them into one of the zippered bags, then dumped the rest of the trash back into the bag and put them back in the big can. He handed the zippered bag to Olivia who stopped recording and took the bag.

Olivia gave him a gentle hug, "I am so very sorry for your loss Mr. Harkins. Jenny seemed like a wonderful woman. If I can do anything for you, please let me know," she gave him one of her cards. She hated to ask for it, since it was probably one of the last things Jenny had touched, but she knew she had to.

"Would you mind if I took the crumply one you found that day that you think Jenny may have hidden behind the plant. It's slightly possible that it could have fingerprints from one of the killers. Even a slight possibility is worth checking on."

He sighed and went inside. He returned shortly, with the bedraggled card carefully stowed in a zippered baggie now that she'd mentioned fingerprints. He handed it to her a little hesitantly, as if it was hard to let it go.

"Thank you, Mr. Harkins. We're going to figure out who killed her and make sure they are locked away, and hopefully find James too." Olivia gave him another little hug. "If you think of anything else that might help, please call me."

"I doubt that I will remember anything, but I will call if I do," he said. "I don't know how you are going to find these people or James either, but somehow I think you just might." He took a deep breath and seemed to gain strength from that thought.

As she drove away, Olivia hoped he was right. So far they had very little to go on as far as where they might be hiding. Knowing who one of them was helpful, but since the one they knew of was from the Boston area, and was obviously up here instead, the helpfulness of the information was limited.

Olivia turned the heat up in the SUV, as she could hear the wind screaming against the car which made it seem even colder than it was. Passing the lake, she was tempted as always to get out and stand by the water in the frigid air, drinking in the grey splendor of the day. If the wind had been a tiny bit less fierce she would have done so, but she knew it would feel too raw coming off the huge expanse of water.

The traffic was sparse and she made good time through

the Lakes Region into Conway. After making a couple of stops for things she needed in town, Olivia headed toward Birchwood. She was looking forward to seeing the neglected old mansion.

As she started up the once stately drive, she could visualize how beautiful it could be with some tender loving care. The weeds had been allowed to flourish and huge patches of wild blackberries with vicious thorns grew rampant over much of the grounds. This time of the year, they were not so bad, as the freezing temperatures had knocked them back a lot, but she knew come spring and summer, walking around the property would be no fun at all unless they were controlled.

She pictured the grounds with freshly seeded or sodded grass, beautiful flower beds and bordered by a much smaller amount of the wild blackberry and raspberry vines, with forest bordering the rest. There were several gorgeous old trees on the property as well as some smaller trees that looked to be of the flowering variety, though this time of the year it was hard to be sure unless you really knew your trees.

When she was about three-quarters of the way up the drive, Olivia could see a white panel truck at the top of the driveway. As she stopped to look, she saw a man walking from behind the house toward the truck. He seemed to spot her at the same time and ran toward the back of the house again. Her senses went on full alert. She studied the license tag for a couple of seconds, as she shifted into reverse, then started backing down the long winding drive as quickly as she could, one-touch dialing Josh's cell phone as she drove. As she reached the bottom and backed into the road to turn around, the panel truck roared down the driveway, clipping the front of her SUV hard enough to spin it around two-hundred-and-seventy degrees, as it turned into the road and sped away.

Olivia was jolted so severely by the impact that her head smacked the side window hard, the cell phone flew from her hand landing in the floor on the passenger side and everything went black.

As the world came slowly back into view, she could hear Josh's anxious voice coming from far away, but was too disoriented to be able to reach for the phone for several seconds. Her head felt like she'd been smacked with a two-by-four and her hand came away bloody when she felt her left temple. Her neck felt like it was on fire. She moaned and tried to sit up straight but everything was blurry and she felt nauseated from the pain shooting from her head and neck.

The seat belt wouldn't allow her to reach the floor, so she struggled with shaking hands to get the buckle to release. Blood dripped into her eyes as she scrambled to retrieve the cell phone, and the pain of bending her head made her gasp. She shoved herself back up into the seat with her free hand, clutching the phone with the other.

"Josh," she panted in a whimper that didn't sound like her own voice. "Car wreck . . . Old Candlewick . . . head hurts," she fought against the greyness that threatened to overcome her again. Josh's voice on the other side of the line sounded panicked, but it was fading as she succumbed to the welcoming darkness.

CHAPTER SEVEN

Josh leaped from his desk, barking at his subordinate Bob O'Brian to follow him and instructing another subordinate to send an ambulance and the local Birchwood PD to the address of the house that on Old Candlewick Road, as he raced out the door to his police car. He peeled out of the parking lot with O'Brian on his tail, both with flashing lights and sirens blaring.

He'd answered the phone and had heard the horrible sound of the crash, then nothing for a few terrifying minutes until finally there was the sound of rasping breath, and he knew Olivia was alive. He'd heard her say where she was and that her head hurt, then her cell phone had disconnected. His heart lurched as he relived the moments when he'd thought she was dead.

He tried calling Olivia's cell phone again while he drove as fast as he dared over the curvy mountains road, but it went straight to voicemail. Bob O'Brian flashed his headlights behind him, reminding him to slow down, as he was coming up on some major 'S' curves. He forced himself to pay better attention, as getting into a wreck himself would definitely not help Olivia.

The two police cars had to slow down through the tiny town, but Josh pushed it as fast as he could without endangering anyone. *Hang on Olivia,* he thought. *I'm almost there. Just hang on.* Cold sweat beaded on his brow and his eyes were moist. *I can't lose you. We've just found each other.* He slammed his hand onto the steering wheel, relishing the pain—needing to drive away thoughts he couldn't bear to think.

As he drove, visions of Susan's pale lifeless face flashed before his eyes, only to be replaced by images of Olivia's face, covered in blood, her hazel eyes wide and sightless. *This can't be happening again,* he thought. *I can't lose Olivia too.*

He slowed at the light, then pushed through as soon as he was sure no one was in the way. He could see O'Brian right behind him. Only a couple more miles to the house. He heard another siren and saw flashing lights coming toward him and quickly called the dispatcher on the radio, confirming that Olivia was in the ambulance. He hung a U-turn and followed closely behind, grabbing the radio again.

"O'Brian, go on up to the wreck site and call for backup from the Birchwood force and check the house. I think we'll find that Cordell Salger and his crew may have been using this place as a hideout. Check the house and the grounds thoroughly. If James Hill is still alive, we need to find him before they get tired of schlepping him around and kill him. I'll be at the hospital. Keep me posted." Josh hung up the radio, and tried to relax his death grip on the steering wheel.

It seemed like hours, but they arrived at the hospital in just over ten minutes, pulling into the emergency entrance that was just for ambulances. The paramedics jumped out and lifted the stretcher out of the back and wheeled it inside as Josh ran up behind them.

Olivia's face was deathly pale under the blood. Josh saw her eyelids flutter as he grasped her hand, while walking alongside the stretcher.

"Liv, you're going to be okay," he said fiercely. "Just hang in there and you'll be fine. I'm here with you now."

He trotted along with the paramedics into an exam room. He flashed his Police ID at the nurse who tried to tell him he couldn't come in unless he was a relative. Being a cop definitely had its advantages and that was one he might miss when he left the force.

As a different nurse put a blood pressure cuff on Olivia's arm, Josh felt Olivia squeeze his hand slightly. Her eyes were open, but she looked disoriented. He squeezed back gently.

"It's okay sweetheart. They're just going to fix you up so you feel better."

A doctor came into the tiny curtained cubicle and told Josh that he would have to wait outside until they'd examined her, as there wasn't enough room for him, the doctor and her assistant. When Josh argued, she sympathetically agreed to let him back in as soon as they were done.

There was no one else in the little waiting room inside the checked-in area of the emergency room. As he was pacing, he walked behind the reception desk and saw that there were a few people in the outer waiting room. Stopping and attempting to relax, he looked at the available magazines, then tossed them back onto the table and resumed pacing.

Josh walked away from the desk, and called O'Brian to see what they'd found at the scene.

O'Brian informed him that they'd found an old summerhouse a short ways into the woods, where the trees were fairly young. There'd been a distinctly new looking trail through the weeds. Apparently Salger and his men had been using it as a hideout. O'Brian figured James must still be alive and had told them about the summerhouse or they'd never have found it.

"Boss, it also looks like they've been searching the big house for something. They knocked a couple holes in the walls and pulled up a few boards in the floor in one of the bedrooms." O'Brian stated. "It's lucky for James Hill or whoever owns it that Olivia came here and scared them off before they did too much damage. I'm really sorry she got hurt Lieu. I hope she's going to be okay."

"I hope so too Bob," Josh's voice came out huskier than usual. "She probably startled them and they rammed her car. It could have been just a hit and run and nothing to do with the house, but that's highly unlikely, so we need to go with our theory of Cordell Salger for now."

"You got it Boss, We've been dusting for prints and checking for DNA and any other clues they may have left behind. Hopefully we'll get something good, since they wouldn't have expected anyone to be here and probably weren't careful."

"Okay O'Brian, keep me posted." Josh hung up and walked back to peek into Olivia's exam room. It was still full of people, so he continued pacing. Flashbacks of his late wife Susan's death from the car wreck tormented him behind his eyes as he walked up and down the hall.

"Detective?" a woman's voice came from behind him.

Josh spun around to see the doctor smiling at him.

"She has a mild concussion and we are keeping her overnight to make sure everything is okay and there are no complications, but I think she's going to be just fine."

Josh let out a pent up breath, "Thank you doctor. Is she awake? Can I see her now?"

"She's awake, but is a little groggy right now. We gave her something for the pain and nausea, so she may be bit incoherent and sleepy." The doctor paused, "She's a pretty tough cookie. That was a hard knock she took on her head. Oh, be prepared for the extensive bruising on her face and don't scare her by looking like you've seen something awful. She won't appreciate it later," she grinned.

Josh smiled back, the relief at the good news flooding his system like a tidal wave, almost taking his knees out from under him. He shook the doctor's hand, and stepped into the cubicle.

She looked so little and defenseless lying there with her bandaged head and a monitor attached to her finger. Josh carefully smoothed her dark auburn curls back from her forehead away from the bandage. Her eyelids fluttered and opened groggily.

"Josh," she whispered. ". . . white panel truck . . .." Her eyes closed for a few seconds then struggled to open. ". . . at the house. . .." her voice faded out and her eyes closed. The pain killers were working.

Josh called Olivia's house on his cell phone to let Sally know what had happened and told her to ask Dave, the security guard to stay over in the guestroom Josh had slept in last night and to tell him that that Josh would make it worth his while to pull the overtime. When he'd hung up the phone, Josh pulled up a chair and sat beside Olivia, holding her hand while she slept.

~~~

The first thing Olivia saw when she woke up the next morning was Josh sleeping awkwardly in the chair with his head beside her on the bed still holding her hand. She fought to remember what had happened. Why was she in the hospital? She lifted her head slightly to look at Josh and a searing pain shot through her temple. She whimpered involuntarily and Josh immediately woke up.

"Livvie, are you okay?" he came to hold her gently. "Are you in pain? Should I call the nurse?"

She took a deep breath, letting it out slowly and keeping her head very still, which seemed to ease the pain. "I'm okay Josh; but my head hurts. What happened? Why can't I remember what happened?"

"You were in a car accident up on Old Candlewick Road just below the house we want to buy. Do you remember anything at all about the wreck?" Josh asked.

"Almost," Olivia winced as her head hurt from thinking. "I must have temporary amnesia. I thought I was going to remember something for a minute, but it was gone before I could grab it. Do you know what happened?"

"You called me on my cell, and right after I answered I heard a huge crashing of metal and glass. Scared me half to death because I couldn't hear you and didn't know if you were even alive," Josh stopped to take a deep breath. "I was so afraid I was going to lose you." He held her tenderly. "That was unthinkable."

Olivia smiled wanly. "My mom always said I was hard headed. I guess she was right."

Josh shook his head and let out a pent up breath. "You have no idea how glad I am for that."
~~~

Olivia laughed weakly, "You'd be the only one, besides me." She put a hand to her head and carefully touched the bandage. "Is the head bump the only thing wrong? After how much it hurt when I tried to move my head, I'm a little wary of moving anything else."

"It's just the head and a bit of whip lash, thankfully, and the doctor said that should heal up pretty quickly—hopefully the concussion and amnesia will too, though she said you were out for so long that she wants to keep you here one more night for observation."

Olivia closed her eyes for a couple of minutes, then they shot open, "Josh, there was a white panel truck. The tag was from New Hampshire, number HJH2124 It was at the top of the driveway when I started up. I saw a guy heading toward it, then he saw me and ran toward the back of the house, and I started backing down the driveway as fast as I could, but before I could get turned into the road I could see him barreling down the driveway straight at me," she paused. "I remember one-touch dialing you then nothing after that."

"You remembered!" Josh smiled and hugged her. "I can't believe you even got the license tag number. You would have been a phenomenal cop."

"It just came all of a sudden like a movie and I saw it all happening again," she sighed. "I still don't remember the actual crash."

"That may be a good thing sweetheart. I almost wish I could forget hearing it. I'm going to go call O'Brian and get them out looking for this truck. You're the best!" Josh kissed her, then grinned and stepped into the hall to call O'Brian.

He was still grinning when he came back into the room.

"Well, Vicki and Andrew will be happy. The stolen highboy was in the summerhouse up on Candlewick, and it wasn't even damaged. They'd opened the secret compartment, and I have a feeling they were not happy to find it empty." Josh sobered. "I hope they didn't take their anger out on James."

"Olivia grimaced, "I just hope he is still alive and in one piece. These guys play pretty rough." She put her hands out to indicate the hospital room.

"Yes they do," Josh agreed. "We need to get them out of commission ASAP. I've got the guys working on the truck angle now and hopefully we'll get a break in the case soon." He smiled at her, "That was a fabulous thing you did, remembering the tag number while fleeing for your life backwards down the hill. I am seriously impressed."

"Josh, are Jimmy and Sally okay at my house? Are Molly and Sheyna doing okay? Dave is still there right?"

"Yes, he is staying in the house, in 'my' room," he laughed, as he made finger quotes in the air. "He is beyond pleased with the arrangement, since Sally is happily cooking all of his meals for him. We may have a hard time getting rid of him once the case is solved."

Olivia smiled, "As long as he is keeping everyone safe, he is welcome to stay. I'm sure Sally is enjoying having another mouth to feed. I really miss Molly and Sheyna."

"The doctor said that as long as you are still doing well, you can go home tomorrow. She doesn't think it was a serious injury. Your CAT scan looked normal."

She sighed, "That's good, but I still wish I could go home now. If my head didn't hurt so much, I would ask them to let me leave early."

"Well, it hurts for a reason. You need to rest and heal and stop worrying so much," Josh smiled and kissed her head gently above the bandage. "Do you want me to stay with you tonight?"

"I'd love to have you stay with me, but I'd rather you stayed with the girls and Sally and Jimmy. Even with Dave there, I'd feel safer if they were with you too," she smiled. "I'm perfectly fine here with the nurses and doctors to take care of me. I'll probably just sleep and be otherwise boring anyway."

Josh laughed, "You'd have a really hard time boring me sweetheart, even sleeping. I'll stay at your house tonight then and come to pick you up in the morning when they discharge you." Josh laughed, "I just realized, I'll be sleeping on the couch since I gave Dave the guestroom I've been staying in."

He leaned over and kissed her and as she put her arms around him, they clung to each other for a moment, both feeling grateful that they still could.

~~~

As soon as the doctor left the room the next morning, Olivia called Josh to let him know she'd be ready to go once they'd finished their paperwork on her discharge.

Her head felt better this morning, but she was still a little woozy when she stood up. The doctor had pronounced her free to go as long as she promised not to overdo it. For a 'Get out of the hospital free card', she was happy to promise almost anything.
~~~

"I heard your wreck happened up by the old Candlewick House," the sixtyish nurse said as she came in to give Olivia some prescriptions and the rest of her discharge papers. "I didn't think anybody even went up there anymore since Edna Hill passed. Most people think the place is haunted or cursed."

"Is the house called Candlewick?" Olivia asked wonderingly. "What a pretty name for it. I guess it is because of the road." She tilted her head, "I wonder why they think it's haunted?"

"No, the house was called Candlewick before the road was. It used to be such a showplace when the Hills lived there. They had huge parties for all the big holidays and invited the whole town," she smiled as she remembered. "I was just a teenager, but I loved those parties—we all did. I danced with my late husband Barton, right there on the front lawn of Candlewick—had my first kiss there that night too. It was the saddest thing when she died. Old Jack Hill just seemed to change overnight without his wife," she paused to reflect. "He went from being a kind, fun loving and generous person to a shell of a man, not wanting anything to do with anyone—not even his own children. Her death is the reason people say it's haunted. There've been tales of folks seeing her ghost." She shook her head sadly.

"How did she die?" Olivia asked.

"She fell down the basement stairs and broke her neck. It was such a tragedy for the family and for the whole town. We all loved Edna. She may have been rich, but she didn't act all hoity-toity like a lot of the rich folks do. She treated us all like we were just as good as she was. Jack did too until Edna died, then he didn't like anybody, rich or poor."

"Wow, that is so sad," Olivia said. "I'd never heard the story before. Is that why Jack moved to the other house?"

The grey haired nurse nodded, "I think he just couldn't be in that house anymore . . . where she died." She paused, "They never could figure out why she was going down in the basement that day. Jack said she didn't have any reason to be down there. She was supposed to have been getting ready to meet him in town for dinner. When she didn't show up, and he couldn't reach her on the phone, he went home and found the basement door open and Edna lying dead at the bottom of the stairs. It still breaks my heart to think of him finding her like that. She was the love of his life." She dabbed her eyes.

Tears prickled behind Olivia's eyes too as she pictured the old man finding his wife's broken and lifeless body. She couldn't imagine the pain of finding Josh like that.

"Was there any question about whether she'd fallen or if someone had maybe pushed her?" Olivia asked tentatively, a little afraid of causing her to stop talking.

"There was a lot of talk," she lowered her voice slightly, "just rumors. A couple of the servants were saying that someone who worked for the Hills had been seen searching the house for something more than once," she paused. "I'm not naming any names, as rumors are all they were. I will say that the ones they were talking about were a bad lot, so it wouldn't have surprised me if there was some truth in it. That's why people think the house is haunted, not only because she died there, but because she was murdered. You'd be hard pressed to find anyone who'd want to live there—that's probably one of the reasons why Jack never sold it."

Olivia glanced at the woman's name tag—Martha Garland. "I'm trying to find out more information about the Hills and the house. The son James is missing and I'm a friend of his son Jimmy, and Sally Tanner, Jimmy's grandmother," she explained. "Would it be okay if I came and asked you more questions if I think of them later? It may be that something from the past is relevant to James' disappearance."

"I guess that would be okay," the nurse said. "I'm not sure how much more I can tell you, but you're welcome to ask if you have more questions," she looked pensive. "I felt sorry for James and Jenny after their mother died. Their father just closed himself off like they didn't exist. James was about twelve then. Jenny tried to be mother and father to him after that, but she was only two years older than he was and was pretty lost herself. James started running with a rough bunch of kids after his mother died, doing drugs and getting into bits of trouble. Is it something to do with all of that, that caused him to disappear now?"

"I think it probably is, yes," Olivia said sadly. "Do you know who any of the kids he was hanging out with were?"

"I can't remember their names offhand, but there were three or four boys and a girl he was running with, all closer to Jenny's age. The one boy was even a few years older than Jenny. They were up to a lot of petty mischief mostly, but some people thought they were behind a few worse things, like vandalism of the school and some burglaries, but they didn't get caught at it, so who knows?"

"If you happen to remember any of the names, I'd be grateful if you'd let me know." Olivia handed her one of her business cards. "Please don't mention any of this to anyone. We think James is in danger and it might be worse if people were talking about it."

"I won't say a word. I always liked both the kids when they were younger and felt bad for how he turned out. Jenny at least, did okay with her life, but poor James on the other hand . . .."

"Thank you so much for talking to me about them. It may help us to find James." Olivia folded the discharge papers the nurse had given her and put them in her purse.

"You're welcome. Anything I can do to help, just ask." She smiled as she left the room.

Olivia sat back down to wait, but Josh walked in before she even had a chance to cross her legs. She stood up and hugged him.

"Hi, sweetheart, thanks for picking me up."

Josh kissed her, "I am so glad to be picking you up, you have no idea!" He laughed. "Molly and Sheyna will be happy too, not to mention Sally and Jimmy."

"Oh, speaking of Jimmy, isn't his surgery scheduled for tomorrow?"

Josh nodded as he helped her into the required wheelchair to push her out to her SUV which he was driving.

"Yes, he is excited and a little nervous I think. Sally is beside herself with both, excitement and worry," he chuckled, "Molly and Sheyna are the only ones not acting a little loony right now. Sally put the sugar in the fridge and the eggs in the pantry this morning—it's a good thing I noticed, because the smell of rotten eggs is brutal."

Olivia laughed, "Oh my, she must be worried to do that . . . I feel for both of them—operations are always a bit scary. I know the doctor you got for the surgery is one of the best in the country, so everything should be fine, not that I'm not a little worried myself."

Josh pushed her wheelchair out the door after they made sure she had everything. They were alone in the hallway and Josh knelt and kissed her.

"You are the most wonderful part of my life. Please don't ever get hurt like this again," he cupped her face in his hands. "Sometimes I'm not sure about the detective agency we're planning. I don't think I could stand losing you."

She kissed him back, ignoring the pain in her head from leaning back. "I'm planning to be very hard for you to lose. Josh, don't let this scare you out of doing what we want to do. Something like this could have happened even if we weren't investigating. I was there to look at the house we want to buy, not hunting for criminals."

Josh sighed and rose to push her down the hall. "You're right. I've just not been so afraid in a very long time." They turned the corner into the lobby of the hospital and he waited for the automatic doors to open before pushing her into the parking lot and up to the SUV.

"I'm sorry to have worried you so, Josh. I can imagine how it must have felt after losing Susan in a car wreck." Olivia hugged him tightly as she got up to climb into the vehicle. "You're not going to lose me, and I'm not going to lose you either. We won't let it happen."

They held each other for a moment, then Josh helped her into the car and closed the door.

"I'm going to stop and pick up some takeout food from the Thai place on the way home. I already called it in, so it should be ready," Josh said as he got behind the wheel. I'm hoping to create a relaxing evening for you, and for Sally and Jimmy too. Sally was already baking up a storm when I left the house, so she can live without cooking lunch too," he smiled. "I would imagine you will be glad to get some non-hospital food into your mouth after being stuck with the stuff they serve there."

"You know it!" Olivia laughed. "Yuck. Hospital food even smells disgusting. I am rather hungry, now that you mention it." She took his hand and leaned back. "I missed you Josh."

Josh smiled at her and brought her hand to his lips, kissing her palm sensually without taking his eyes off the road.

"I missed you too sweetheart—more than you can imagine."

She sighed contentedly, caressing his face with her hand.

Josh parked and went inside to get the food. Olivia idly looked out the tinted window of the SUV while she waited.

It was a chilly day with a hint of snow in the air and she could see a lot of people in the village shopping, probably for holiday gifts. As her mind was wandering over what to buy Josh for Christmas, she saw her best friend Abby walking down the street on the other side, so she rolled down the window and yelled to her.

Abby ran across the road, narrowly avoiding a poor unsuspecting bicyclist who fought to control his bike while shooting her dirty looks. Abby threw her hands over her chest in a gesture of apology and he wobbled, but kept going, shaking his head.

"Oops," Abby said, looking embarrassed. "I almost creamed that poor guy. "Well, it does say pedestrians have the right of way, but yikes!" she laughed. "We all know how dangerous I can be, even on foot."

Olivia got out and hugged her friend. "It's great to see you. Ooh, I love that coat. When did you get it?"

"I just found it the other day on sale and had to snag it. It doesn't clash with my hair. Isn't that amazing?" she laughed.

"Your hair is gorgeous and you know full well it doesn't clash with much at all . . . only a few colors that aren't that attractive anyway." Olivia said staunchly, smiling at her friend.

"Well, at least you know what I go through, even though your hair is more brown than red, it's still got enough red to cause major fashion clashes once in a while." Abby laughed. "Remember that bright orange and white sweater my mom knitted for you for Christmas because she thought it would be nice with your reddish brown hair, even though she and I can't wear that color?"

Olivia laughed, "I will always remember the look on her face when I tried it on. I felt so sorry for her. She'd put so much work into it and it looked absolutely hideous on me. It went even worse with my hair than it did with yours. She looked devastated, but tried so hard to act like it was no big deal. Your mom is a total sweetheart."

"Hey, what happened to your face and head? I almost missed seeing the bandage you have sticking out from under your hat, and those sunglasses are doing a good job of hiding your poor scratched and bruised face." Abby looked concerned. "Did you take a fall on the ice?"

"No, I was in a car wreck, but I am okay. I'll tell you all about it over dinner next week if you'll come," Olivia smiled, blithely changing the subject. "There is someone we wanted to introduce you to."

"Uh oh, you mean like a blind date?" Abby put her hands in front of her to ward off evil. "The last blind date I went on was way too memorable for me to want to do that again."

"Come on Abs, he's a really nice guy. Very good looking in a slightly scary sort of way, but he's not scary at all, or weird or anything. He's just really nice and I think you'll like him." Olivia coaxed. "Look, if you don't like him, we'll all be at the restaurant together and you can let me know when we go to the restroom or something. Then we can make an early night of it when we're done eating and all leave together so you're not stuck with him."

Abby made a face, "How do I always let myself get talked into these things? I should know better." She laughed, "All right, this is the last time though . . . and if he's a creep or I just don't like him, we leave right after we're done eating, right?"

"You've got it!" Olivia beamed. "You've heard me talk about Tiny, right? He was involved in the murder investigation a couple months ago. He's a big, tough looking biker with tattoos and leather, but he's the sweetest guy and I think you two might just hit it off really well."

"Well, I do like guys with a few tattoos, and leather looks pretty great on a guy that knows how to wear it." Abby looked a bit more interested. "Is he muscular, or just big?"

Olivia laughed, "I didn't feel him up Abs, but yes, I think he's built quite nicely and not at all hard on the eyes. He looks more like a biker you'd see posing for a calendar, than one you'd see guzzling beer in a parking lot."

Josh walked up carrying bags of steaming hot take-out food with tantalizing aromas that made Olivia's stomach rumble audibly.

She laughed, "Gee, I knew I was a little hungry, but that was just way too loud." She took the bags from Josh and put them in the back seat, as he hugged Abby.

"How have you been Abby? Did this wild woman tell you what dangerous escapades she's been having?" Josh looked teasingly at Olivia.

"Only that she was in a wreck and that she's been busy trying to set me up with her friend Tiny," Abby laughed. "She promised to tell me all about the wreck at dinner, so I agreed to a blind date because of bribery or extortion, whichever that was."

"That would have been bribery, but since you aren't an elected official, I'll let you both slide on it." Josh chuckled.

Olivia laughed and put her arm around Josh. "You'd better let us slide sweetheart, because I think you might be more than a little complicit in this one yourself."

He hugged her, "There is that. So Abby, I take it we will be all having dinner together next week. It'll be fun and I'm looking forward to getting to know you and Tiny both a little better, so it isn't only a matchmaking event."

"I'm looking forward to that part too, and who knows, maybe Tiny will turn out to be a friend at least, if nothing else happens, since you both like him so much." Abby grinned. "You can never have too many friends."

"We should get the food home before Mrs. Tanner and Jimmy starve on us," Olivia said, hugging Abby again. "I can't wait for our dinner together. Oh, and speaking of dinner, Can you and your mom come for Christmas dinner, and can you fix your famous turkey for the meat eaters as usual?"

"Definitely!" Abby grinned. "Do you think I'd miss our holiday dinner if I could help it? I'll bring the turkey and cook it at your house as usual, so what else can I bring?"

"Just yourself and your mom." Olivia smiled, getting into the SUV. "I'll pick up the things for the stuffing and get it all ready for you to put half of it in the turkey. I'll make the other half vegetarian. Sally Tanner is baking pies, and I've got the rest covered."

"Call me when you have the dinner scheduled with Tiny, if he wants to go." Abby waved and darted back across the street, taking care not to scare any cyclists this time.

Olivia and Josh laughed as he got behind the wheel.

"Abby is so much fun," Olivia said, still chuckling.

"I can see that. I really am looking forward to getting to know her . . . and Tiny too. He seems like a great person, very courageous too."

"Ooh, it's snowing," Olivia smiled in delight. "Not sleeting, raining or wintry-mixing, but actually snowing."

Josh grinned at her enthusiasm, "I think I will grill veggies and veggie burgers on the patio grill tonight and we can all eat dinner in front of the fireplace and have some hot cocoa afterwards and maybe play Monopoly or something to help Jimmy and Sally relax." He squeezed her hand, "We can look out the sliding glass doors and watch the snow falling against the holiday lights outside."

"It sounds wonderful and very romantic."

"Livvie, tomorrow I want to take you to the house so you can look around again if you feel up to it. I know you didn't get a chance to see it the other day with Salger and his guys there."

"Oh Josh, I was talking to the discharge nurse this morning and she told me a lot of information about that house, including its name. It is called Candlewick, like the road," Olivia said in excitement. "Jack Hill's wife was named Edna, and it's possible that she was murdered. Though it was ruled accidental at the time, there were a lot of rumors and many people thought an employee may have pushed her down the basement stairs. The nurse said that other employees had seen a certain employee searching the house more than once, apparently looking for something they thought was hidden there. I wonder if it was the shoe bank."

"Why did they think this employee might have killed her?" Josh asked.

"I'm not sure Josh. The nurse just said there were a lot of rumors running around about it and the other workers seemed to suspect that one of them had pushed her. Maybe she surprised the person while they were searching and they panicked? Do you think you could get hold of the old police files from back then? It was almost thirteen years ago now."

Josh nodded slowly, "If they are still around, I'll check them out and bring them home. It would be interesting to see if there is anything about who the workers suspected, and what people thought they were searching for." He looked thoughtful, "It's possible that it was just idle rumors you know, so don't get too wrapped up in that theory yet, until we know more. If that little bank is worth as much as Vicki thinks it is, it's not hard to imagine two people being murdered over it though, unfortunately."

"Josh, if that's true, Jenny and her mom were both murdered and maybe James too. Is someone killing off the whole family, one by one for a stupid toy bank?" Olivia shook her head. "That's insane. I love antiques, but none of them are worth killing over."

Josh sighed, "It is insane. Some people are so driven by an obsession with money or possessions that nothing else matters to them."

"What I don't understand is that if someone killed Edna, it couldn't have been Cordell Salger. He would have just been a teenager then." She paused to reflect, "I suppose a teenager could have done it actually, but would he have been working at the mansion then? If he's Jenny's age, he'd have been fourteen or fifteen back then. Do you know who his parents are? Maybe they were working there."

"His father, Frank Cordell, Sr. died several years ago and his mom, Wendy moved away shortly after that. We haven't been able to track her down yet to see what she can tell us about her son. She never left a forwarding address and until now, we hadn't had a reason to wonder about her. Frank had been in trouble with the law a few times before he died and Wendy was arrested for shoplifting a couple of times. The whole family seemed to think they were owed something by everyone else and weren't above stealing, cheating or brawling to get it." Josh looked disgusted. "It seems Cordell is just following along in Daddy and Mommy's footsteps. I'll look into who was working on the estate back then and see if they were on the list of suspects."

Josh pulled into Olivia's driveway and got out and opened the door for her, then as she retrieved her little overnight bag he'd taken to the hospital for her, he took the bags of Thai food from the backseat and closed the car doors.

CHAPTER EIGHT

Sally Tanner opened the front door before they even reached it and enveloped Olivia in a warm hug.

"I am so happy to see you back and looking so well, Olivia. Your man here was beside himself with worry," her eyes twinkled. "Jimmy and I were pretty worried too, but after he saw you yesterday, Josh insisted that you were doing well and that we should stay here and wait to see you instead of coming to the hospital," Sally was her usual talkative self. "Oh, while you were gone, Josh, I answered the house phone and the hospital called to say that Jimmy's surgery was postponed until Thursday next week, because the doctor has been delayed due to an emergency in his family and he isn't arriving until the evening of next Tuesday. They said he needs to have a whole day here to go over everything with the other doctor and be ready."

"Thanks Sally, I'll give them a call after lunch to make sure they'll have it all together." Josh smiled.

Josh set the food on the table and Olivia put out plates and silverware. Jimmy and Sally hadn't had Thai food before and they both enjoyed it. Olivia had added it to her list of favorite foods a while back, and, you could tell Josh liked it from the occasional expressions of bliss that crossed his face as he chewed.

"Josh, I'm feeling much better now, after the real food and the pain pills. Do you think we could go out to Candlewick House today?" Olivia asked. "I am not sure I'm up to driving there yet, but since you took the day off work, would you mind taking us all up there? I'd love for Sally and Jimmy to see it too. We can take Molly and Sheyna and walk them on lead."

"That is a great idea, as long as you're sure you feel up to it. I want to see that summerhouse, as well as the damage done to the main house."

"As soon as I get the kitchen cleaned up, we can go then."

Josh laughed, "Do you seriously think we're going to let you clean the kitchen? I'm agreeing to going for a drive and little walk around the house, because I know it will be enjoyable and relaxing for you, especially as curious as you are about the house, but you are supposed to be resting and healing, not doing housework." He got up and stood behind her, leaning to kiss the nape of her neck. "Let me help you upstairs so you can get ready, then I will clean the kitchen." He looked up and grinned, "No Sally, you're not cleaning today either. Just relax and enjoy the day. It is now an official holiday for women and children in this house."

He walked Olivia up the stairs, and they snuck in a few kisses once they were alone and out of sight at the top.

"Yell down if you're ready to come down before I come back up. I don't feel comfortable with you on the stairs alone yet," he kissed her again and closed her door so she could change.

Olivia looked at her bandaged head in the vanity mirror, tried on a couple of different scarves, then decided to go back to the hat she'd worn home from the hospital, as it was comfortable and hid most of the bandage. Much of her face was a lovely shade of purple, with some beautiful bright red scratches and cuts highlighting it. The oversized sunglasses hid the worst of it, but she still looked like she'd lost a fight with the Whomping Willow from the Harry Potter movies. Truth be told, she felt like it too—her neck and back were very stiff and sore, but there was no way she was telling Josh that, because she was dying to see Candlewick again.

Finally dressed in a comfortable pair of faded, slightly ripped blue jeans and a soft fleecy aqua colored top, Olivia put on warm socks and her snow boots and opened her bedroom door. Josh wasn't upstairs yet, so she decided to write a list of Christmas presents she needed to get for various people while she waited.

There was Josh of course, and she was having a really hard time figuring out the right present for him. She'd never before had to shop for someone who could afford to buy half the town if he wanted to. It was proving to be a challenge.

For Sally Tanner, she was thinking of a nice set of vintage solid copper baking molds or Jello molds and cookie cutters that she'd seen in a little antique shop in town. The molds would look adorable hanging in Sally's kitchen and she was sure they would get plenty of use as cake molds.

She had been trying to put together a really nice art set that contained pencils, pastels, charcoals, acrylic paints and some large notebook style art paper for Jimmy to draw on. She wrote 'canvasses' on the list for Jimmy as well. For a five year old, he was a pretty amazing artist, and she thought he would only get better and better.

Her pen paused, what on earth should she do about Josh's father? Josh had been trying to arrange for them to meet, but so far, she and Josh had just had way too many things going on lately. She decided to ask him if he thought it would be appropriate and a good idea to invite his dad to come up for Christmas.

Wow, she thought, *how can I put him up here in this little house when he is used to a mansion on Lantern Knoll? He will think Josh is marrying a pauper. Hmm, I guess he is, relatively speaking.* She sighed then shook herself. *You already figured out that his dad is not like that. He isn't going to judge you for not having tons of money, so get over it.*

She wrote Abby's name, then stopped and chewed on her eraser for a moment. "Oh, I know," she muttered to herself, "I'll get her that gorgeous old Tiffany style stained glass lamp I saw last week in Littleton if it's still there."

"You know what they say about talking to yourself, right?" Josh grinned from the doorway. "Did I ever tell you how adorable you are?"

Olivia smiled, "You did, but you're welcome to tell me that anytime, as long as you don't mind me saying the same thing about you. I totally, madly adore you, Joshua Abrams." She stood carefully and kissed him, wrapping her arms around his neck.

He gently lifted her into his arms and kissed her back, leaning against the doorframe. Molly ran into the room and sat in front of them on her haunches, lifting her front paws in the air. Josh laughed and set Olivia down so they could both hug Molly.

"You want to be in on all the hugs, don't you Molly?" Josh asked scratching her behind the ears. She woofed her agreement and wagged her tail contentedly.

Olivia knelt to kiss her on the nose, then rose carefully, not letting on that the change of position had made her slightly dizzy.

Josh put his arm around her and they walked down the stairs with Molly prancing ahead of them excitedly, seeming to know they were taking her somewhere.

Sally and Jimmy were already sitting in the kitchen waiting for them. Sally had packed a little basket with cookies and a thermos of hot cocoa for them to take with them in case anyone got hungry.

They all took warm jackets and Olivia put Molly's and Sheyna's harnesses on them, so they'd be all ready to just snap on their leads when they arrived at Candlewick.

It was still snowing lightly and the roads were a little slick, so Josh drove carefully, keeping his distance from other cars and they arrived without mishap. The snow in the long winding driveway was untouched, and Josh and Olivia both sighed in relief that there didn't seem to be anyone at the house. Josh might have loved a chance to catch Cordell Salger and his crew, but not with Olivia, Sally and Jimmy in the car.

Sally and Jimmy were in awe of the huge mansion. Even in its dilapidated state, it was a stunning place, and with the newly fallen snow, it had been transformed into a slightly spooky and mysterious fairyland.

Josh told the others to wait for a minute while he checked to make sure there wasn't anyone hiding in the house or in the summerhouse. He motioned that it was safe to come out, as he came back and opened the doors for Olivia and Sally.

They snapped the leads on Molly and Sheyna and everyone headed toward the house. Even though it was technically still a crime scene, the police were finished with it, and Josh decided to allow them all to go inside the house with him, since it had been processed, explaining that even though the house had already been dusted for fingerprints and thoroughly checked out, they were to be very careful not to touch anything, and they were to stay with him. Sally explained it to Jimmy in their own special sign language. Josh handed out latex gloves to everyone so that just in case they inadvertently touched something they wouldn't leave their prints.

It was the first time Olivia had been inside the huge mansion and she was a bit awestruck. The foyer was as big as her bedroom and she could see a delicate Victorian loveseat with intricately carved legs sticking out from under a drop cloth and a sweet little Victorian table with two lamps on the other side of the foyer. There was a stunning, though dusty and cobweb covered crystal chandelier hanging overhead. The floor was granite and marble in a beautiful star pattern leading into an absolutely awe inspiring double staircase that curved to form an upside down U, meeting at the top. Between the two sides of the staircase, she could see through to what was probably the living room with more drop cloth shrouded furniture.

Olivia felt as though she'd been transported to the middle of a Victorian romantic suspense novel. She glanced at Josh to see if he had somehow turned into a nineteenth century lord of the manor, but was relieved to see her handsome fiancé looked like his normal self. Of course she had always thought that he looked like a lordly type of man anyway, but at least his clothes were still from the twenty-first century.

Sally and Jimmy stood in hushed awe as well.

Josh broke the silence with a sneeze.

Olivia laughed, "Yes, as stunning as it is, there's definitely a lot of dust in here. It needs a major cleaning job and I would so love to be the one to tackle it." She looked at Sally, "When we find James, do you think he would be willing to sell this house to us?"

Sally was still gaping at the magnificent chandelier over her head.

"Yes, I do," she said coming back to earth. "James has never been into this sort of life. He grew up wealthy, but after his mother died he just wanted to leave it all behind him and I don't think he ever looked back. He seemed to partly blame her death on being wealthy. He'd sell it in a heartbeat, is what I think."

Olivia took Josh's hand and he hugged her. The four wandered through the spooky hallway, past the stairs and into the living room beyond. Every chair and loveseat was covered with drop cloths, but Olivia could tell that the furniture was high quality and probably all antique, just from lifting a corner of the cloths to peek under a couple of them.

She admired the gorgeous fireplace on one wall with the buildout and cladding made from beautiful glittery mica infused river rock and the hearth and mantle from flagstones. There were paintings under cloths on the walls, and beautiful dainty figurines graced the inside of a large glass enclosed curio cabinet. Olivia was completely enchanted.

Josh's eyes twinkled at Olivia's rapturous expression as he led them into the dining room, complete with huge wooden table and gracefully carved wooden chairs, all shrouded in the ubiquitous drop cloths. Another lovely fireplace inhabited part of one wall. Olivia spotted what she was sure was a genuine Tiffany lamp hanging over the table. She was amazed that it hadn't been stolen by Salger and his cohorts.

"Oh Josh, I have no words!" she gasped. "This house is like something out of a dream I had when I was a little girl—where I was a princess, living in a great castle." She twirled around laughing and fell into Josh's arms, hiding the wince from the pain that her impromptu spin had caused her abused neck and back muscles.

"I think I remember having that same dream when I was a child," Sally laughed. "Probably most kids that didn't grow up wealthy had it at one time or another."

Josh chuckled, "Well, having grown up as a rich kid, I never really had that one, but I know I was one of the lucky ones. My parents were rich, but they never let me feel like I didn't have to work or that I was better than the kids who weren't rich." He smiled, "I didn't always appreciate that when I was a kid, but I am so grateful now that I was made to have a strong work ethic, and not allowed to feel like I was entitled because my family had money. Many of the kids I grew up with weren't so lucky, and at least a couple of them are now such pompous, pretentious adults that I can't stand being around them."

Olivia laughed, "I think I may have met them when I was teaching at the ski slopes. There were a couple of people like that now and then." She sobered, "Seriously though, it really is sad when people teach their children to feel either superior or inferior to others, for any reason. We're all human and doing the best we can to make it through life. Josh, I am so glad you had great parents." She hugged him again.

Sally smiled, "You really were lucky Josh. Growing up in a wealthy family can be a wonderful thing, but all too frequently, it is the exact opposite."

Josh nodded his head, "There were a lot of fantastic experiences I had because we were wealthy, but even I had a few not so nice ones. The prejudice runs both ways. It took a lot of difficult explanations from my mom and dad to help me understand why some kids hated me and were cruel to me just because I had money."

Jimmy jumped up and down suddenly, smiling brightly. He motioned to his grandmother and she smiled and motioned back.

"He left his art notebook and pencils in the car, and wants to get them so he can draw the house," Sally explained. "I'll just run and get them and be right back." She told Jimmy in their special sign language to wait with Josh and Olivia, and walked quickly toward the front door.

Josh, Olivia, Jimmy, Molly and Sheyna moved on into the kitchen. It was just as elegant and beautiful as the rest of the house, though Olivia could tell that some of the appliances were outdated and might need repair or even replacement, depending on their working condition.

The kitchen, though a bit old fashioned, was large, and Olivia could so easily imagine herself cooking huge festive holiday dinners in it. Maybe she and Josh could bring back the tradition that Edna and Jack Hill had kept many years ago, of inviting the whole town for an outdoor Christmas party.

She ran her fingers over the dusty white marble topped counter and pictured it all sparkling clean and a matching island in the center of the kitchen with extra storage inside it and a couple of chairs on the other side so she and Josh could sit and eat breakfast while looking out the large windows at the spacious backyard.

Sally came in carrying Jimmy's notebook and the little box with his pencils and he grinned broadly. He took them from her and motioned that he wanted to draw in the dining room.

"Sally, would you mind staying with him, as I really can't leave him unsupervised because of my job? I'll show Livvie the rest of the house then one of us can watch Jimmy while the other takes you around." Josh looked slightly awkward asking.

"I understand perfectly, Josh," she smiled. "There's no need to even ask. You are already doing more than you should by letting us come in, and I'm grateful that we got to see it. Jimmy doesn't know this belongs to his family, but maybe someday he will."

Olivia hugged her, and followed Josh into the stunning library. Three walls were covered in floor to ceiling bookshelves, with a movable ladder on wheels attached to each wall of shelves. Some of the shelves were enclosed in ornate beveled glass doors. Almost every shelf was filled with books.

Olivia gasped to see so many books in one place. "Josh I think there are more books here than in the whole North Conway Library, and there are a fair number in there. This is incredible!" She walked around the room reverently, "I'll bet most of these Classics behind the glass are First Editions."

Josh was checking out the rest of the room, "You know, I think you're probably right. This room, so far is the only one without a fireplace. It seems to have centrally controlled air and heat, and they most likely had it regulated to best suit the books." He smiled, "My parents had their libraries set up like that too. They didn't want the smoke and humidity getting to the rare books and causing damage. My dad has an electric fake fireplace in his libraries, both at home and on the island too, now that look pretty real and lend a cozy atmosphere without hurting the books."

They wandered into the den next. It looked like it would be a very comfortable room in which to read if the drop cloths were removed and the place cleaned up. Another fireplace, though this one, as well as the whole wall into which it was built was red brick. The cladding was of beige colored flagstones. Josh seemed to be awed by the pair of antique snowshoes hanging above it in an upside down V shape, and Olivia loved that they had placed a large wreath of dried flowers in the center between the lower part of them. The other three walls were covered in white tongue and groove paneling. One side of the room was designed more as a game room, with a pool table under another Tiffany hanging lamp.

Sheyna leapt onto the drop cloth that covered the pool table and meowed loudly. Josh laughed and picked her up. She leaned against his chest and purred.

"Josh, the Hills must have been so happy here—before the tragedy. I feel so bad for James and Jenny, and for their father too. Edna's death must have completely broken him," Olivia's face looked troubled. "Such a horribly sad thing to happen. I hope we can find James, and then maybe somehow Jimmy and Sally can rescue him from himself."

"If anyone can save him emotionally, I think those two could do it, but I wouldn't get my hopes up too high. Drug addiction as bad as his apparently is, is really hard to cure." Josh said somberly. "Remember that he basically cut all ties with his son and Mother-in-Law."

"I know, Josh, and I also know it wouldn't be easy, but people can change and they can start over and make it, so I'm not giving up hope for him yet." Olivia said staunchly. "He may surprise everyone."

Josh hugged her as tightly as he could without hurting her, "And that is one of the many reasons I love you so much."

Olivia hugged him back, then holding his hand, she led the way back through the house to the foyer, smiling at Sally, who was sitting next to Jimmy on a drop cloth covered dining room chair, watching him sketch.

CHAPTER NINE

Josh carried Sheyna, and Olivia held Molly's lead as they ascended the left side of the staircase, marveling at the gracefully carved wooden banister. When they reached the top where the banister curved to form the bottom of the U shape joining the other staircase, they stood for a moment, looking down into the foyer from the small balcony.

"It's so beautiful the way the stained glass side lights of the door reflect little rainbows of color all over the room," Olivia breathed in delight. "I didn't notice it when we came in. I guess the sun wasn't in the right place, but oh my, look at it now."

"It's beautiful," Josh agreed. "This house is so lovely and was obviously built well and with wonderfully imaginative forethought. It is a shame to see it so neglected. If we are able to buy it, it'll be great to restore it to the happy, well loved home it once was."

He led the way to the left of the stairs along the straight part of the balcony, and opened the first door they came to. It was dark inside, so Josh strode across the room and opened the dusty curtains to reveal a teak four poster bed, with an enormous drop cloth covering most of it. He lifted one corner of the cloth carefully to find that it was beautifully carved.

"I wonder if this was Jenny's or James' room as a child, or if it was a guestroom?" Olivia mused aloud. She peered into the closet and the bathroom. "Hmm, I think it looks too small to have belonged to a family member in this huge house, so I am guessing that it was a guestroom." She laughed, "It's still bigger than my master bedroom at home."

Molly woofed her agreement, sniffing around the inside of the closet, and Olivia and Josh both chuckled.

They moved on to the next bedroom which was near the end of the balcony. As soon as they stepped inside, and Josh had opened the curtains, it was obvious that this room had belonged to Jenny. The drop cloth that covered the white canopy bed had slipped a little, showing a slightly moth-eaten filmy material that had once been a gorgeous faded pink canopy. The white wooden bed looked to be in perfect condition, and Olivia touched one of the posts with reverent fingers.

"I can barely picture Jenny as the little girl who lived in this fairy tale room, all pink and white and girly." Olivia sighed sadly. Poor Jenny, she'd gone from being a beautiful little princess to a scared, shy little mouse of a woman, who'd been murdered over an antique toy from her childhood, that hadn't even belonged to her.

Josh was wandering through the huge bedroom, when he stopped and called to Olivia. She walked over to see what he had found.

On the drop cloth covered nightstand was what had to be an old picture of Jenny and James with their parents. All four were smiling brightly. Jenny was about thirteen and James about eleven.

"This must have been taken shortly before Edna died," Josh said. "They all look so happy."

Olivia sighed as she took the picture from Josh. "Aww, they really did look happy. I would never have recognized Jenny." She wiped the picture with her sleeve. "She and James both look full of life and confidence here, and Jack and Edna look so proud. You can tell they were a loving family. How could even Edna's death have changed Jack so drastically that he emotionally abandoned his kids after that?"

Josh was thoughtful, "I wonder if he knew something about it that he never told anyone, or if someone threatened him."

"Was he feeling guilty because he wasn't there to protect her?" Olivia sighed again. "There are so many possibilities for his actions. The only person that is hopefully still living, that might know and tell us is James. We have to find him, then we might have a good chance of unraveling this mystery as well as catching Jenny's killers."

Olivia asked Josh if he could keep the picture for a while, and maybe make a photocopy so Jimmy could have it someday.

He agreed to make a copy, since the crime scene had already been processed. He put it in his coat pocket and retrieved Sheyna from the top of the canopy where she had climbed to peer down at them while the tattered silks fluttered around her like Rapunzel's flowing tresses. She purred as he scratched her ears.

The human and animal foursome left Jenny's old room and passed the guest room, then crossed the staircase they'd come up earlier and the intersecting hallway between the two staircases, then finally crossed the top of the other staircase and entered what turned out to be another guestroom. It was fairly similar to the first one, so they didn't spend time looking around much, but headed on to the next door off the balcony.

The master suite was even larger than Jenny's room had been, and the master bath was enormous. Olivia loved the bathroom. There was a separate room with a Jacuzzi that she thought would be incredibly romantic, not to mention how good it would feel to her sore muscles right now. She laughed at the walk-in closet that was divided into 'his' and 'hers'. 'Hers' was almost twice as large as 'his'.

Josh laughed, "I could give you half of the 'his' portion of this closet to go with the 'hers' and still have enough room for my clothes."

Olivia grinned, "I think we could both fit all of our clothes into the 'his' part."She thought for a second, "Though, if we put all of our winter clothes, hiking clothes and everything, we might need at least some of the big side too. I know I have quite a lot of my winter stuff in the closet in 'your' guestroom."

"Yeah, I think you're right. I store some of my winter stuff in the living room closet in my apartment." Josh chuckled.

Josh opened the French Doors that led into a music / sitting room and Olivia and Molly followed him in. There was a Baby Grand Piano near the center of the room under a big drop cloth, easily distinguishable from its shape. Another large fireplace graced the wall on the right and the far wall was more than half glass, with beautiful French doors opening onto a large roofed balcony.

"Oh my stars!" Olivia breathed. "Josh, look at the view of the grounds and the valley. I could look at it for hours."

"It's breathtaking." Josh agreed. He set Sheyna down in the sitting room so she could play with the drop cloths she found so amusing. Molly was busily sniffing the whole room. Sheyna meanwhile had climbed onto the piano and was filling the room with a weird discordant symphony. After a few seconds, Molly joined in, sitting back on her haunches and singing/howling along in great exuberant woo-woos, then deciding to dance to the strange, almost eerie music, while continuing to howl.

Josh and Olivia grinned as they watched Sheyna patting the keys under the cloth, then striding across the keyboard, and stopping to listen to the weird dissonant music, as though she were trying to play the piano on purpose.

"Wow Liv, remember when I said we needed to teach Sheyna to dance? Forget dancing, she can play the piano, while Molly sings and dances." Josh laughed.

Olivia giggled, "They are quite the pair all right. Who'd have thought I'd have musical animals. I don't have a shred of musical ability myself."

Josh picked Sheyna up from the piano. Molly stopped howling, looking displeased that the music session had ended, and they all moved back into the bedroom where he set Sheyna down on the bed. She sniffed the bed and sneezed, then Olivia sneezed too, as the dust rose. She and Josh both laughed.

There was a slight rustling noise from under the bed and Sheyna catapulted herself under the bed faster than Josh or Olivia could react. Molly barked and Josh and Olivia knelt to see what Sheyna had found under there.

A tiny mouse darted out from under the bed and ran beneath a dresser on the other side of the room with Sheyna in hot pursuit. Fortunately for the mouse, he or she had picked a piece of furniture that was too low for Sheyna to squeeze under. Sheyna batted the drop cloth in frustration, finally grabbing the corner of it and lying on her back kicking it furiously with her hind feet. Molly was sniffing the drop cloth, and Josh, who had been trying to catch Sheyna, was sitting on the floor, convulsed with laughter.

"Josh, come see this," Olivia interrupted his merriment with a serious sounding voice. "I don't want to touch it until you see it."

Josh knelt down next to Olivia and saw a small packet of papers sticking out from between the box springs and mattress. He pulled his phone out and took several pictures of it where it was, then carefully lifted the edge of the mattress and removed the packet from the bed with his gloved hands. It was made of several folded papers with an almost completely disintegrated rubber band semi-attached to the paper in pieces, probably melted on from the heat of thirteen summers without air conditioning in the abandoned house.

Olivia's eyes were wide as she watched Josh gently separate the papers. He painstakingly unfolded the first one to reveal a spidery handwriting in faded blue ink. Josh read it aloud while Olivia peered over his shoulder.

"'Dear Mr. Hill, I am writing this letter to warn you that your daughter Jenny was seen by someone when she pushed her Mama down the stairs. If you don't want her to be arrested, you need to leave a box with ten-thousand-dollars in the woods behind your summerhouse on Monday evening. If anyone tries to catch the person picking it up or follows them, the police will be notified about your lovely little murdering daughter and your family will be ruined.'"

"Oh Josh, he was being blackmailed, and they were saying that Jenny killed her mother. It couldn't have been true!" Olivia gasped. "I absolutely don't believe it."

"Neither do I," Josh stated as he looked at the next letter. "Look Livvie, the handwriting is different, but not quite different enough. I think someone was trying to make him believe Jenny was guilty in order to blackmail him, but maybe even more to keep him from looking at anyone else as a suspect."

Olivia looked at the second letter, "You mean the murderer sent these letters?" She read the letter out loud to Josh.

"'Deer Mr. Hill, I have nolege about yur girl Jenny. She was the one what killed her mother. Her baby brother wached her and laffed. All The Best, A Well Wisher.'" Olivia paused, "Lots of misspelled words and poor grammar in this one, unlike the first one, but yes, I see what you mean. The capital H is exactly the same in both letters, as is the capital I and the lower case k, l and m. The rest of the letters are somewhat different, but the whole letter looks too carefully written, as though the writer was trying to make it look a certain way, I would suppose because they were trying to disguise their handwriting."

"Exactly," Josh agreed. "They were obviously much better at getting away with murder than at disguising their handwriting, if our theory is correct."

"Well, if we're right, we won't let them get away with it any longer." Olivia said firmly. "So many lives destroyed for money! We have to solve this one Josh and save James too. Whoever killed Edna and wrote those letters ruined or changed way too many people's lives to get away with it."

"You're right Liv. I want to get them too." Josh looked angry and determined. "Little Jimmy grew up without a father, poor James has been a train wreck since his mother's death and Jenny seems to have tried so hard, but she couldn't raise James by herself and she probably felt so guilty over that failure that she could never get back to being the confident person she once was." Josh sighed heavily.

"These letters are the first tangible clues to what was most likely a murder, and they may ultimately prove that it was, as well as who did it." He carefully folded the letters back and put them into a baggie he took from his pocket. "We'll read the others when we get to your house. I don't want to keep Sally waiting for too long especially after Molly was howling and barking; she'll think something happened to us."

Olivia smiled, "Are you ever without gloves and baggies? I suppose I should start carrying them in my pockets too actually, if we're going to be partners in this investigating business."

Josh laughed, "Years of police work has thoroughly taught me the Boy Scout motto of 'Always be prepared'." He slid the envelope into the breast pocket of his jacket, where it would be safe and scooped up Sheyna, who was still stalking the poor little mouse that was hiding under the dresser.

Olivia laughed and picked up Molly's leash. Molly gave one last sniff at the dresser and obediently led the way out of the room.

"Unfortunately, I really should get these back to headquarters as soon as possible, so we can start work on fingerprinting these. I'll make photocopies to bring home with me so we can look at them and see if we can get any more clues, but we will have to cut our visit here short today," Josh said apologetically.

"No worries sweetheart," Olivia smiled, as she started carefully down the staircase opposite from the one they'd ascended earlier. "I'm glad I'll still get to see what the other letters say and how they look though. Just don't get yourself in any trouble over it."

"Well, the way I see it, is that you're working for a PI agency even though it technically isn't open yet, so if anyone asks why I showed them to you, you're a consultant," Josh laughed.

Olivia beamed. "I think it's going to be so much fun working with you."

"I'm just hoping it isn't too dangerous," Josh grinned ruefully. "You seem to have a knack for always landing right in the middle of the action."

Sally looked worried as she and Jimmy met them at the bottom of the stairs.

"I heard strange music and Molly howling and barking. Is everything okay?"

Olivia hugged her and laughed, "Sheyna surprised us by playing the piano when she walked across the keyboard, which made Molly howl, then Sheyna discovered a mouse and she and Molly had great fun chasing the poor little thing under a dresser. I'm sorry you were worried."

Jimmy showed them the unfinished drawing he had made of the dining room, and it looked like he'd drawn enough that he might be able to finish it from memory.

"Jimmy, that is awesome!" Olivia hugged him, then held up both thumbs to convey her approval of the drawing.

Josh clapped him on the shoulder gently, and also gave him a thumbs up. Jimmy glowed with pride and ran back into the dining room to draw as much as he could before they had to leave.

"Sally, we found some letters under the mattress in the master bedroom that make it look like Jack was being blackmailed. Someone was telling him that Jenny had killed her mother, said that James laughed about it, and was also threatening to go to the police and to ruin the family." Josh told Sally, carefully turning so that Jimmy couldn't see his face if he came back into the room, just in case he was able to read lips a little.

"That must be why he turned against Jenny and James. If he started believing it, even a little, it could have done enough damage to ruin his relationship with them permanently." Olivia said sadly. "I think it would have been really hard, knowing it was likely his wife had been murdered, and never knowing for sure who did it, especially if people were saying his daughter was guilty and his son complicit. It might have been enough to push him over the edge of sanity."

"It's a wonder Jenny didn't turn out even worse than James, if she knew her father suspected that she had killed her own mother," Sally said. "That would explain a lot. I knew both of the kids were troubled—James had his dark moments even while he was married to Joanie, though he was so happy with her and baby Jimmy that he mostly handled his issues well, at least until Jimmy went deaf—that just took him apart at the seams. Jenny seemed to me like a scared little girl, too shy and insecure to ever be comfortable in her own skin."

"Well, Sally I'm sorry, but I'm going to have to renege on my promise of showing you the rest of the house right now," Josh said. "I need to get these letters to headquarters right away, but we'll come back soon and you and Jimmy can see the whole house for sure."

"That's okay Josh," Sally smiled. "I just hope you can catch whoever did this to Edna and caused so much misery to so many people." She paused, "I remember hearing the rumors that Edna had been murdered back then, but I never heard any rumors that Jenny or James had been involved. I'd heard that it might have been someone who worked for the Hills. I figured that's why James blamed his mom's death on being wealthy. Talk was she'd probably interrupted a worker who was stealing from them. I could never figure out why he seemed to also blame himself. I guess this explains a lot. Jack must have treated them very differently than he did before if he had come to believe that they'd been responsible for Edna's death."

Josh perked up, "Did you ever hear any names mentioned, when people spoke of the worker they suspected?"

Sally scrunched her face in thought, "I seem to remember people saying it was one of the men who worked there that they suspected, but I don't recall hearing a name, no. I'm sorry Josh; it was so long ago."

Josh smiled, "Don't worry about it. It was a long shot that you might have heard it anyway. Just from finding these letters, we're way ahead of where we were yesterday." He walked into the dining room to let Jimmy know they were ready to leave. Jimmy cheerfully closed his notebook, packed his pencils back into their box and followed Josh, reaching up to pet Sheyna, who was riding on Josh's left arm.

"Josh, do you think you'll be home in time for dinner?" Olivia asked as they locked up the house and headed through the snow to the SUV.

"Yes, unless something unexpected comes up, I should be." He let Sheyna down on the ground on her lead, then opened the car doors for Olivia and Sally. Once they were in, he and Jimmy walked Molly and Sheyna around for a couple of minutes then put them into their crates in the back.

When everyone was in the car, Josh turned it around and they all had a last look at the house and grounds.

"It's interesting how it can still be beautiful when it is so neglected and spooky looking," Olivia said. "I guess beauty really is in the eye of the beholder."

"I wonder why Jack Hill held onto this house all that time instead of selling it if he couldn't stand to set foot in it." Josh mused aloud.

"I think I can answer that one," Sally replied from the back seat. "At least I have a good guess. It was the place where he'd lived so long with his beloved wife, where they'd spent most of their wonderful years together, so he couldn't bear to part with it, and know that strangers were living there, yet he couldn't live in it, because it was also the place where she'd died, possibly by violence."

Sally's voice was sad, Olivia knew she must be thinking of her late husband Albert, and how hard it was living without him.

"Even if he had put it on the market, I doubt if it would have sold. There were too many rumors that Edna had been murdered, even though there was no proof, and there were a lot of tales told of a ghostly woman walking around the property, and lights appearing in the windows and things like that. Not too many people want to buy a huge old run down mansion like this anyway, but a haunted one . . . not likely."

Josh pulled into Olivia's driveway and opened the doors, then helped Olivia get Molly and Sheyna inside. He handed her the keys to her SUV and picked up his patrol car keys from the hall table.

"I'm going to rush off so I can get back in time for dinner," he said pulling Olivia close and kissing her as Sally and Jimmy headed to their guestroom to put away their coats and change into indoor clothes.

"Drive safely sweetheart and I'll see you when you get here."

"I will," he kissed her again and walked out, closing the door behind him.

CHAPTER TEN

Three days later, on Tuesday, Olivia woke up early. She'd had a fun time after dinner with Josh, Sally and Jimmy. They'd played the old game "Twister" until she, Josh and Jimmy were a tangled exhausted mess on the floor. Sally had wisely designated herself the one to call the positions. Sheyna and Molly had enjoyed the game too, slinking through the middle of the humans and knocking them over once in a while.

Sheyna had thought it was almost as fun as helping Olivia with her Yoga by climbing on her while she tried to hold complicated positions. Molly tended to prefer helping her with Aikido, as it was much more exciting to help Olivia to inadvertently practice her rolling falls.

The alarm clock was playing soft music, and Olivia rolled over and stood up gingerly, still feeling a very slight soreness in her neck and back from the accident, turning the clock off on her way to the bathroom. She yawned widely, as she brushed her teeth. Looking in the mirror she was pleased to see that most of the swelling had gone down in her face. It was still quite colorful; she could see purple, green, red and yellow, but at least the shape and size were almost back to normal. A hot shower helped ease the stiffness and she found that she was able to move better than she had since the wreck. The Twister game had been a little like Yoga and may have done some good in stretching her muscles.

She kept thinking about the other letters that had been in the little packet under the mattress at Candlewick. There had been six letters altogether and four of them appeared to have been written by the same person, trying to disguise their handwriting, and it was probably a woman, as there was something feminine in the writing on all four. The other two, Olivia thought, were written by a male with very poor handwriting and grammar. There had been no attempt to disguise the writing and both letters were obviously written by the same person. All of the letters accused Jenny of killing her mother, and three of them mentioned James laughing while it happened.

As soon as she was dressed, Olivia headed to the kitchen to make a pot of coffee. Josh walked into the kitchen with his hair still damp from the shower and Olivia noticed there was something different about his handsome face. He kissed her and she melted against him.

"Mmm, are you going back to the beard and mustache? I think this look is wonderful on you too—just a hint of facial hair."

Josh laughed, "If you like it, I can keep it this way for a while, shave or go back to a little bit more hair, but it was only because I didn't have time to shave this morning, not a hair decision."

"Oh no! You have to run off already?" She kissed him and nibbled his lip teasingly.

"Oh . . . when you do that, I really wish I didn't have to, but I got a call from Pete Turner, the ex-cop I have staying at Sally's house. Someone . . . he's pretty sure it was Cordell Salger . . . tried to break in at five o'clock this morning. Pete almost caught him, but Salger or whoever it was had a gun and the advantage of being awake, and he got away. I have to get over there and talk to him while his memory is still fresh."

Olivia hugged him, "The coffee is almost ready. I'll pour some into a couple of travel cups so you have extra for the road. You're going to Headquarters after that, right?"

Josh nodded, "Yes, I put out an APB on the car Salger was driving already, but I'm still hoping for something from the lab on those letters. I told you the only fingerprints they found weren't in the register, and probably belonged to Jack Hill, but they are checking to see if there is any DNA on them."

Olivia handed Josh two travel mugs filled with steaming hot coffee. The wonderful aroma filled the room and was almost enough of a wake up without even tasting it.

"Thanks sweetheart. I'm sorry to run off so early, especially after that delicious kiss, but at least I shouldn't be late getting here this evening."

"Drive safely and call me when you can." Olivia hugged him again and he set the coffee cups down and kissed her so fervently that her toes curled.

Josh grinned as she staggered slightly when they stepped apart. "I'll be remembering that all day."

Olivia laughed a bit breathlessly as she handed Josh his coffee mugs. "You aren't the only one."

After Josh had gone, she drank her coffee and read the newspaper until Sally joined her in the kitchen.

Olivia told her about the attempted break-in at her house, and Sally was relieved to know that he hadn't actually gotten in and that Pete wasn't harmed.

"Sally, was there anyone that you ever suspected might be guilty when Edna Hill died? Did you believe she was murdered or that it was an accident?"

Sally thought for a minute while she poured her coffee and took a sip, "I'm not really sure what I believed. There was a lot of talk going around—you know how even though we are living in a bunch of very small towns, that are separate, they're all still connected, so it's really more like one slightly larger small town and the rules of gossip work pretty much the same as any other small town." She paused for breath, "All I really remember is that the most popular theory at the time was that someone who worked on the estate had been searching the place for something valuable and she caught them at it, so they pushed her down the stairs."

"Do you remember if there was a specific person they suspected the most and who it was?"

"There was a specific person, yes, but I can't remember what his name was anymore, if I ever heard it." Sally shook her head. "It was an awful tragedy, and everyone felt really bad for the family, but I don't think there was ever any proof that it wasn't an accident, so in the long run, that's what they decided to call it I guess."

Olivia sighed, "Well, it looks like the gossip may have been right this time, at least that she was murdered, if not who the murderer was." She paused, "Did you ever hear anyone say they thought the Hill children were involved in it?"

"Never! Trust me, I would have remembered that, especially once Joanie started dating James."

Olivia smiled, "Yes, I guess you would have. So that leads me even more to think the murderer wrote those letters to Jack Hill to try to deflect suspicion away from himself or herself." She started as a thought struck her, "Sally, did anyone ever suspect a woman or was it always a man they thought killed her? Four of the letters really looked like they'd been written by a woman."

"It seems to me that I remember something about a woman being involved somehow, but I just don't remember how it all went anymore. There were actually several theories floating around, and they've gotten a bit mixed up in my memory after all these years."

"I'm not surprised," Olivia smiled. "It's been a long time since it happened."

"I wish I could tell you who might remember more, but I can't think of anyone right now. If I do, I'll let you know," Sally said as she poured herself and Olivia both another cup of coffee.

"I'm taking Sheyna and Molly over to the retirement home to visit today. Do you and Jimmy want to come along? I'm planning to stop at The Wall for breakfast on the way, since the girls can sit outside at the table with me."

"Thanks for asking, but I think I'd rather stay here today. Jimmy's surgery is day after tomorrow if they don't postpone it again, so I want to just hang around here with him and enjoy the time peacefully. I'd love to go next time, but the retirement home is too similar to a hospital, and he'll be in the hospital soon enough." Sally chuckled. "Don't get me wrong, I am more than excited that he is getting the implant, but I'm going to hate seeing him in the hospital."

"Oh, I know, I will too." Olivia said smiling ruefully. "He's such a little cutie and it's going to be hard to see him all bandaged up and hurting."

Sally sighed, "We're just going to have to remember what it's for and that the month that he is suffering from the surgery will go by quickly and he'll be able to hear for the rest of his life, if it all goes the way it should."

"Yes, he will!" Olivia said as she washed her coffee cup. "He's a strong little boy and so determined, that I think he's going to have a complete success with this."

"Have a good time and I hope Molly and Sheyna cheer everyone up over there. I'm sure the people must love it when they visit."

Olivia smiled, "It's almost hard to say who loves it more, the people or Molly and Sheyna." She picked up her car keys and grabbed the leads for the girls, "I think I am going to stop at all the thrift stores on the way home to see if there is anything interesting, so I'm not sure when I'll be back. Do you need anything from anywhere in town?"

"I can't think of a thing I need right now," Sally smiled. "Have a fun day and good luck with the thrift stores."

Olivia put their coats on and loaded the girls into the SUV. Her cell phone rang as she pulled out into the street.

"Vicki! Long time no hear. Are you guys okay?"

"Yes," she answered. "Everything is fine and Bob O'Brian brought the stolen highboy back to us this morning. He said Josh okayed releasing it, because they'd already processed it. I was calling because there is something you need to see, Miss Nancy Drew."

Olivia could hear the grin in her voice. “What did you find Vicki?” she asked excitedly. “You sound way too much like the cat that swallowed the canary.”

“You’ll just have to wait and see until you get here, but I promise you’ll like it,” she chuckled mischievously. “Can you come over now?”

“I’ve got Molly and Sheyna with me and was going to stop for breakfast on the way to the retirement home. If you’ll fix me breakfast, I’ll be there in ten minutes,” she laughed. “I’ll return the favor next time you’re in my area and want breakfast.”

“You’ve got it. I don’t suppose Josh is with you.” she said with a question in her voice.

“No, he’s gone to Headquarters, why? Is it something he should see?”

Vicki laughed, “No I just wanted to see his face when he sees what I found, because his guys missed it. I’m cruel that way. I’m just kidding; it was only sheer clumsy luck that I found it.”

Olivia laughed, “You . . . clumsy? Never! I’ll be there almost before we hang up. Bye sweetie.”

Olivia ended the call still laughing. “Molly, Sheyna, Aunt Vicki’s making breakfast. You girls lucked out this morning.”

Molly woofed from the back. She loved Vicki and Andrew, and they always gave such yummy treats when they visited.

Seven minutes later Olivia pulled into the driveway and got the girls out of their crates. Vicki opened the door and let them all in, giving Olivia a hug on her way in. Olivia handed Sheyna to her and she cuddled her, scratching her ears until she was purring like a motorboat.

Molly sat at her feet and lifted one paw to nudge her leg. She grinned and petted her too, lowering Sheyna to the floor.

"Okay Ladies, breakfast is served!" she announced grandly, leading the way to the little breakfast nook in the kitchen.

Olivia sat at the cute little round wooden table while Vicki presented her with a plate filled with a lovely miniature, one-portion sized frittata, surrounded by fresh fruit and blueberries. She put two small bowls on the floor for Molly and Sheyna, with some delicious handmade treats that she bought from the fancy pet store in town.

"Oh Vicki, this looks almost too pretty to eat! But it smells too yummy not to." She took a bite and her taste buds were flooded with the sweet spiciness of red bell pepper and fresh basil, topped off with zucchini in the silky egg concoction. "Oh, so much better than eating at The Wall," she said, taking a second bite, as Vicki handed her a glass of hand squeezed orange juice and joined her at the table with her own plate.

"So, I was oiling and buffing the highboy to rid it of all the nasty fingerprints and bad energy from the hoodlums that had stolen it. I had one of the drawers open and was polishing the sides of the drawer, when I noticed a slightly rough spot on one side." She paused to let the suspense build.

"Oooh, you are cruel Vicki!" she laughed. "You know you've got me hooked already. Give it up!" she waved her fork at her friend in a mock threat.

She laughed, "Okay, okay, I rubbed the spot a bit harder with the rag and it turned out that it was a button which released the front of the drawer and a shallow secret drawer that is underneath the main drawer. It just pulled away from the main drawer and exposed this adorable little hidden drawer. Now you have to wait until you're finished eating and I will show it to you," she said teasingly. "This one was much better hidden than the one that had the letter. It merely had an extra space behind the back of one drawer that was a bit obvious if you had two drawers open at the same time."

Olivia refused to eat the delicious frittata too quickly, and savored it, along with the fruit and berries, but she was dying to see what she'd found.

"You're killing me Vicki!" she said making a face at her as she finally swallowed the last bite.

"It's so rare that I get a chance to surprise you with something that I just can't resist prolonging the moment for as long as I can."

Vicki swallowed her last bite as well and stood to lead the way into the den where she'd been working on the highboy.

It stood grandly in the center of the room with all its secrets chastely hidden from view.

"Vicki, this piece is simply splendid! If you ever want to sell it, you could get a ton of money for it." She touched it reverently, "If I could afford it, I'd buy it myself, and just sit and look at it all day. You've done a brilliant job with the polishing. It is stunning."

Vicki smiled broadly at her praise, "I've enjoyed every minute of work on it. I finally understand your fascination with refinishing antique furniture. It's like watching something that was dead come back to life under your hands, isn't it?"

"That's it exactly. It's a wonderful feeling and worth all the hard work when it turns out to be something beautiful like this." Olivia thought for a second, "In a small way, it's like rescuing an animal or person that is injured or abandoned and giving it a second chance. I know furniture isn't alive, but some of these old pieces are amazing works of art that might have been lost forever if someone didn't rescue them and fix them back up. The wood almost feels alive sometimes, once it's been restored."

"I hadn't thought of it like that, but it makes sense."

"I'd certainly always choose to help an animal over a thing, no matter how beautiful the piece, but old things call to me too. I love my job!" Olivia said, her eyes shining. "Okay, let's see the secrets this beautiful highboy holds, Vic. No more teasing."

Vicki opened the drawer on the left, in the center section of the highboy, then as Olivia watched closely, she pressed a small almost invisible spot on the side of the drawer near the bottom. The front of the drawer sprang out, separating itself from the rest of the drawer and revealing a fairly shallow second drawer under the main drawer. The main part of the drawer still looked the same except that the wood on the second front that was still attached to the drawer was unpolished on the front.

Olivia peered into the secret drawer and gasped. "It's a key!" her eyes danced in excitement. "Vicki, it's a key! That's got to be to open the place where the piggy bank is hidden."

"That's what I think," Vicki said looking proud of herself. "Now we just have to figure out where that place is."

Olivia wrinkled her nose, “You had to mention that part, didn’t you?” she laughed. “We’ll find it yet. Just look how far we’ve come already.”

“You’re right, we’re definitely getting closer. I want you to take the key and keep it somewhere safe, so if you find anything that looks likely, you’ll be able to try it right away.”

“Okay, that makes sense, though I promise to call you as soon as I find something that it fits, before I even look inside it.” Olivia said warmly, giving her a hug.

“Mwah”, Vicki planted a noisy kiss on her cheek. “You’re the best, Liv!”

Molly sniffed at the bottom of the highboy and barked, then whimpered.

Olivia and Vicki looked at each other in puzzlement, then as Molly continued to sniff the piece, they knelt and peered underneath the highboy. They didn’t see anything at all.

“Okay, now we need to check out that drawer above where she was sniffing,” Olivia said, shaking her head. “Dogs have amazing noses. They can smell things that you’d never dream they could smell.”

Vicki opened the drawer and they both started touching it and running their finger over it trying to find anything that might cause something to open.

After an exciting few minutes, they were becoming frustrated at their lack of progress.

“Maybe she was just barking because she smelled the scent of someone she didn’t like,” Vicki suggested.

“That’s possible, I guess, but I don’t think so. They must have touched the whole piece, not just one corner on the bottom," Olivia mused. "Molly, what is it, girl?" she asked.

Molly sniffed the same area and whined.

Olivia lay on the floor and looked up at the bottom of the highboy, then started running her fingers all over the area Molly was interested in. While Vicki looked on hopefully, she pushed against a tiny depression on the back of the bottom runner and the bottom of the highboy slid smoothly out at the back, revealing itself to be a large fairly shallow drawer.

Olivia slid out from under the highboy and she and Vicki were both almost jumping up and down in excitement.

"It's your highboy, you look first. " Olivia grinned.

"I think it's big enough, we can both look." She laughed, pulling Olivia around the tall chest with her as she went.

Inside the drawer was a small package of letters and an old rather fragile looking little book with a decrepit leather cover.

"Oh my, she must have smelled the leather," Olivia breathed, carefully lifting the little book and opening it gently. "It's a journal." She carried it over to the desk and laid it down so they could both see it. Molly sniffed the book for a moment, then, bored with it, lay down beside them.

The writing was old and a bit faded, but they were able to read most of it.

"'*January 16, 1894,*'" Olivia read in an awed voice. *'"Dear Diary, Momma has said that I am to have a new tutor starting next week; that I am old enough to put away my toys of childhood and take a more active interest in learning to be an educated woman in our new society. I'm thankful that I'm not to be sent away to school in Boston after all, as I dreaded the thought of never being able to go to Papa's work with him. I believe Momma feels badly that she didn't have the grand opportunities for education that I will have, and I am grateful to have them, my dear diary, though only you may know that I would trade them gladly for a chance to work as an engineer on the railroad, driving that rumbling, behemoth down the tracks to faraway places I may only ever be allowed to dream of seeing on my own. I know that Papa would take me anywhere, but is it so wrong of me to want to take myself, and to make my own way in a job I know I would love?'"*

"Oh Vicki, she was born into a time where women could finally become well educated, but she was still born way too early to be allowed the freedom to do the work she craved," Olivia said sympathetically. "I forget how easy we have it nowadays. She was from a wealthy family and she still wasn't allowed to do what she really wanted to do with her life." She continued reading.

'"January 18, 1894, Dear Diary, I do like it much better here in Birchwood, though I find that I miss Hildy and Thomas dreadfully. Momma said that perhaps Hildy could come and visit me sometime, but that it wouldn't be suitable for Thomas to visit unless his parents came, as we are no longer children, and that it is doubtful they could afford to come anyway. Dearest Diary, I don't mind giving up my childhood toys, but I truly don't understand why growing up means giving up my childhood friends.'"

"How sad," Olivia said, "Though I guess it isn't as different as we might think now. I'm quite sure that if my family had moved away when I was around her age my male friends wouldn't have been welcome to come and spend a week with us, the way my female friends would have been. My parents would have thought it inappropriate also, even thought it would have been entirely innocent."

"Yes, I'm sure they would have. They were, as I recall, even a bit concerned about you and our old friend Jake Latimer, who was such a gorgeous boy that all the little girls were drooling over him even in kindergarten—except for you and I. You and I were playing sword fights and Olympic medalists with him instead, though I did my share of drooling when I was a little older. You never did, did you?" Vicki laughed.

"He was like my brother. How could I drool over my brother, silly?" Olivia laughed. "I was astounded when you started crushing on him and acting all awkward around him. He took it in stride though. I think he was so used to everyone treating him like he was a movie star that he barely noticed one more devotee."

Vicki grinned, blushing slightly, "Yeah well, at least I had a lot of company in my silliness. He was a really nice guy though, which is surprising considering his popularity. Most people would have let all that adoration go to their heads."

"You're right," Olivia smiled. "Okay, back to the diary. *'January 24, 1894, Dear Diary, It's been too long since I had time to write to you, as I have been so busy with my new studies. Besides spelling, reading, handwriting and arithmetic, my new tutor is teaching me composing, rhetoric, philosophy, Latin, algebra, geometry, history, geography, astronomy, chemistry, biology and logic. How shall I ever have time for anything besides studying?'*" Olivia paused. "Wow, it sounds like people were being much better educated back then than they are now." She continued reading.

"'*January 25, 1894, Today was my birthday and Papa and Momma surprised me with a darling puppy! I have named her Beauty, as she truly is a little beauty. Papa said she is a Maltese. I adore her and Momma has promised that she can sleep in my bedroom. Aunt Aggie sent me a shiny new silver dollar for my piggy bank, which I have put with the others she has given me. My sweet little bank has become quite heavy and full from all of my birthday dollars, and my darling Aunt Aggie sent me a new piggy bank that she said I must start using next year. I have put the full one into my little chest in the play house hidden behind the sleds and skis and locked it up tightly.*'"

Olivia and Vicki both squealed in excitement, "Playhouse! Vicki, I have to tell Josh and see if we can go and search the summerhouse. That must be what she meant. Oh no, look how late it is! I'm supposed to be at the retirement home in fifteen minutes."

"You call Josh on your way to the home and I will keep reading in the meantime to see if she mentions the piggy bank again—plus I have to know how it all turned out for her now." Vicki smiled. "It's like reading a good book—you simply have to finish it."

Olivia laughed, "You're right about that, and I want to read the rest of it later too. Let me know if there is anything else that is helpful." She hugged Vicki goodbye and rounded up Molly and Sheyna, snapping their leads on quickly. "Call me later Vic!" she grinned, leaving her friend immersed in the old diary.

CHAPTER ELEVEN

Once they were on their way, Olivia called Josh and told him what they'd found. He agreed to take her to search the summerhouse, as soon as possible and reminded her that Jimmy's surgery was set for tomorrow, so perhaps the next day or two would be better. She hung up feeling a bit shocked at herself.

Oh my, she thought, *finding that diary drove everything else right out of my head. Tomorrow is a day to be there for Jimmy and Sally, not playing treasure seeker, Livvie.* Giving herself a mental shake, she focused on parking in between two cars that had both been pulled in crookedly.

"Wow, the place is packed today girls," she muttered to Molly and Sheyna as she clipped their leashes on. "I hope it's not a madhouse."

Pam was in the lobby, and greeted Olivia with a hug. "What happened to your face?" she exclaimed in surprise, holding Olivia away to look at her more closely. "You're all bruised."

"I was in a car wreck five days ago, but I'm okay now." Olivia smiled, "I just look awful, but I feel fine."

"Wow, that must have been some wreck." Pam shook her head. "Don't tell me that you're involved in another murder or something! Are you?"

Olivia grinned ruefully, "Well . . . yes I guess I am, though I didn't discover the body this time at least. This time it's all Vicki's fault that I'm involved," She laughed.

"Oh dear, what has she been up to now?"

Olivia smiled and put her finger to her lips, "I am sworn to secrecy. I can only say that it went from being a treasure hunt of sorts to a kidnapping and murder investigation and Josh is in charge of the whole thing now."

"Wow, Liv, you are never boring, that's for sure!" Pam laughed, picking up Sheyna and kissing her head. "Let's get you guys started for now, and maybe one day you can tell me all about it." She led the way to the first room on her list for Olivia and the girls to visit.

Molly trotted happily over to the elderly woman in the wheelchair by the window and sat patiently while she petted her and told her how pretty she was. The older woman smiled as she rubbed Molly's head with her gnarled fingers. Molly gazed up at her sweetly with her soft brown eyes, loving the attention.

Olivia and Pam smiled at each other and Olivia sat in the chair by the door petting Sheyna while Molly visited with her old friend. Sheyna purred and kneaded Olivia's lap in content, waiting until it was her turn to visit one of the residents. Olivia found it interesting that some of the people wanted to talk to her almost as much as they wanted to visit with the animals, while others only wanted to see Molly and/or Sheyna, and would pretty much ignore Olivia's presence.

After a little while, Olivia gently led Molly out of the room, assuring the old woman that she would bring her back to visit again next week. The old woman nodded her understanding, but her eyes stayed glued on Molly, as they left her room.

Olivia sighed, it was so hard to take the girls away from them sometimes. She knew that many of the residents had left pets behind and missed them acutely. She really needed to figure out how to make the idea she and Pam had talked about work out. They'd come up with it a while back when she and Josh had been in the middle of trying to solve a murder and she really hadn't given it the time and thought she should yet to make it happen.

I'll have to talk to Josh and see if he has any ideas too, she thought, as she walked down the sterile hallway. *I honestly think that having people foster or adopt the residents' pets when they moved in, with the agreement that the residents could come and visit them, with the help of volunteers is a very viable and practical solution to the dilemma that many elderly people faced upon admittance to a retirement home or nursing home. I just really need to get it figured out and working before anyone else loses their beloved pets because they have to move to assisted living.*

Olivia silently resolved to get the ball rolling on it before the first of January, as she brought the girls into the next room on her list and handed Sheyna to the elderly man in the bed. Molly sat beside him too, so he could pet her too, since he loved cats and dogs both.

Molly and Sheyna both seemed a little tired after they had completed all their visits and Olivia felt a bit emotionally tired as well. She and Pam waved to each other as she backed out of the parking lot, after promising to get together soon.

The girls were sleeping when Olivia reached the first of the two thrift stores she wanted to check. She felt bad to wake them, but she no longer felt safe leaving them alone in the car for more than a minute, no matter what the weather was, as it seemed that all over the country, even in small towns like Birchwood, there were stories of cars being stolen with pets inside, and those stories seldom had a happy ending. In fact, her own car had been stolen not long ago, and her first thought had been how thankful she was that Molly and Sheyna had not been in it at the time.

Olivia loved how pet friendly so many of the shops

were in the area. She had friends who lived in other states that were amazed that she could take Molly and Sheyna with her to so many stores, parks and even some restaurants, as it seemed there were few pet friendly places in most states.

She carried Sheyna, and led Molly into the tiny thrift store. As she closed the door behind her, a cute, feisty little Chihuahua came running up to Molly barking and wagging her tail. Molly responded by wagging her own tail and going into a play bow, with her elbows on the ground and her rear end in the air.

"Hi Twiggy," Olivia said, "Give me a second to unhook Molly's lead and put Sheyna down and you guys can play." She quickly lowered Sheyna to the floor and snapped Molly's leash off. All three animals ran into the next room, chasing each other happily under furniture and hanging clothing.

Olivia laughed as she greeted the large friendly woman who was both manager of the shop and the person owned by the adorable Chihuahua.

"Hi Diane, it looks like the girls are up to their usual game of tag. There isn't anything they can hurt is there?"

"No, they're fine. All the breakables are on the shelves, and they're really good about staying away from those," she smiled. "Oh, you know what I have for you? Take a look," she reached behind her desk and pulled out a beautiful antique quilt.

"Oooh," Olivia said gasping. "Look how strong the colors are. Someone has taken such care with it. It's absolutely beautiful!"

"I knew you'd love it, that's why I kept it aside for you," Diane said with a wink. "Darleen Blackmoor was in here this morning asking for quilts and I made sure it was nowhere in sight. That woman is so domineering and just plain irritating. I couldn't let her buy this beauty, knowing how much you'd like it."

Olivia smiled widely, "Oh that's what her name is; I couldn't remember it to save my life last time I saw her. Boy, I'm going to be on her hit list for sure now if she finds out about this. I managed to get ahead of her in the line for the Pendergraft estate sale and I got all the beautiful quilts that Melinda's Grandmother had, and Abby got the cedar chests they'd been stored in. She positively glared at me when she saw me with the quilts, all marked sold." Olivia was chuckling. "I'm normally not so quick to gloat over getting something someone else wanted, but she *always* gets into the estate sales first, it has to be because she either has cronies in the management staff or she is paying someone off; I'm not sure which. I was floored that I actually got in before her for once."

Diane laughed, "Maybe she had a falling out with her cronies. Personally, she drives me crazy when she comes in here, as she always wants to pay less than things are marked, and you know how cheaply everything is marked, but if it's priced at one dollar, she'll ask for it for fifty-cents. I mean it's all for charity, what's an extra fifty-cents to her?"

Olivia sighed sadly, "It's for such a good cause, it's a shame when people who can afford it so easily, try to pay less than everyone else." The only time she really felt justified in gossiping was when it might help solve a murder investigation, so knowing that Diane loved to gossip, she quickly changed the topic of the gossip to one she felt more comfortable with. "Diane, I know it was a long time ago, but do you happen to remember any of the details about Edna Hill's death?"

Diane frowned in thought, "That *has* been a while. I know everyone thought she'd been shoved down those stairs, including the police. They never did figure out who did it though."

"Was there anyone in particular that people suspected?"

"There were a couple of people's names being tossed around at the time—they both worked for the Hills. Hmm, let me think on it," her frown deepened as she concentrated. "There was a man who worked as a mechanic, part time, and used to go up to take care of their cars when they had problems. I think his name was Richie, or something like that . . . He was a bit simple-minded, but really good at fixing cars, and there was a married couple who worked there . . . I'd heard they were bad news. I think they had a kid who was a mischief maker . . . I'm sorry Olivia, I just can't think of their names. It's been too long," Diane said regretfully.

"That's okay Diane, what you've told me is a big help. I'll hopefully be able to find someone who remembers who the couple was, and this Richie guy too." Olivia smiled and went to check out the rest of the little shop.

Finally, laden with one adorable large coffee mug that read 'Who rescued who?', a cute stuffed rabbit toy that Molly had found with floppy ears and a ping pong ball with a bell inside it for Sheyna, Olivia paid for all her finds and the lovely quilt. Diane put the stuff in a bag while Olivia collected Sheyna from the top of a clothes rack and snapped the leads on both her and Molly.

"If I remember anything more about Edna's death, I'll let you know," Diane said with a smile, hugging Olivia as she handed her the bag. "You have a good day sweetie and I'll see you and the girls next time you're in town." She picked up Twiggy so she wouldn't follow Molly out the door.

"Okay girls," Olivia said as she pulled into the road, "I'm making one more stop to see if Joy has any old unfixable chairs that I can make towel racks from, then we'll head home."

The Twice Over Shop was empty, like the other thrift shop, as Tuesday wasn't usually a busy day for the thrift stores. Olivia parked right in front of the door and brought the girls in on lead.

"Hey Liv, Hi Molly & Sheyna," the tall, thin woman sitting behind the counter said, pushing her reading glasses up onto the top of her short blonde hair as she put her book down. "Haven't seen you for a while. What happened to your face?" she peered closely, pulling her glasses back down to see better. "Are you kidding me? Was that you that got hit by a truck a few days ago? "Cause that's exactly what it looks like happened to you!"

"Hi Joy, yeah, that was me," she laughed it off, "I'm doing okay now though and thankfully the girls weren't with me when it happened. It was up by Candlewick, the old Hill mansion in Birchwood—you know it, right?"

"Oh yes, I've never seen it, but I remember hearing so many stories about that old place and the parties they used to throw. I think almost everyone in town went to them back in the day," she paused. . . "Wasn't the wife murdered up there?"

Olivia was disappointed that Joy didn't seem to know anything more than she did, "Yes, there were apparently rumors that she was. I was away on a foreign study program when it happened and never even heard about it until recently. Do you remember hearing anything else about it?"

"Not much. I was too busy dealing with a new baby at the time. That was a couple of months after Donnie was born and I was feeling too overwhelmed between him keeping me up all night with colic and two-year-old Dana running me ragged in the daytime to worry too much about anything else," she laughed. "I remember there was a rumor that it might be a teenager, and I heard another rumor that someone who worked for the Hills killed her because she caught them stealing. No one ever really knew for sure . . . except for whoever killed her, I guess."

"A teenager? Do you remember who it was they suspected?" Olivia asked in surprise. "I've heard the rumor that it might have been someone who worked there but nothing about a teenager being involved."

Joy shook her head, "I really don't remember anything else. Not sure if I ever heard the name—if I did, it didn't stick in my head. It was a teenage boy. That's all I remember."

"Oh, you just gave me a great idea! I should ask some of the guys around town who are in their late twenties or early thirties now, because they'd have known the guy then and probably heard any gossip going around about him back then." Olivia smiled excitedly. "If a teenage boy did it, he might have even bragged to his friends about it."

"Yeah, teenagers, especially the 'bad boys'", she made finger quotes in the air, "have a hard time keeping quiet when they've done something evil they could brag about. Trust me on this one—I married one of them—it was not my smartest move, though I did get two wonderful kids out of the deal. They, on the other hand got a deadbeat dad who moved away and finally got himself killed by someone he ripped off in Chicago."

Olivia hugged her, "They also got a fabulous mom, who loves them to death and is raising them to be as wonderful as she is."

Joy hugged her back, "Thanks for that. Sometimes I don't think I did them any favors, but I couldn't live without them, so I wouldn't change anything if I could."

"Well, I need to get home and I shouldn't be keeping you from your work, so let me take a quick look around and I'll get us out of your hair," Olivia picked Sheyna up and led Molly toward the back of the store.

"No hurry, and I wasn't working anyway. It's been

dead slow today," Joy laughed as she reached for her paperback and sat back down.

Olivia went through the shop quickly, not finding anything she was interested in, and was ready to leave when a well dressed young woman entered the store carrying a pair of old wooden snowshoes. Olivia's eyes widened and she promptly turned back toward the counter to see if the woman was trying to sell the snowshoes.

Ten minutes later and thirty dollars poorer, Olivia said goodbye to Joy, and led Molly and Sheyna out to the SUV, clutching the snowshoes in one hand and the leashes in the other. She struggled to open the back without losing her hold on anything. Once the girls were situated in their crates, she stowed the snowshoes on the floor under the back seat, so Josh wouldn't see them if he happened to get home before she could put them away.

"Well girls, Josh should love these snowshoes for his collection, don't you think? When should we give them to him?"

Molly and Sheyna ignored her question in favor of snoozing. Olivia laughed at how riding in the car always made animals so excited for the first few minutes and dozing off almost immediately afterward. They'd done enough riding today that the excitement had long since worn off.

Josh's patrol car was nowhere to be seen when Olivia pulled into the driveway, so she got the girls inside and hurriedly unloaded the snowshoes and hid them in her closet until she had time to wrap them.

Sally and Jimmy were playing cards in the living room and waved as Olivia ran through. Molly followed her upstairs, but Sheyna went to check out the card game and get some pets from Jimmy.

"I see someone is getting a nice little present," Sally chuckled when Olivia and Molly joined them at the folding card table in the living room. "Where did you stumble across those beauties?"

Olivia laughed, "Joy had a lady come in to sell them while I was there. She paid the lady fifteen dollars for them, I paid Joy thirty, and everyone was happy. I think Josh will be too."

"I'm sure of it. You were moving pretty fast, but they looked like a nice pair from here."

Before Olivia could answer, the front door opened and Josh walked in, calling out a cheerful 'Hello', causing Molly and Sheyna to race to the door, followed closely by Jimmy.

Olivia and Sally burst out laughing, and Olivia ran the back of her hand across her forehead, while mouthing a silent 'Whew' of relief.

Josh picked up Jimmy and swung him in a circle, then knelt to pet Molly and Sheyna as he put him down.

Olivia smiled at the scene. *What a fantastic man he is, she thought. How did I get so lucky?* She joined him at the door to the living room and he picked her up and spun her around too. She laughed as she heard Jimmy giggling.

"How did your day go sweetheart?" she asked, hugging him and pulling his parka off, brushing the snow from it onto the rug. "Oh wow, it's snowing again?"

"Not too much yet, but I heard we're going to get a few inches tonight."

"Uh oh," Olivia grimaced, "We have to have Jimmy at the hospital by seven am. Are they fairly sure it won't be more? I'm sure they won't be plowing up here that early and we can't be late."

"Well, there's no way to know for sure, as you know, but the forecaster seemed pretty confident. Most of the snow is supposed to be south of us." Josh kissed her, as he reached for a pot to make some hot chocolate. "I know I shouldn't encourage him to have cocoa before dinner, but it's a special occasion. Do you think Sally will mind if I corrupt him?" he grinned, waving a bag of tiny multi-colored marshmallows.

Olivia laughed, "I'm sure she won't mind tonight. Here, I'll do it; you go shower and get changed. She took the bag from him and hugged him. "Even your clothes are cold."

He chuckled and headed to 'his' room.

Olivia quickly started the cocoa heating and decided she was going to make a couple of huge pans of roasted vegetables with lots of spices, and a big pot of brown rice for dinner. *Tonight should be quick and easy for everything so we can all get to bed early. Morning will come way too soon tomorrow.*

Sally came and asked if she could help fix dinner, but Olivia laughingly shooed her away, telling her to have fun with Jimmy and keep him relaxed.

Olivia was all done with chopping the veggies by the time Josh emerged, his hair wet and tousled from the shower. True to his word, he still hadn't shaved off the stubble from his face and Olivia thought he looked wonderful in a bad boy sort of way, not that she like bad boys, but he really did look hot.

"Hmmm, I can't decide whether you're sexier when you've shaved, when you really have a little beard and mustache, or all rough and rugged like this," she murmured, smiling, as he wrapped his arms around her and kissed her neck from behind. She handed him a fragrant cup of hot chocolate.

Josh set the cup down and kissed her, "I may look a bit better this way, but I have a feeling you might get tired of the scratchiness pretty quickly." He rubbed his jaw experimentally, "I think it'll start feeling like sandpaper rubbing your face every time I kiss you, and I plan on kissing you every chance I get."

Olivia laughed and kissed him back, "I could learn to love sandpaper. I definitely love your kisses, scratchy, fuzzy or smooth."

She poured herself a cup of the foamy chocolate and Josh took a sip of his own.

"Delicious!" he exclaimed, licking the foam off his upper lip. "I'll take some in to Sally and Jimmy. It's perfect for a night like this."

Olivia put the pans with the vegetables in the pre-heated oven and stirred the rice on the stovetop, then Josh returned to the kitchen and helped her set the table.

After dinner, they played Monopoly for a short while, then went to bed early. Molly slept with Olivia, and Jimmy fell asleep with Sheyna's tail draped across his neck.

CHAPTER TWELVE

It was still dark when the alarm clock woke Olivia the next morning. Fighting the urge to hit the snooze button, Olivia forced her eyes to focus and sat up yawning. As usual, a hot shower did the trick and she was wide awake by the time she joined Sally in the kitchen. Molly followed her and head butted Sally for pets, wagging her tail when she received them.

"I heard Josh singing in the shower, as I passed by his room," Sally laughed as she petted Molly "Rather nice double bass he has there."

"Oh my, I will have to sneak over and listen some morning," Olivia smiled. "I love the sound of his voice even when he talks," she confided, blushing a little. "Yes, I am biased, but he does have a lovely deep velvety voice, doesn't he?"

Sally laughed and handed her a mug of coffee, "Yes, he actually does have a beautiful voice, even to me, and I'm not in love with him. A deep bass has always been my favorite."

Olivia grinned, "Is Jimmy up? Did you guys sleep well last night or were you too nervous?"

"Jimmy slept like a baby. I was the one who was tossing myself around all night like a caber at the Scottish Highland games."

Olivia laughed, "Okay, now I'm picturing Josh in a kilt, lifting you like a caber and tossing you in the air, then running and catching you before you land. I'd love to see him in a kilt."

Sally laughed and yawned at the same time. "I'm too old to be thinking of Josh's legs, though I'm sure he'd look quite fine in a kilt, but right now, the thought of me spinning through the air like that is almost enough to put me off my breakfast . . . and actually, that's probably a good thing since we can't eat until Jimmy is under sedation in the hospital or we'll make him hungry."

"Yes, that wouldn't be nice at all," Olivia smiled. "He's going to be a little hungry and thirsty anyway until he's knocked out."

Josh entered the kitchen with Sheyna and Jimmy on his heels.

"Good morning everyone, I smell coffee," he kissed Sally's cheek, then kissed Olivia's lips, hugging her as he reached around her for a cup.

Olivia kissed him back, then tousled Jimmy's hair and gave him a hug, which he returned briefly before squirming out of her arms and running to hug Molly. He asked in his own sign language if Molly and Sheyna could go to the hospital with them. Olivia's face was sympathetic as she shook her head, no.

"You know what?" Josh did some fast thinking. "Let's bring them so he can cuddle with them until we get there. I'll follow behind in the patrol car and take the girls home on my way to work after you go in. Does that make sense?"

"Perfect sense. Thanks Josh," Olivia smiled happily. "I'm sure he will feel more relaxed with the girls to hug, and speaking of hugging . . .,"she threw her arms around him and enveloped him in a warm hug.

"Josh, you really are an angel," Sally patted him on the back. She signed to Jimmy that the girls could ride with them, but would come home once they went inside. Jimmy's little face lit up and Josh blushed.

It didn't take long to arrive at the hospital, thanks to the early morning lack of traffic. Olivia waited in the SUV with the animals while Josh went with Sally and Jimmy to make sure his admittance went smoothly. When he got back, they led the girls to his patrol car and he kissed Olivia goodbye before driving off toward her house and she went inside to find Sally and Jimmy.

They'd already taken him to his room to await sedation and he was sitting in his bed wearing a hospital gown with race car designs on it. For the first time, he looked a little scared. Olivia gave him a hug and handed him a new Teddy Bear that was wearing a fake speech processor that looked like the real one Jimmy would be getting to allow him to hear speech and sounds once he was healed. She and Josh had bought it for him from the cochlear implant manufacturer as a pre-surgery present. He took the bear, touching the processor and smiling, then he put the bear beside him on the pillow.

"It's time for him to go to pre-op now," said a young blue eyed man wearing scrubs and a surgical mask, as he strode into the room.

"Oh my, that was fast," Olivia said and gave Jimmy a hug, quickly moving aside so Sally could hug him too. "How long before the actual surgery?"

"It'll be real soon, but I need to hurry and get him there so they can prep him; I'm already running behind," the orderly hurriedly wheeled Jimmy's bed from the room, giving Sally only time for a quick hug. Jimmy looked frightened, but clung to his new bear and didn't cry.

"Can we go with him?" Olivia asked his back.

"You'll see him after the surgery," he said, continuing briskly down the hall. "Just wait here for now."

Olivia turned to see Sally resuming her seat in one of the chairs. *Well, that guy seemed less than friendly, Olivia thought to herself. Even if he was running late, he could have been nicer to a little kid. Someone like that had no business working with patients in a hospital.* She sat in the chair next to Sally and pulled her phone out of her purse to call Josh to let him know Jimmy had gone in.

"We're going to be taking him into the pre-op soon now," said a cheerful female voice as a woman and a man entered the room wearing hospital scrubs.

Olivia gasped, but she didn't stop to ask questions. She raced down the hall in the direction the orderly had gone with Jimmy, leaving Sally to explain that someone had already taken him. Another man in scrubs rushed after her and she told him what had happened as they ran. He peeled off and ran to the nurse's station to call security.

Olivia kept running, watching closely for any signs of the mobile bed. As she turned a corner, she saw the orderly pushing the bed several yards ahead of her, and she sped up as fast as she could.

The guy with the bed must have heard her running behind him because he glanced over his shoulder, then started running, pushing the bed wildly down the hallway.

Olivia could see Jimmy sitting up and hanging onto the bed, laughing like he was enjoying the crazy ride. She ran faster, trying to get to him before he realized the man wasn't running for fun.

Seeing two nurses coming toward them, from the opposite direction, Olivia yelled as loud as her heaving chest would allow.

"Stop him! Stop him!" she stumbled and bounced off the wall, catching herself before she fell, losing speed, but struggling to regain it before he got away. "Kidnapper!"

The women tried to stop the man, but he rammed the bed into them, knocking them both down, then realizing that Olivia was right behind him, he abandoned the bed, picked Jimmy up, flung him over his shoulder and ran for the stairs.

Olivia was silently lamenting her shorter legs, as she chased the tall, thin guy. Even carrying Jimmy, who had obviously realized by now that it wasn't a game and was screaming and hitting him in the back, he was moving wicked fast. Luckily for her, he didn't seem to be in very good physical shape. She could see him faltering a little and it looked like he was getting short of breath. She pushed herself harder, closing the gap.

A door on the left side in front of them opened and someone stepped out, causing the kidnapper to have to dodge around, losing speed, just as Olivia closed on him and grabbed his flapping scrubs, ripping a huge piece of the thin material off and yanking him to an abrupt stop.

The panicked kidnapper whirled, threw Jimmy at her and fled down the hall. Jimmy's unexpected weight knocked Olivia over backward and as she fell, her Aikido training caused her to instinctively tuck her head, and hold Jimmy tightly in her arms to protect him from the fall.

She felt the breath slam out of her chest as her back hit the hard polished floor and Jimmy's added weight thudded onto her chest. She was stunned for a moment, trying just to breathe, then she felt Jimmy wriggling to get out of her grasp and she loosened her death grip.

They sat up together and Olivia could see that Jimmy was crying. She wiped his face and held him gently to her chest, rubbing his back to soothe him. People were coming from all directions to see what the screaming was about, and as Olivia looked down the hall, she saw a security guard leading the kidnapper in handcuffs toward her.

Olivia stood up and picked Jimmy up protectively, turning him away from the kidnapper.

"Ma'am, can you tell me what happened here? Is this the man someone reported having kidnapped a child from his room?" the security guard asked, walking through the circle of people that was starting to form around Olivia and

Jimmy. He held the handcuffed man firmly by the arm.

"Yes sir, that's him," she replied, recognizing the pale eyes and greasy brown hair of the man even though the surgical mask was still covering the lower half of his face. She could see the tattered remnants of the ripped scrubs fluttering at his back and she displayed the piece she held to the guard in case he had any doubts he'd caught the right man.

The guard reached up and pulled the mask down, revealing a sneering mouth in a sallow, unhealthy looking face. Olivia guessed him to be around thirty years old.

"Why did you kidnap him?" Olivia asked angrily. "You scared him half to death, and he's just a little boy."

"I ain't tellin' you nothin'," he spat, giving Olivia a nasty look. "Cordell'll fix you good for getting' in his business." He seemed to realize that he'd said more than he intended and shut his mouth firmly, refusing to say another word. The security guard led him away to wait for the police to arrive.

Several of the hospital staff who'd gathered to see the excitement escorted Olivia and Jimmy back to his room where his grandmother was frantically waiting. Jimmy reached down from Olivia's arms and grabbed his bear from the abandoned bed as they passed it, burying his face in it as he sobbed softly.

Sally clutched Jimmy to her and cried. Olivia had tears in her own eyes as she watched their reunion, while explaining to the Sally and everyone in the room what had occurred. Sally was so intent on Jimmy that Olivia knew she probably wasn't hearing much of it.

As soon as the excitement died down a little, Olivia called Josh to make sure he knew what had happened so he could come and question the kidnapper himself, since it was obviously connected to the case he was in charge of. He told her he would be there in half an hour or less, as he had just dropped off Molly and Sheyna and was barely on the road to Headquarters.

Olivia asked the nurse who was still in the room to please let the security people know that Josh was on the way to interrogate the suspect.

By the time Olivia had finished talking to Josh and the nurse, Sally was sitting in the chair holding Jimmy in her lap. He was looking much calmer, though he still had an occasional hiccupping sort of sob escape. He was holding tightly to Sally and his Teddy bear.

Olivia sank shakily into the other chair, her legs giving way as the adrenaline rush wore off. They'd come so close to losing Jimmy. Olivia realized how much she'd grown to love him and Sally. They'd become family. She got up and went to Jimmy and Sally and patted him on the back gently. He reached up and hugged her, then settled back in his grandmother's lap.

"Thank you Olivia. I don't know how I would have gone on if something bad had happened to him. He's all I have left," Sally spoke softly, tears still trickling down her cheeks.

"He's going to be okay Sally," Olivia petted her arm. "We're going to be on our guard every minute now that we know for sure they are trying to kidnap him."

"Here you go folks," an orderly came in pushing a portable bed like the one Jimmy had been in before and rolled it into place. "Someone should be along in a few minutes to talk to you."

Olivia thanked him and Sally stood up, carrying Jimmy to the bed. She tucked him in and sat on the edge of the bed beside him, so he wouldn't be afraid.

"He's been through so much, going deaf, then losing his mama and then having his dad leave him. I just want things to go right for him for a change." Sally sighed. "We were both so hopeful about this surgery, even though I knew it would be rough on him, but I never expected something like this to happen."

"I know, I didn't see it coming at all," Olivia said sadly. "We knew Salger might be after him; that's why we moved you guys to my house, but I guess we just got so excited about the surgery that we forgot to be cautious. I don't think any of us thought the hospital might be dangerous."

"I sure didn't," Sally shook her head. "There are so many people, it never crossed my mind that he could be in danger here."

"Well, I have a feeling Josh will be making sure there is a guard on duty 'round the clock, now that we know. I'm also hoping he can get some information out of that guy."

Jimmy finally dozed off as Sally gently brushed his hair off his forehead over and over in a soothing motion. She rose carefully, and moved back to the chair so she wouldn't wake him.

The door opened to admit Josh, followed closely by a male doctor and a nervous looking man in a business suit.

"I am so very sorry that something like this occurred in our hospital," the man in the business suit said, taking Sally's hand and pressing it. "I'm Ralph Weathers, a hospital administrator. You can be assured that we will be taking every precaution to protect your grandson and keep him safe while he is under our care." He rubbed his bald spot as if to reassure himself, "We've never had anything of this nature happen here before. I'm shocked and extremely sorry for the trauma you all went through."

Sally was her usual gracious self, "It wasn't your fault; you had no way of knowing someone might try to kidnap Jimmy. I don't hold the hospital responsible for this; don't worry."

Josh moved closer to Olivia while Sally and the Administrator were talking.

He surreptitiously took her hand and squeezed it. "Are you okay? I heard you got knocked down hard," he questioned softly.

"I'm fine, just had the wind knocked out of me, since Jimmy landed on me too," she grinned wryly. "Thank goodness he's small. I won't have more than a bruise or two thanks to my Aikido training."

Josh looked angry with himself, "Seems like you're always getting bruised. I should have thought that something like this could happen—that's my job."

"Don't beat yourself up over it, we all knew he was at risk, but none of us thought of it. We were too excited about the surgery."

"Are you sure you're okay?" he rubbed her palm with his thumb. "I need to go and take custody of the kidnapping suspect, and I will need for you to identify him, as well as Jimmy and Sally later probably."

"I'm fine Josh, truly. I've gotten worse in Aikido practice." She smiled and squeezed his hand. "Go ahead and do your job. I'll come and ID him whenever you tell me to. Oh, do you know what is going to happen with Jimmy's surgery now? Will they still do it this morning, or postpone it?"

"I'll find out. It may be partly up to Sally as well—whether she thinks they should wait, since he was put through so much already today."

"I think they should go ahead and sedate him now, while he is asleep, so that when he wakes up, the surgery will be all over and he won't have to worry about it anymore," Olivia said, speaking a little louder than they had been speaking, so Sally could hear too.

Sally nodded her head, "I agree with that. Can you still do the surgery now?"

The administrator looked at the doctor, who nodded and smiled, stepping over and shaking Sally's hand.

"I'll get the staff to get him under and prepped right away."

The two men left the room and a nurse entered almost immediately to place a mask over Jimmy's nose and insert the IV into his hand. He fluttered his eyes half open for a second and went right back to sleep.

"Josh, go ahead and do what you need to do, just call me and let me know what is happening when you can," Olivia said kissing him quickly.

"Before I forget to tell you, I have the old files from the investigation of Edna Hill's death. The Salgers were working for the Hills and were definitely suspects at the time, but there was no proof that she'd been murdered, so eventually it was ruled an accident and the case was closed. I am going to try to officially reopen it, and have started putting out feelers as to the whereabouts of Wendy Salger, Cordell's mother, who moved away shortly after Edna Hill's death." He gave her a quick kiss on the lips, "I have to get going, sweetie, I'll call you as soon as I can." Josh turned to the nurse, "I need for Olivia to be allowed to go with the patient right up until he enters the operating room, as he was almost kidnapped a little while ago."

"I understand sir," the nurse answered. "The doctor told me someone might be going with him, and that I should let you know there will be extra security on hand as well."

"Thank you." Josh turned back to Olivia and Sally. "I'll call you soon. Keep me posted please. I am sending O'Brian over for the rest of the day, and I'll have someone replacing him for the night shift. Don't worry, Sally; no one is getting to him again." His expression was stern as he left the room to head toward the security office.

"I'd let you go with him Sally, but I think I can run faster, plus I am studying Aikido, which makes me the best one to go," Olivia said sympathetically.

"No it's okay, I know you should go with him Livvie, I'm sure you'll keep him safe. You already saved him once." She hugged the sleeping boy and sat back down in the chair twining her fingers together to keep them from shaking.

"I'll be right back," Olivia said, as a male nurse, an orderly and a security guard entered the room together.

The orderly wheeled the IV stand, while the male nurse pushed the bed and the female nurse and security guard walked alongside with Olivia, keeping their eyes peeled for anything suspicious. Another security guard waited in a chair outside Jimmy's room.

The Pre-op room had a few other patients in various stages of sedation, though most, like Jimmy seemed to be completely out. Olivia sat in a chair and waited until they finished prepping him, shaved the area around the ear and above, and the doctor looked him over again.

"The surgery should take several hours and you can ask for progress reports at the nurses' station, though they won't know much unless there is a problem, which I don't anticipate," the doctor smiled. "Don't worry, everything should go smoothly. Your son is a healthy little boy and obviously a brave one too."

Olivia smiled, but didn't correct him, as he was already heading toward the operating room. *Jimmy makes me wish I had a child sometimes*, she thought to herself. *He is such a sweet little guy, and so much fun to be around.*

Olivia walked back to Jimmy's room and asked Sally if she wanted to go with her to get some breakfast, but Sally was too nervous about leaving until he was out of surgery, so Olivia offered to go pick something up for both of them, since they hadn't had breakfast.

She grabbed a couple of egg salad sandwiches from a deli, after a bit of thought as to what sounded good. It was still fairly early in the day but so much had happened that it seemed more like supper time than late breakfast to early lunch time.

Josh called to report that the prisoner was refusing to talk, but they had figured out who he was, because he had his driver license in his wallet.

"His name is Eddie Perkins, and he actually worked in the hospital part-time as a janitor," Josh explained. "Apparently he was an old buddy of Cordell Salger. Salger must have figured out somehow that Jimmy was having the surgery and since Perkins worked at the hospital, I guess it seemed too easy not to try kidnapping him there."

"I am so glad his timing was bad," Olivia said shuddering. "If the real prep team hadn't come along immediately after him, he would have gotten away with it and who knows what would have happened to Jimmy. The thought scares me silly."

"It definitely wouldn't have been good," Josh said grimly. "I don't have a good feeling about the state of James' health either," he sighed. "Anyway, I should be at your house by 5:30 if nothing else happens before I get off duty. Should I pick up something for you and me for dinner?"

"That sounds like a good idea Josh, or I can pick it up. Sally is staying at the hospital in the extra bed tonight, thanks to your generosity. After all that happened today, I'm quite sure she would have slept in the chair or even on the floor if you hadn't arranged for the private two-bed room."

"It was my pleasure. She's had a rough go of it losing her daughter and having to start over raising a deaf child late in life. So, what should I grab for dinner?"

"We're having egg salad for lunch, so anything but that I guess. Whatever you're in the mood for," Olivia answered, feeling more cheerful than she had all day, "Surprise me."

"Sounds like a plan," Josh laughed. "I can give you a massage too, since you may be feeling a bit sore after your heroic race through the hospital, not to mention being body-slammed by a five year old as you hit a hard floor."

"Mmm, I'll be looking forward to that for the rest of the day," Olivia said smiling. "I'll be home as soon as I can leave Sally and Jimmy. See you tonight sweetheart."

She parked and carried the food through the hallways to Jimmy's room, finally feeling famished by the time she got there.

"That looks divine," Sally exclaimed. "I didn't even realize how hungry I was." She cleared off the bedside table so Olivia could set the food down.

They both dug in quickly and Olivia thought the egg salad on seeded rye was the best she'd ever tasted.

"I knew I was hungry, but this still tastes incredible," she moaned, before taking another bite. "I've never tried that deli before; it's better than even my homemade."

"Better than mine too," Sally said. "I'm seriously impressed." She grinned weakly, taking another bite, as she started to look more like her normal self.

Once they'd polished off the sandwiches, Sally announced that she was going to take a nap for an hour, since Jimmy wouldn't be back from surgery for at least another two hours. Olivia decided to use the time to go and try to talk to the nurse, Martha Garland, who she'd met when she was in the hospital to see if she'd happened to remember anything else about Edna Hill's death. She promised to call Sally and wake her up in an hour.

CHAPTER THIRTEEN

Olivia went to the nurses' station to ask if Martha was in today and found that she was working in the ICU department, but would probably be going to lunch soon. The nurse behind the desk suggested that she'd be likely to find her in the cafeteria by the time she could get to it.

Olivia spotted her sitting at a table by herself, as soon as she walked in.

"Hi Martha, I'm Olivia, do you remember me from the other day?" Olivia smiled, walking up to her table. "You were telling me about Edna Hill."

Martha smiled, motioning to a chair, "Yes, I remember. Have a seat. How are you feeling? Your face looks much better."

"It feels much better too," Olivia laughed, sitting down. "I felt like I'd been used as a punching bag for a couple of days."

"If you've come to ask if I remember anything, I really haven't."

"I'm here with a friend and her grandson. He's in surgery to get a cochlear implant right now. His name is Jimmy and he's James Hill's son."

"Oh . . . the little boy is deaf?" she asked. "How old is he?"

"Jimmy's five. He's a very smart and sweet little boy," Olivia smiled. "Someone tried to kidnap him from his hospital room this morning."

"That was him?" Martha asked in astonishment. "Were you the one who chased down that Eddie Perkins?"

"Yes, the real prep team came in right after he took Jimmy, and he'd seemed so out of character for someone working with people in the hospital that I was already a little suspicious, so I knew immediately what had happened and just ran," Olivia ginned wryly. "Thank goodness pushing the bed around corners and obstacles slowed him down or I'd have never caught him. Boy is he long-legged!"

Martha shook her head in dismay, "I should have told you everything when you asked me before, but I didn't want to carry tales unless I knew they were true. I just never dreamed something like this would happen."

"What is it that you know?" Olivia asked intently.

"It's not anything about Edna's death, but when you asked me which kids James had been hanging out with, I said I didn't remember, because I didn't want to cause trouble for anyone. One of the kids turned out to be a fine person and a valued member of the community. Two of the kids later moved away and the other one was Eddie Perkins," she said worriedly. "I always had a feeling he was still up to his old tricks, and every time anything comes up missing around here, he's the first one that comes to my mind."

"Would you tell me the names of the other kids?" Olivia asked softly. "I'll try not to do anything to be too much of a bother to the one who still lives here. I'd just like to ask him about the others."

"Her . . . the one who still lives here is a woman. She was a wild child, and very rebellious when she was a teenager, but she was a good person at heart, a very smart girl, and fortunately she grew out of her rebelliousness quickly. Her name is Hannah Marsh, and she's a doctor here at the hospital."

"Dr. Marsh?" Olivia's mouth dropped open. "Why, I know her! My friend Abby redid her whole downstairs and I was the one who found the antique dining room set for her. She's a sweetheart! It's hard to imagine her ever being into the kinds of mischief they were in back then. Wow!"

Martha laughed, "Yes, she really went a bit overboard on the teenage rebellion. Fell in love with the ultimate bad boy and tried really hard to turn her parents' hair grey fast." She sobered, "It might have worked too. Her father had a heart attack shortly after she told them she was pregnant."

"She had a baby?" Olivia was still in shock. "I never heard about any of this. I was in Europe on a High School foreign study program. I left here shortly before Edna Hill died and was gone for three years. It seems I missed an enormous amount of excitement while I was gone."

Martha shook her head, "No, she never had the baby, she had a miscarriage. In retrospect, that might have been the kindest thing for all concerned. Like I said, her dad had a heart attack and almost died, she felt completely responsible for that, and between getting pregnant and her father almost dying, she snapped out of her rebellious phase real quick."

"When did she miscarry, before or after her dad's heart attack?" Olivia asked. "I'm glad he didn't die; that would have been a lot of guilt to carry around."

"You're right, and it might have done the opposite of turning her around if he had. She might have thrown everything away and ended up like James Hill or worse," Martha's left eyebrow raised and her voice turned slightly acerbic. "She had the miscarriage after her dad's heart attack. She went back to tell the baby's father that she was going home to her family and she slipped and fell, somehow landing on her stomach and face. She miscarried right away."

"Wow, isn't that a bit odd?" Olivia asked, startled.

"Seems like a lot of falling going on back then."

"Hmph," Martha scoffed. "We all knew he'd beaten her, but she refused to admit it, so there was nothing anyone could do about it. The finger shaped bruises on her arms were from him trying to keep her from falling, she said." Martha blew out an angry breath. "I was one of the people who treated her when she had the miscarriage."

"Who was the father of Hannah's baby?" Olivia asked. "It wasn't James, was it?"

"No, James was the youngest of all of them, at least a couple years younger than Hannah. He was also definitely the nicest of the four boys. CJ, the father of her baby was the oldest, and the cruellest of the bunch. He was already nineteen or twenty by then, so technically it was statutory rape. Once she'd miscarried, they may have felt it was better to let it go, so she could get on with her life without airing everything in public." Martha, made a wry face. "As much as I hated to see him get away with it, I have to say, I think that was for the best. Having it all dragged through the press if her parents had pressed charges would not have been in Hannah's best interests."

"So this CJ was one of the boys who moved away? Do you known his last name?" Olivia questioned. "Who was the other boy that left town?"

Martha sighed, "I can't remember CJ's last name, nor the other boy's either, though his first name was Ward, I think. It's been too long since either of them was around. I only remember Hannah and Eddie Perkins because they work here—well, Hannah, I'd remember anyway—she left an impression on me that night. All bruised and bleeding when she came in to be treated for the miscarriage, yet insisting that she'd just fallen, when the truth was so obvious." She ran her fingers through her hair, "At the time, I thought she was just acting in a typical manner for an abused woman, but now looking back and knowing how strong she is, I think that those boys had probably threatened to hurt her family if she talked. That CJ was mean as a rattler."

"Wow, poor Hannah, that must have been a nightmare for her," Olivia said sadly. "Thank goodness she was strong enough to get out of that situation and get her life back on track." She paused, "Do you think she would mind talking to me about it? She may remember CJ's and Ward's last names, and that could be helpful."

"I think she would be willing to talk to you, but unfortunately she is on a skiing vacation in Colorado right now and won't be back for another week," Martha answered. "I'm really sorry I didn't tell you about all this the last time you asked me, but I never dreamed that any of those kids were involved in James' disappearance. It was a long time ago."

"I don't blame you for not saying anything then. You obviously aren't someone who likes to gossip about people, and that is usually a very good thing," Olivia smiled. "I'm just glad you told me now. I will have to wait until Hannah is back from her vacation to talk to her, but in the meantime, I guess I'll keep trying to find someone else who knew that group of kids and might remember all the names."

"I hope you find someone, and I promise I'll get in touch with you right away if I think of anything more."

"Thanks Martha. I'd better get back to Jimmy's room now, he should be getting out of surgery soon." She grinned, "You don't think I could bring a certified therapy dog in to visit him tomorrow do you? I think he would feel better instantly if he saw her."

"Hmmm, I think that might be a problem. If she was his service dog, yes, they would have to allow it, but unfortunately, because of potential allergies of other patients, I don't think they'd let you bring her."

"Yeah, I had a feeling that would be the case, but figured I might as well ask you," Olivia laughed.

"What kind of dog is she? I'm thinking about adopting a dog myself but haven't figured out which type or size makes sense for me."

"Well, Molly is a female Golden Retriever, which is sort of medium large. She sheds a lot, and is pretty well medium energy. Oh! I have a thought. Pam McAllister, who is the manager at the retirement home and I are trying to start something to help future residents that have pets, since pet aren't allowed at the home," Olivia said excitedly. "We are hoping to find people to adopt or foster their pets when they move into the home, and let the residents come to visit them occasionally. We would find volunteers to bring them to each new home and make sure everything went well. Would you be interested in participating in that?"

Martha's eyes twinkled as she smiled, "That is a fabulous idea! Sign me up! I think I will rely on you to help me choose which dog will fit with me too, if you don't mind."

"I'd be happy to help you with that. You are the first person I've asked to be involved and now I'm even more excited about it."

"Just let me know when there is a dog available in the program so I can meet him or her. I'd be fine with bringing the owner to my house or bring the dog somewhere to meet them too if that would make it easier," Martha volunteered.

"Wow, you are a marvel! I'm so glad I thought to ask you about bringing Molly. You made my whole day!"

"Here is my cell number. Call me anytime," Martha handed her a paper with her number scribbled on it. "I've got to get back to work or I'll be looking for a new job instead of a new dog," she laughed as she went to put her lunch trash in the garbage can. "Talk to you soon, and good luck on finding James."

Olivia put the paper in her purse, and after buying herself and Sally each a cup of hot spiced tea, she called Sally to let her know an hour had passed, then headed slowly back to Jimmy's room, calling Pam and leaving a message on her cell phone to let her know the good news about Martha volunteering to be on their list to adopt a dog. Just as she hung up, her phone rang.

Sally was in the chair reading when Olivia got back, and took the tea gladly.

"Any word on when he'll be out of surgery?" Olivia asked.

"Actually, a nurse stopped in a minute ago and said things were going well, and they think he will be out of surgery in another hour or two," Sally answered smiling.

"That's great news," Olivia beamed. "Josh just called me and said he took some time off today and would like to meet in town and look for a new car right now, if everything is going well here. We haven't had time to look yet and the old one was totaled in the wreck. If we do it now, we'll both be close by and can come here as soon as we find something, or sooner if you need us."

"That's a good idea," Sally agreed. "I shouldn't need you for anything as long as things go the way they're supposed to, and they said Jimmy will be flat out of it when they bring him back, so there's no rush on getting back until you find what you're looking for."

"Okay, call me if you need anything at all. We'll bring you food when we come back so you aren't stuck with hospital food," Olivia grinned. "Call me if you have any special requests, otherwise I will just surprise you."

"I'll opt for the surprise I think. You guys have fun and I hope you find him a nice car."

"See you soon," Olivia called as she closed the door.

The sky was cloudy, but the snow had stopped and the wind was fairly calm when Olivia stepped outside. She zipped her parka and adjusted the scarf around her neck as she stood in the crisp, cold air waiting for Josh to pick her up. She smiled as she felt the slight crunch of the snow under her boots. *I love winter,* she thought. *However cold and damp it may be, it is so beautiful.* She looked up at the ice coated twigs and branches on the trees that sparkled in the sunlight and took a breath of pure joy.

Josh pulled up next to her and got out. He walked around the car and hugged her before opening her door.

"What's the news on Jimmy?"

"He's still in surgery, but the nurses told Sally that he's doing well and should be out in a couple of hours." Olivia sat in the passenger seat and Josh closed the door.

"So, I thought we'd try the dealership on the south end of town first. I know we may end up in Berlin after all, but it's worth a look." He pulled around the circular drive and drove down toward the main road.

"I'm glad the roads aren't too icy. This curvy hill can be interesting when they are," Olivia chuckled. "I once saw a guy in an old VW bug spin out and go sideways all the way down almost to the road before he managed to get it under control. I nearly bit my fingernails off watching."

"You know, the driveway at Candlewick may be a bit challenging in icy weather too," Josh mentioned thoughtfully. "The road up to it isn't any worse than your road, or not much, at least, but the driveway is a little on the steep side. I wonder if we will have to rebuild it, if we buy the house?"

"I don't know Josh, the Hills lived there and

apparently had winter parties and all that, so maybe it isn't as steep as it looks, or it doesn't ice up too badly."

"Ah, I think you hit the nail on the head with both of those thoughts. The driveway faces south, and is in the clear, so it gets both the morning and afternoon sun, I'm betting, and it does have a pretty decent curve to it, so the steepness may actually be less than it seems even though it is sitting on a high hill."

After a fairly short time of looking, Josh spotted a pretty silver Buick Enclave with all wheel drive and leather interior that they both liked a lot. They would be able to remove the last row of seats and put the girl's crates there, and the leather wouldn't attract hair too badly, so it was perfect. The both test drove it and loved the way it drove, so Josh negotiated on the price, paid for the SUV and the extended warranty and arranged to pick it up later.

He hugged Olivia as they stepped outside. "That was a lot easier and quicker than I expected. I thought for sure we'd end up at several dealerships before we found the right one."

"I know, right? I can't believe we found it at the first one. That has to be a record of some kind," Olivia grinned, leaning against him as they walked back to his patrol car.

They stopped and bought a large tub of vegetarian chili, salad and grilled cheese sandwiches from a restaurant in town for an early dinner for Sally and themselves on the way back to the hospital.

"I'm starving," Josh laughed, as the delicious smell of the chili filled the car. "I forgot to eat lunch today and didn't even realize it until I walked into the restaurant and the aromas hit me."

"Poor Love," Olivia murmured, brushing his hair back

from his forehead with her fingers. "You work too hard to miss eating lunch. Speaking of working, how did you manage to get the rest of the day off today?"

"Lucky for me, it was a slow day in the criminal world, and the temporary Captain was in a great mood, since he just found out that he's going to be a father. He actually spontaneously offered me the day off to look for a vehicle and believe me, I jumped at it. It is a bit of a drag to have to drive the patrol car all the time," he laughed. "I feel like I'm on constant duty. I'll have to find a nice gift for him for the baby to express my gratitude."

"Well, tell him thank you for me too. It was such a nice surprise to be able to spend this time with you today."

When they arrived at the hospital, Jimmy was sound asleep in his bed sporting a huge gauze bandage wrapped around his head like a turban.

"Awww, he looks so tiny and pathetic with that big bandage," Olivia got her phone out of her purse and snapped a picture. "He probably won't remember much of this, but he can have the picture to show his friends when he's older."

Sally smiled, "He'll love that. He woke up for a few minutes when they first brought him back, but he was in a lot of pain, so they gave him a shot that knocked him back out." She looked worried, "I didn't realize how badly he would hurt after the surgery. The doctor said the first three weeks will be rough, but he's prescribing plenty of pain medicine, so Jimmy will mostly be doing a lot of sleeping."

"That's good, because his body will need a lot of rest to heal from the surgery. It's a pretty traumatic operation," Josh stated. "I read up on it intensively when Olivia first told me about Jimmy. Rest is very important, as well as keeping his head elevated and icing it to help prevent swelling."

"Oh, a friend of yours, Nora stopped by to see you, and said she'd give you a call soon," Sally informed Olivia. "She seems really nice. She was part of the surgical team, and she said the doctor did a great job on Jimmy."

Olivia smiled, "She *is* very nice. She's the one who told me about the organization that helped make Jimmy's insurance cover the surgery."

Josh and Olivia served the food into the plastic plates and bowls the restaurant had provided and everyone dug in hungrily.

"Yum," Olivia said happily. "Just the right amount of spice."

"Sally, is there anything you need for the night? We're leaving the leftovers here for you in case you get hungry later, since we ate so early. I'm thinking it would be a good idea for me to drive your car over here and leave it in the lot so you have it in case you need it for some reason. I have to pick up my new car, so Liv can follow me here, and drop me at the dealership afterward," Josh said. "Does that sound like a good idea?"

"That sounds perfect Josh. Thanks for that. I doubt I'll need anything, but it always feels safer having a car available, just in case."

"Okay, that's the plan then," Olivia smiled. "We're going to head out now and do the car switches. It'll be after visiting hours by the time we get back probably, so we won't try to come in. If you need anything, call us."

Josh and Olivia decided to bring Molly and Sheyna with them to drop off Sally's car and pick up Josh's new SUV.

Everything went smoothly, with Olivia following Josh in his new car back to Birchwood. As they passed by the smaller of the two houses that Jack Hill had left to James, Josh suddenly pulled over to the side of the road next to the trees just past the house, made a U-turn and parked beside the trees. Olivia did the same and pulled in behind him.

After a few seconds, he got out of his car, closing the door quietly, and walked back to Olivia's car. She rolled the window down to see what was going on.

"I saw someone walking past the big window downstairs just now," Josh said softly. "Back up enough so that you still can't be seen easily from the house, but make sure you have enough room to get out of here quickly if you need to. I radioed Headquarters for backup, but I'm afraid whoever's in there may run before they get here if they spot us, so I'm going to try to sneak up and keep an eye on them." He looked at her sternly, "You need to promise me that if anything looks dangerous—anyone comes toward you besides me—you will get out of here immediately and go somewhere safe. If you're not worried about yourself, remember you have Molly and Sheyna in the back in their crates."

"Josh, please be careful and don't let them see you," Olivia drew in a sharp breath. "It may just be a vagrant, but if it is Salger and his gang you could be in a lot of danger."

"I'm more concerned about you Liv. I have my service weapon," he kissed her quickly. "Keep your eyes open and your doors locked."

Olivia watched worriedly as he melted into the trees, moving stealthily in the direction of the house. She peered hard into the forest alongside the property, trying to force her eyes to adjust to the camouflage created by the waning late afternoon sun filtering through the shadows and the trees.

It seemed like forever, but was really only about fifteen minutes before Molly started growling softly and Olivia heard distant shouting, then short, shrill chirps from a police siren, and a muffled voice from a bullhorn and a battered white panel truck went racing down the road in the opposite direction from her car. She started the engine and was ready to take off if she needed to. Molly barked and moved restlessly in her crate.

Olivia started to pull around Josh's SUV to where she could see the house but before she had a chance a state police car barreled down the driveway and spun out into the road in pursuit of the truck, flashing lights on and siren blaring.

She pulled her car up the road toward the house, watching carefully for any signs of movement. There was nothing. *Oh my, I hope Josh was in that patrol car with the other cop,* she thought to herself. *If I didn't have the girls with me, I'd go and make sure he's not lying somewhere hurt.*

She turned off the engine again, waiting and trying not to bite her nails in worry. Molly whined softly, sensing Olivia's fear. "It's okay Mols," Olivia crooned, trying to ease her own nerves more than Molly's. "Josh knows what he's doing."

She'd almost succumbed to the nail-biting urge when Josh appeared in the driveway by the house, walking toward her, looking unharmed. She let out a pent up breath that was almost a sob of relief.

Josh motioned for her to drive up the driveway, and she quickly obliged, jumping out of the car to hug him as soon as she put it in park.

"Are you all right?" she asked breathlessly. "I was so worried when the cars raced off and you didn't come back."

"I'm fine sweetheart," he kissed her and held her for a moment, seeing how worried she'd been. "By the time I'd made my way through the trees to the house, Salger and another man I didn't recognize were loading James into the truck. He had his hands tied behind his back, and he looked pretty beaten up, but he was still alive, though he didn't seem to be able to walk on his own, even though he was awake. I snapped a couple of pictures on my phone. Both of the men had guns, and since they were holding James, I couldn't risk his life by trying to attempt an arrest without backup. Something must have alerted them to my presence though, because another man came running out of the house and took off on foot through the woods and Salger and the other guy threw James in the truck and roared off. I went after the man who was on foot, but he had a head start and I lost him."

"Well at least we are now completely sure that he is their prisoner, not their accomplice," Olivia remarked. "Who was in the patrol car chasing the truck?"

"Michael Fallon," Josh said grinning. "He's young and eager, and for all that he isn't as experienced as some, he's turning out to be a fine Trooper." He radioed for more backup, so hopefully by now O'Brian or Hendricks is assisting him in the chase. I need my radio." He laughed, "I was in the patrol car almost all day and nothing exciting happened, but as soon as I've got my personal car with no radio, we have a whole batch of trouble going on."

"Olivia laughed as she got into her SUV and turned it

around. Josh walked down and retrieved his new car, backing it up the driveway and parking just in front of Olivia's car.

His cell rang as he exited the little SUV. The conversation was brief.

"Liv, I'm going to be stuck here for a while, so you might as well take the girls and go on home. I'll come as soon as I can, but we have to search the house and see if they left any clues to where they may be headed, so it may be pretty late when we're done."

"Okay Josh, just be careful and let me know when you're coming back." Olivia hugged and kissed him and got back into her car.

She'd gotten the girls fed, made sure Dave, the security guard had eaten and had fixed herself a cup of tea when Josh called to say that they'd found some things they needed to take back to Headquarters and process. Unfortunately the truck with Cordell, James and the mystery guy had given Fallon the slip and gotten away. Josh was going to meet Fallon at Headquarters and just spend the night at his apartment once he'd gotten his work done for the night, so he didn't disturb everyone coming in late.

Molly and Sheyna followed Olivia upstairs and jumped on the bed. *It feels strange with no one in the house except me, and the girls,* she thought. *Well, the guard is on the couch, but that's not the same. With Josh, Sally and Jimmy all staying here the last few days, it's felt like having a family,* she curled up in the bed hugging Molly with Sheyna purring in her sleep against her neck. *I think I could get used to that.*

CHAPTER FOURTEEN

Olivia was drinking coffee when Josh called the next morning.

"Good morning sweetheart," he said in his sexy voice. "I wanted to let you know that I arranged for Jimmy to spend another night in the hospital, as they said he was still in a lot of pain. They will be able to regulate his medications easier there."

"Hi sweetie," Olivia answered. "Poor Jimmy. I hate to hear that he's hurting so much. I'm sure Sally is worried sick."

"Actually, she seems to be doing well. She said the doctor said it was perfectly normal for him to be in a lot of pain, and as long as he was on the strong pain medication and being well taken care of, he should be fine and barely remember it once the swelling and pain subside. I think we should set up a nurse to live in the guestroom I've been using until Jimmy is healed enough to not need her."

"Wow, is he that bad off?"

"It's not that he's bad off, just that he is hurting, and the swelling from the surgery seems to be giving him vertigo, which makes him throw up a lot, so he needs a lot of care for the next couple of weeks."

"I feel so bad for him. He's such a little boy."

"I know, I do too. You know, it might be better for him if I rent them an apartment closer to the hospital for a month, that way there is room for him and Sally, as well as the nurse and the security guard," Josh said thoughtfully. "He's going to have to go for checkups every few days for the first two weeks and fifteen to twenty minute car rides each way from Birchwood will be miserable for him with the vertigo. What do you think?"

"Josh, that's a great idea. I'll miss having them here, but I can't imagine riding that far each way with vertigo," Olivia shuddered. "I've only had it once in my life and that was way too many times."

"Okay, I'll make some calls right now. By the way, we found some DNA on a shirt that was at the house last night. Unfortunately, it was James'. There were four different fingerprints found in the house, I figure one is probably James', but aside from Cordell Salger's, the other prints don't match anyone registered in AFIS, so it doesn't tell us who the other two guys are, but when we find them, we'll be able to prove they were at the house with Salger and James, so it wasn't a waste."

"You took pictures too, right?"

"Yeah, I got Salger and one of the guys with James in handcuffs, but I didn't get a picture of the other guy because he came running out of the house and into the woods too fast. He spooked his buddies badly. I think he must have seen me from the window somehow," he shook his head in disgust. "I couldn't even chase him until the other guys had taken off in the truck because I was afraid they'd kill James if they saw me."

"Listen Liv, I'm going to go to Boston today to pass these pictures around in person to the guys at Boston PD.

Maybe someone can tell us who this other guy with Salger is. I'm planning to stay over at my dad's house for the night. He called me this morning and said he had something he wanted to talk to me about, so I figured I might as well go to the Boston PD too. We haven't been able to trace Wendy Salger yet, so I thought I'd try to see if there were any signs of her living in Boston, since Cordell ended up there. I'd asked over the phone, but sometimes the results are better in person. Are you okay with that? The guard will still be there with you until tomorrow, when I'm going to send him to stay with Sally and Jimmy in the apartment. Yikes, as you say, I still have to arrange that before I go," he laughed. "It's going to be a busy day."

"I'm fine with it Josh. I'll miss seeing you though," Olivia let out a little sigh. "Oh, don't forget we are supposed to have dinner with Tiny and Abby tomorrow night at the Christmas Tree Inn. Abby agreed yesterday when I called her and Tiny said he was looking forward to it."

"I won't forget sweetheart." Josh laughed, "I have a feeling Tiny is a lot more excited about it than Abby is."

"I know, right?" Olivia chuckled, "She's had a few blind dates that were awful on an epic scale, so I think she's expecting more of the same."

"Hopefully she'll be pleasantly surprised this time. Sweetie, I've got to run so I can get to Boston early enough to talk to some people. I wish I had time to come by and kiss you before I leave. I love you Livvie. I'm going to miss you," he said in his sexy voice. "I'll call you tonight."

"I love you too and you know I'll miss you Josh," Olivia said with a touch of longing in her voice. "Drive super safely and give your dad a hug from me, even though we haven't met."

Josh laughed, "I know. It's insanely hard to get us all together right now. I'd ask you to come now, but since he wants to talk about something, it might be better if I went alone this time. He sounded a little worried and I want you to meet each other under good circumstances, not when he is distracted over something."

"That sounds good to me. I'm still the tiniest bit nervous about meeting your dad anyway, so yeah, better not when he's upset," Olivia laughed softly.

"Okay love, I'll call you tonight. Stay safe and please don't go exploring any houses while I'm gone," Josh half joked as they hung up.

Olivia sighed as she broke a couple of eggs into a pan with sizzling hot butter. *I will be so glad when we're married and I can snuggle with him every morning when I wake up,* she thought. *It's funny how much I miss him when I can't see him for a whole day. Well, I'll be busy enough going to see Jimmy and Sally and it definitely wouldn't hurt to think about all the points in the case. It feels like we're just spinning our wheels sometimes.*

It was starting to snow lightly when Olivia arrived at the hospital. Jimmy was sleeping and Sally looked exhausted.

"Was it a rough night?" Olivia asked sympathetically.

"He woke up several times during the night, either crying or throwing up or both. I just didn't realize how awful this would be for him. I know the doctor said he won't even remember a lot of it because of the pain meds, but it's so hard to see him like that," Sally confided. "He seems to be sleeping better today than he did last night, so I think I'm going to try to get some shut-eye myself while I can, if you don't mind."

"That sounds like a great idea. I'm so sorry he's having such a hard time," Olivia said sadly. "Josh has arranged for you guys to spend another night here, so just get as much sleep as you can whenever you can. He is going to call you later to tell you the rest of his plan and make sure it is okay with you."

"I'm sure it will be, dear; you two are so wonderful. Go have a fun day for yourself and I'll call you later after I've gotten a bit of sleep and can make sense," she chuckled sleepily.

Olivia decided to ignore the case for one day and spend it getting some work done on her poor neglected antique business, so she happily turned and headed home.

~~~

"Abby, if you try to cancel on me now, I will come over and drag you here," Olivia laughed as her friend tried to come up with an excuse to cancel the dinner date three hours before they were supposed to meet at Olivia's house. "You are being silly now. We already worked this out, so stop getting cold feet."

"Is Josh back from Boston yet?" Abby asked in a slightly whiny voice. "What if he doesn't make it in time?"

"He called ten minutes ago and said he'll be here in an hour and a half, so put your big girl panties on and get dressed in something nice," Olivia hung up laughing.

"Come on Molly, let's get you and Sheyna in your harnesses and take a walk around the neighborhood before Josh gets here," Olivia hugged Molly and went to collect the leashes and harnesses. Sheyna flew into the room at the rattling sound of the tags on the leashes.

"You are such an unusual cat Sheyna, my sweet. I'm
~~~

so lucky to have you girls," Olivia hugged her as she put the harness on and clipped the leads on both animals.

"Dave, we're only going up the hill and back, so if we're not back in half an hour send in the cavalry," Olivia joked with the security guard.

The sky was still spitting snow, though not enough to cause any worry for their evening plans. Sheyna and Molly set the pace, with Olivia following, taking care to not let the leads tangle.

I love living here in Birchwood, Olivia thought. *It's so beautiful, and until lately it's always been a pretty safe and peaceful place. We've got to catch these guys, rescue James and solve this case. Dave is nice, but I'm getting tired of needing a security guard in my own house.*

As they reached the top of the hill, Molly dove into the snowy bushes after a chipmunk and Olivia called her back quickly.

"Okay, Mols, no chasing chipmunks today. You'll have to save that energy for the park," Olivia laughed as Molly gave her a glum side look. "We'd better head down guys. I don't want Dave getting worried," she turned back down the hill, with Molly and Sheyna following on her heels, looking around and sniffing the ground cheerfully.

Back in her bedroom, Olivia searched through her closet to figure out what to wear for the double date. Molly and Sheyna watched from the bed as she chose one outfit after another, held it up to the mirror and put it back to look for yet another.

Finally, she decided on a pale blue blouse with a super soft white wool sweater and white pants. *Understated femininity,* she thought. *Capable but soft.* "Girls, does it make me look taller?" she asked hopefully.

Molly tilted her head from side to side as she pondered the question. Sheyna licked her paw and ignored it.

Olivia took a quick shower, dressed and put on some light makeup. She was just finishing taming her hair when Molly and Sheyna jumped off the bed and ran to the door and Josh knocked.

Olivia opened the door and Josh lifted her in a warm embrace, kissing her thoroughly as he slowly spun her in a circle. She felt her toes curl as the kiss ignited her senses.

"I've been wanting to do that since yesterday morning," Josh breathed against her hair, setting her down, but not releasing her. "Do you know how much I missed you?"

"Mmm, maybe almost as much as I missed you," Olivia replied breathlessly, snuggling into his arms and standing on tiptoe to kiss him again.

"Was everything all right with your father?" she asked.

"He's okay, but there's a story to tell there. Unfortunately, I don't think we have enough time before Abby gets here," Josh checked his watch.

"I'm just glad he is all right, I was a little concerned."

"I was too. He sounded worried on the phone, but it isn't his health or anything of that nature. I'll tell you all about it tomorrow, or after dinner if it doesn't run too late," he smiled. "We'd better get downstairs and feed the girls and Dave before Abby gets here."

Josh mixed the food and set it down for Molly and Sheyna after Olivia put it in their bowls, while she put the bags away and put a thawed casserole in the oven for the security guard for his dinner.

The guard was starting to move his stuff from Josh's guestroom to Sally's and Jimmy's for the night, but Josh stopped him.

"Dave, you're moving to the apartment tomorrow morning, so you might as well stay in the room for now. I'll sleep in my apartment tonight and move my stuff over tomorrow."

"Okay Boss, works for me," Dave replied cheerfully. "I hope you folks have fun tonight. Me and the girls'll watch some TV and I'll hit the sack early unless you need me to wait up until you get back."

Josh clapped him on the back, "No Dave, you enjoy your evening too. We'll try not to wake you when we come in."

Olivia was washing Molly's and Sheyna's bowls when they ran to greet Abby at the door, before she'd even had a chance to get out of her car.

Josh grinned, "It's uncanny how well they hear."

Molly barked and wagged her tail enthusiastically as she and Sheyna escorted their friend Abby into the kitchen.

Josh and Olivia both gave Abby a hug, then Olivia held her at arm's length to see what she'd chosen to wear.

Abby laughed, "No I didn't deliberately wear something awful to sabotage it." She twirled slowly to display the lovely emerald green dress she was wearing under a fashionable black coat.

"Nice Abby!" Olivia hugged her again. "You look fabulous. That's your very best color and I love the cut of that dress."

Abby beamed then looked worried, "I so hope we like each other. You've actually managed to get me excited about this Liv. What if we hate each other on sight? You said he looks like a biker. He's not a Neanderthal is he?"

Olivia and Josh both howled with laughter, "Tiny?"

Olivia gasped for breath between gales of laughter. "Did I tell you about the lovely china tea set he served us tea in last time we visited him? No, he isn't gay either," she anticipated the next question, and started laughing again. "He's just a nice handsome straight guy, who loved his mom, and happens to love preserving beautiful things. Guys like that are hard to find. If I wasn't so in love with Josh . . .."

Josh reached to tickle Olivia playfully, "He's a good guy, Abby," Josh agreed. "If I thought he was a whack job I'd never be encouraging you to go out with him, and neither would Liv, you know that."

"Yeah, I know. I'm just afraid to get my hopes up," Abby made a rueful face. "I know my luck with guys."

"Okay, I get that," Olivia smiled, sobering a little. "You guys may not hit it off at all as a couple. Maybe you'll just end up friends, but friends are good too, right?"

"Yes, they are, and I'll focus on that and try to stop worrying," Abby smiled. "Let's get this show on the road. I'll follow you in my car."

Tiny was just parking his car when they drove up. He was dressed nicely and it was obvious from the start that there was an attraction between him and Abby. Olivia was thrilled to notice that as the evening went on, they also seemed to have a lot in common. She and Josh smiled and shared a conspiratorial wink.

The two couples decided to forego dessert in lieu of a walk around the lovely property. It was decorated beautifully with all the bare trees covered in tiny clear lights that twinkled gently in the crisp night air. Soft music sounded faintly from hidden speakers.

Josh put his arm around Olivia's shoulders as they

walked, slowly drifting behind Tiny and Abby, allowing the two some privacy to talk and get to know each other.

Josh stopped at a little gazebo on the side of the path. He led Olivia up the two steps and pulled her into a warm embrace. They slow danced to the soft sensuous music, the coolness of the air making them cuddle even tighter. Olivia found herself wishing the song could last forever.

All too soon though, they heard Tiny and Abby returning along the footpath, talking softly.

"I'm sorry to be a drag," Abby chuckled ruefully, looking disappointed. "I am not dressed for being outside, and even though Tiny was sweet enough to offer me his coat, this dress was a huge mistake. My feet and legs are frozen."

Tiny sighed, "She wasn't even letting on that she was cold, until I went to hold her hand and realized it was like ice and she was shivering all over."

Olivia and Josh noticed that he was still holding her hand, and they both smiled.

"I never even thought about that Abs," Olivia shook her head in remorse. "You looked stunning and I simply didn't think about how cold you'd be in that outfit if we went walking after dinner. Some friend I am."

"It's my own fault Liv," Abby grinned, I was trying to look good, and didn't think about the temperature." Her eyes sparkled as she looked up at Tiny, who smiled at her as if mesmerized.

The group headed down the path toward their cars with Josh and Olivia in the lead.

Olivia heard a weird hissing noise and Josh grabbed her, throwing her and himself into Tiny and Abby, and knocking all four of them to the ground.

"Someone is shooting at us," he said in a quiet but terse voice over their yelps of surprise. "Stay low. We need to get to the restaurant. There's nowhere to hide out here." He showed them his service revolver, "I'll cover you. Stay as low as you can and run as fast as you can—no arguments."

He motioned for them to run, and Tiny and the two women all took hands and ran, heads low, with Josh coming behind with his gun raised. He fired in the air once to let the shooter know he was armed, not daring to aim toward the shooter, as he couldn't see him and could possibly hit an innocent person in the parking lot where he could hear someone screaming, as it was directly behind the area in which the shooter was hiding. He heard a bullet whizz by him and ricochet off the side of the stone building as they ran, but they made it into the restaurant safely. A vehicle screeched out of the parking lot just as they made it in the door. Josh figured it was probably whoever had screamed, as the shooter couldn't have had time to get to his car after the last shot.

All four were panting and shaken as they piled in the door, slamming it behind them. Josh immediately called for backup and ordered the restaurant staff to lock all the doors. The sound of Josh's gun firing had been heard loud and clear and the frightened staff obeyed quickly. Restaurant patrons, their dinners forgotten, were starting to gather in huddled groups away from the windows, as it became apparent that someone really had been shooting outside.

From inside the restaurant, Olivia and Josh heard the sound of a car peeling out of the parking lot and roaring away. Josh let out a pent up breath.

"Okay, everyone, my name is Detective Lieutenant Josh Abrams. I think the shooter is probably gone, but we need to stay calm and remain inside where we're sure we're safe until the police arrive."

The noise level rose as the people started discussing what had happened.

"Please, everyone, I need for you to remain calm and quiet until they arrive. I need to be able to hear if there is anything going on outside." Josh held his hand up and used his sonorous double bass voice to be heard over the din, effectively quieting the crowd of diners and staff.

A few brave and hungry people ventured back to try to finish their dinners, as it seemed the crisis was over and no one had actually been shot, but the rest vied for positions closest to the bar where they could more easily duck behind it for cover, or at least get a good stiff drink to calm their nerves.

In the midst of all the chaos, Olivia looked around and saw that Tiny had his arm protectively around Abby's shoulders and she didn't look at all displeased with the arrangement. Josh was busy talking on his phone to someone at Headquarters, but he hadn't left her side since they came in.

"Okay everybody," Josh spoke up loudly. "The police are here. Please everyone take your original seats. You'll all need to be interviewed briefly before you leave. Sir, can you please have the staff unlock the doors now? My people are here." He turned to Olivia, Tiny and Abby. "We're going to have to walk the guys through what happened from the time of the first shot, when I knocked you all down. Hopefully you can all go home after that. I think I'm going to be here for a while."

Olivia squeezed his hand and gave him a sympathetic look.

"Josh, I hate to be a pain, but if I have to be walking around for very long out there, my feet are going to be wicked unhappy," Abby grimaced, wiggling her still half frozen toes. "Do you think they can make it quick on the outdoor part? I can volunteer to go into the barracks or Headquarters or wherever tomorrow after work if I need to."

"Oh, right. I forgot about that Abby. Yes, I'll make sure you don't have to be out there long. There were four of us, so you can do your part first to get it over with, and I'll tell the guys to make it quick. Then you can leave or come back in where it's warm and relax until Tiny and Liv are done."

"Thanks Josh," Abby smiled, tucking her hands into her coat pockets and going with Josh to greet O'Brian and Hendricks.

It didn't take very long for the detectives to finish with Abby, Tiny and Olivia, so after giving Josh a quick and slightly surreptitious hug, Olivia caught a ride home with Abby. She happily noticed that Tiny and Abby shared a quick kiss goodnight through the car window and that they were both smiling a bit shyly while their hands continued to touch as he backed away until their fingertips finally couldn't reach each other.

CHAPTER FIFTEEN

Josh was tied up for the next several days on a convoluted criminal court case two counties away where he'd accidentally been the first responder when he'd heard the call come through as he was leaving a friend's house a block away from the incident almost a year ago. The trial was so time consuming that he'd barely had time even to talk with Olivia on the phone except at night.

The town where the trial was taking place was three hours away from Birchwood, so he was staying in a motel for the duration. He'd arranged for a policewoman he worked with and knew well to stay in the guestroom at Olivia's house. She would be working in the daytime, but at least she was there at night. She and Olivia liked each other on sight.

In the meantime, Olivia had been visiting with Jimmy and Sally every day and getting some work done on refinishing an antique upholstered chair she'd found that needed to be sanded down and reupholstered. It had been peaceful and there had been no sightings of Salger, James or anyone connected to the case.

"Well Molly me girl," she sighed late Thursday afternoon, brushing the dust from her hands and laying the sander down, "I think it's time to go play some Frisbee.

What do you think? Sheyna, are you up for it?"

Molly jumped up and down and woofed her enthusiasm. Sheyna blinked her pretty amber eyes and yawned, stretching her legs and all her claws.

Olivia laughed, "Okay, I'll take that as a yes from both of you. Let me get changed into something a bit less dusty and we'll head to the park."

After a nice romp through the mostly brown leaves, Molly and Sheyna seemed to have had the edge taken off their boundless energy, so Olivia loaded them back into the SUV and headed home. *It's amazing how much I miss Josh after not seeing him for a few days,* she thought wistfully. *I hope the trial is over soon.*

Olivia was pleased to arrive home to find the house smelling of pizza and garlic bread, and Julie, the policewoman, setting the table for them.

"I passed by Cipriano's on the way here and couldn't resist," Julie smiled cheerfully. "I hope you're in the mood for pizza."

"Always!" Olivia grinned. "There is never a bad time for eating pizza or chocolate, though I try not to do either that often. You just made my night."

She fed the girls their kibble and changed their water dishes quickly, while Julie ran the pizza cutter through the pizza to completely sever each slice.

"Are you up for the next Harry Potter movie after dinner?" Olivia swallowed a bite of crunchy garlic bread. "We still have the last two to watch."

"Definitely. I know you want Josh to hurry back, but I'm going to miss our movie nights," Julie laughed. "Since I started working as a cop, I haven't really had much time for my old friends and they are all married and having kids, so we don't have as much in common as we used to. I'd kind of forgotten how much I missed having a girlfriend to hang out with."

"Yes, I can imagine. Well, you and I have a lot in common, even though I'm not a cop, since I'm engaged to one, and I'm learning to be an investigator, plus we like the same movies, so I hope we'll stay friends and have lots of movie nights even after this job is over for you." Olivia hugged her new friend warmly.

~~~

Olivia slept in a little and woke up to the sound of her cell phone ringing.

"Good morning Josh," she answered happily. "I love waking up to the sound of your voice. Where are you?"

"On the way back finally. The trial is over and I'm all done with it. I have a lot of catching up to do at Headquarters today, and I'm pretty tired, so I'm planning to just go home and crash after work today. Do you have plans for the weekend?"

Olivia laughed, "Well, after hearing that you're back, I'm hoping I'll have some with you."

"And I was hoping you'd say that," Josh said with a grin in his voice. "I want to take you and the girls to Boston to meet my dad if you're up for it."

"Yay!" Olivia chuckled. "I was seriously starting to think he would be my father-in-law before I ever met him."

"I'm going to ask Julie to stay on at your house for now since you are getting along so well. It's probably not a good idea to have it empty over the weekend anyway with Salger and his guys on the loose."

"That's a great idea Josh. It really wouldn't be fun to come home to find all my things trashed. Actually, I was
~~~

thinking about asking Julie if she'd like to be my roommate until you and I are married, and maybe I could rent her the house fairly cheaply afterward. I think she's lonely and she can't have any pets in her apartment and really wants them. She keeps saying how much she loves being here. Oh!" Olivia cried. "I'll bet she would be perfect for the program at the retirement home. She could foster or adopt and I think she'd be happy to have the residents visit their former pets. She's such a sweet person."

"She really is, and I think that's a wonderful idea. All of those ideas actually," he laughed. "You're on a roll sweetheart."

"I'm so excited now," she laughed. "You're coming back, I'm finally going to meet your dad and I think Julie will really like these ideas. It's going to be a fabulous day."

The day actually flew by, quickly. Olivia spent a good deal of it going through her clothes to figure out what to take on the weekend trip.

For all that she was mostly convinced that Josh's dad would be a great person and not snobbish, part of her still felt a tiny bit intimidated by the thought of meeting him. Josh was the only billionaire she'd ever known personally, and since she hadn't realized in the beginning that he was rich, it hadn't been an issue for her. Knowing in advance that his dad was so incredibly wealthy made it a little scary.

Finally she settled on a classic 'little black dress', a pair of nice wool pants with a pretty blouse and cardigan and a couple of extra outfits, just in case. She chose a thin gold chain with a pearl for her necklace and a couple of Bakelite bangles for her wrist. *Yikes,* she thought. *I hope I'm taking the right things. I want to look classy, but not over done. I hope he's as down to earth as Josh says he is. I don't have the wardrobe for 'rich and fancy'.*

Molly tilted her head as if asking why Olivia was so worried. Olivia dropped to her knees and hugged Molly, laughing. "What would I do without you girls to keep me sane?"

Sheyna came over and stood on her back feet, nuzzling Olivia's chin to get pets too. Olivia played with both animals for a while, then took out the grooming box and gave them both a good brushing. "Now you are both looking even more beautiful than usual," she kissed them and put away the grooming stuff.

Before closing her small suitcase, Olivia wrapped two of the First Edition classics she'd found to give Josh's dad and tucked the package into the suitcase between her clothes. She decided to hold onto the other books she'd found, in hopes that he would be able to come up for Christmas. So far, those books were the only things she'd been able to think of to give him. *Oops,* she thought, grabbing her prettiest swimsuit, and tucking it into the full suitcase, *I almost forgot Josh told me to bring this. It will be wonderful to get to swim in a heated pool in the middle of the winter.*

Molly nudged her with her nose to let her know it was time to go outside and then have lunch. "Girls, we're going to get to meet your future grandpa tomorrow. What do you think of that?" Olivia zipped the suitcase and led the way downstairs.

After lunch, Olivia locked the girls in the house and drove quickly to the small grocery store down the hill. *It's hard to decide which is less dangerous,* she fretted, *leaving them home alone or leaving them in the car. That's the only thing that I really don't like about trying to solve mysteries*

—having to worry that someone will harm Molly and Sheyna to get back at me.

Luckily, everything was fine when she got home, though Molly did look a bit disappointed that she had been left at home. As Olivia put away the groceries, Sheyna levitated herself onto the counter to make sure Olivia had gotten everything she was supposed to, and Molly sat waiting hopefully, to see if anything fell to the floor that needed picking up and eating.

Just as she was done, her cell phone rang, showing Abby as the caller.

"Hey girlfriend, long time no hear," Olivia teased.

"That's because I've been busy," Abby answered rather smugly.

"Oh yeah?" Olivia chuckled. "What have you been up to now? Do I want to know?"

"You bet you do!" Abby laughed. "It's all your fault, **and** you even get to say 'I told you so'. After that wild fiasco of a double date, Tiny called me the next morning and asked me out for dinner again. We had a blast, and then the next day, I took off work and we went for a ride on his motorcycle over to Gorham and even checked out the thrift stores while we were there. He is so much fun!" Abby squealed, "Thank you so much for making me go on that crazy date! We've been talking and emailing each other every day."

"Yay! I knew you guys would like each other. Is it more than a friendship kind of liking, or do you know yet?"

"Oh, it's definitely more than a friendship kind." Abby sighed sobering. "It's scaring the skin off me already. How can I like someone this much after only a week? That's not even possible, right?"

"Sure it is, Abs. Josh and I fell in love so quickly it scared me half to death," Olivia assured her, laughing. "I'm not even surprised . . . delighted, but not surprised. You guys have a lot in common and he's such a great guy. I am so glad you like each other!"

"Me too! We're going out again tonight and I'm so excited. I haven't even had a second date in ages, much less a fourth," she laughed. "We're going to play pool after dinner too, which is way cool."

Olivia laughed, "Yes that does sound way cool. I hope you have a blast. Oh, before I forget to tell you, Josh is taking me and Molly and Sheyna to meet his dad in Boston this weekend, so we'll be gone until late Sunday night. Julie is staying here though, if you need anything from my house. You can't have the antique clothes irons, but anything else you need from the storage room is fair game."

"Great! Hey, so he's finally taking you to meet his dad, huh? Are you nervous?"

"Yeah, a little. He sounds wonderful, but . . . he lives in a whole other world from me." Olivia's voice was soft. "What if he doesn't like me? I mean, I'm marrying his son. It's going to be awful if my father-in-law hates me. You know how much I value family."

"How could he possibly not like you?" Abby remonstrated. "You're the most lovable, kind person I know. He's going to adore you Liv. Stop freaking yourself out."

"Thanks sweetie, I needed that. When Danny left me without a word two days before we were supposed to get married, my self confidence took a beating. I thought I'd managed to bounce back, but apparently there's still a little self doubt in there, ready to hit me over the head once in a while," Olivia sighed. "It's funny, I am not even very afraid of Josh leaving me, which surprises me, because after Danny, that was a big issue for me for a while, yet perversely, I am still afraid something else will go wrong that could ruin everything."

"It won't," Abby said warmly. "You should tell me when you need a pep talk. You're always there for everyone and so strong and confident, that I'm constantly surprised when you need reassuring about anything. I guess I sometimes forget that you can get scared and hurt like the rest of us."

"Aww, you're making me blush now," Olivia laughed. "I think we can adjourn this meeting of the mutual admiration society now. I have to straighten up the house and clean the bathrooms and such before I start making dinner.

Oh, I know I asked you if you wanted to move in with me ages ago, and you said no, but I wanted to make sure you hadn't changed your mind, because I am thinking of asking Julie if you're sure you don't want to. How do you feel about that? You're my very best friend and I don't want to ever risk hurting your feelings."

"Thanks for making sure Liv. No, I love my apartment for the most part. It's closer to town and more accessible to my mom and all the shops and everything. I think it's a great idea for you to ask Julie. As often as you get involved in dangerous situations, the more cops you know, the better," she laughed. "Julie seems like a fun and nice person. I'd like to get to know her better myself."

"Okay, I'll ask her tonight then," Olivia said happily. "You need to call more often and let me know how things are going with Tiny. I want to hear all the good stuff!"

"You've got it Bestie! Have a fun weekend and say hi to Josh for me."

Olivia grabbed the vacuum and chased it through the house before tackling the bathrooms. Once everything was cleaned and straightened up, she took Molly and Sheyna for a walk around the neighborhood then started fixing dinner.

By the time Julie opened the door at 5:30, the aroma of fresh broccoli soup and spiced roasted vegetables filled the kitchen.

"Yum, that smells delicious!" Julie smiled, walking in and placing a bag with freshly baked croissants from the bakery on the table. "Here's the bread to go with it."

"Ooh, great idea. Thanks for thinking of it," Olivia opened the bag to peek inside.

"I'm going to run and change out of this uniform. Be right back," Julie, took off her heavy 'duty belt' as she headed toward the guestroom where she was staying.

Olivia set the table and poured them each a glass of wine to go with their dinner, then went to put another log in the fireplace. Molly brought her a small log from the rack and watched as she placed it on top of the partially burnt ones, then fetched another for her.

"Wow, she is so smart," Julie said from the doorway. "How did you teach her to do that?"

"Actually, it was easy. She loves to bring things to people, so I just showed her a few times and she got it right away. Whoever had her before she ended up at the shelter, obviously worked with her a lot, and yes, she's wicked smart too."

"That's for sure. She and Sheyna both seem smarter than your average bear to me."

"Listen, I've been thinking," Olivia started as they walked back into the kitchen. "You have said a couple of times that you miss being able to have pets, so I was wondering if you'd be interested in being my roommate until Josh and I are married, and then maybe renting the house afterward."

"Seriously?!" Julie's mouth dropped open. "You have no idea how much I would love that!" She paused, looking crestfallen, "I don't think I could afford the rent by myself once you move out though. My little apartment is only six-hundred dollars per month, and I can barely afford that and the utilities and still be able to eat."

"I would rent it to you for an affordable price, so no worries. My mortgage payments are very low. They are only four-hundred and fifty per month, and I wouldn't charge you more than that, so you'll actually have more left over to live on, and though it may be bigger than your apartment, at least it's heated by wood not electricity, so your bill shouldn't be any higher," Olivia smiled at Julie's stunned expression. "I love this house and want to see it lived in by someone who will appreciate it and take good care of it. I really don't want to sell it, at least not right away, and I'd be afraid to rent to someone I didn't know. You would of course have first dibs whenever I do decide to sell it."

"Are you sure about this?" Julie's eyes shone. "I mean, because I'm ready to move in right this minute!" She laughed and threw her hands over her heart, "I can't believe it. WhooHoo! Goodbye tiny apartment! I'm so glad I don't have a lease."

"You are more than welcome to move in tonight, if you want," Olivia laughed, "But it might be easier to start all that in the daytime, when you can see."

Julie laughed and sank into a chair, "Once you and Josh are married, will I be able to have pets here? I know you do, but they are yours and it's your house."

"Oh, yes, of course you can have pets. That's another thing I wanted to talk to you about. Do you remember I told you about the plan my friend Pam and I had for trying to keep the retirement home residents' pets in homes where they could visit them once in a while? Would you be interested in being a part of that—adopting or fostering a dog or cat and letting their elderly previous owner visit them?"

"Definitely, you can sign me up right now. Well, at least once I'm living here, I guess," Julie smiled. "Or once you and Josh are married, as I guess you probably don't want another animal here before you leave."

"As long as they get along with Molly and Sheyna, I wouldn't have a problem with it. We can sign you up now if you want." Olivia gave a huge sigh of relief and contentment. "I think we're going to have a lot of fun being roomies. I don't even know when Josh and I are getting married at this point, but it's looking like it will be in the spring after all, since I don't see us being able to get the venue and everything else put together by Christmas like we had hoped. It's just way too much to do in too little time."

"I'm sorry you can't have a Christmas wedding, but it'll be a lot warmer and you won't have to dress like you're in Antarctica either," she laughed.

"You're right," Olivia chuckled. "That would have put a crimp in my style for sure. How on earth I would have planned the clothes for the wedding party, I have no clue.

Oh, will you be one of my Bridesmaids? Abby is going to be my Maid of Honor and I'm hoping my friends, Vicki and Nora will be Bridesmaids too."

"I'd love to be a Bridesmaid. Can you believe I'm twenty-seven and I've never even been to a wedding before?" She laughed, "I am so excited by all of this! A fantastic new friend, a wonderful new place to live, the possibility of finally having pets of my own again and now I'm going to be a Bridesmaid. Just Wow!"

Olivia hugged her, "I'm so relieved that you want to live here. I'd thought of asking Sally Tanner if she wanted to rent it after I move, but she's used to a much bigger lot, with chickens and everything, so it really wouldn't be right for her, besides, she has her own house, which she'd have to sell to do it, so it didn't make sense. I was starting to worry that I might have to sell the house after all."

"Well, I'm still stunned by my sudden change of fortune," Julie grinned. "I've gotten so spoiled staying here for the last week that I was dreading going back to my teensy little apartment. If you're positive you want me to move in, I am giving my thirty days notice tomorrow."

"Please go right ahead and give notice. Actually, now that your job for Josh is over and he won't be paying you to stay here, how would you feel about moving in right away, and I won't charge you any rent until I move out, as you would be still helping to protect me and the girls? That way you could move right in while you're still paying your last month over there," Olivia smiled. "You'd be doing me a favor moving in, since I really don't want to go out of town and leave the house empty with Salger and his crew around and you living here isn't going to raise my mortgage payments."

"That sounds wonderful to me! I'll start moving my stuff over tomorrow. I'm so happy!" Julie was almost jumping up and down in delight. "Where are you going?"

"Oh my, with all the excitement, I forgot to tell you. Josh is taking me and the girls to meet his dad in Boston finally. We should be back late Sunday night I think."

"That's great! I'm glad you're getting to meet him finally. It sounds like a fun trip, but maybe a little nerve wracking meeting a future in-law, right?"

"Yes, a little," Olivia smiled. "I'm less worried now than I was before though, so hopefully it will go well."

After dinner, they cleaned up the kitchen together and watched the last two Harry Potter movies, back to back, then Olivia yawned sleepily and said goodnight.

As soon as Molly had done her business, she and Sheyna followed Olivia upstairs. *I shouldn't have stayed up so late watching the second movie, but it's hard to stop when they're so good,* Olivia chuckled to herself as she drifted to sleep, dreaming of magical swords and powerful spells.

CHAPTER SIXTEEN

The sound of the alarm caught Olivia in the middle of a dream and for a moment, she thought Voldemort had just used the death curse on James, before her brain woke up.

"Yikes, girls, those Harry Potter inspired dreams were wild. I hope I wasn't kicking you all night," she yawned, stretching and hugging Sheyna and Molly. "I really hope the part about James wasn't some kind of premonition."

She stood up and stretched again, "Okay sweeties, we're going on an adventure this weekend, and Josh is coming to pick us up in a couple of hours, so I guess we'd better get up and moving."

Olivia dressed in a pretty black and white dress after her shower and grabbed her suitcase and headed down to fix breakfast. Julie was sleeping in after their late movie night, so Olivia wrote her a quick note, reminding her that they'd be back on Sunday night. *I'd better get the girls' bowls, kibble and coats and stuff ready to go as soon as they finish eating,* she nudged herself, as she was still feeling a bit scattered after her dramatic dreams.

Once she'd fed the girls, eaten her own breakfast and washed the dishes, she quickly packed Molly's and Sheyna's stuff and made a couple of sandwiches for her and Josh in case they got hungry on the trip and didn't have a good place to stop for lunch.

Molly jumped up and ran to the front door just before Josh knocked. Olivia hurried to open the door for him and he picked her up in a bear hug, kissing her breathless before setting her down.

"Why are you knocking? Did you lose your key?" she asked, hugging him tightly.

"No, I just felt that it was better, since Julie is staying here too. I didn't fancy getting shot first thing in the morning," he laughed. "She's an excellent markswoman."

"Ooh, I hadn't thought of that," Olivia laughed. "The perils of having your own live-in bodyguard."

"I missed you so much Liv," Josh kissed her again, then knelt to pet Molly and Sheyna who were almost as excited to see him as Olivia was. "Yes, I missed you too, girls."

"So we're all ready to go, unless you'd like some more food or anything before we leave," Olivia smiled. "I know you said you were eating breakfast before you left your apartment, but in case you didn't . . .. Oh, I also have a thermos of coffee for each of us and some sandwiches."

"We're all ready then. Thanks for fixing the sandwiches and coffee. I know they will come in handy." Josh picked up her suitcase and the little bag with the girl's things in it and took Sheyna in his other hand.

Olivia let Molly do her business quickly while Josh loaded Sheyna into her crate in his SUV. He had the bags stowed by the time Olivia and Molly came back, so once Molly was securely in her crate, he opened the door for Olivia, then got in and pulled out of driveway.

Olivia leaned against him for a moment, breathing in his scent and just feeling happy.

Josh squeezed her hand, "I never got the chance to tell you what my dad had wanted to see me about the last time I went down. Apparently, there are some mysterious things happening around his vacation home on Mary's Orchard that he wants me to look into. Of course, now that I've told him that we're starting our own detective agency, he wants to hire us to look into the situation."

"Oh wow! We have our first official client?" Olivia was thrilled.

"Well, not quite yet. He has friends staying in the house until next month, so we can't go until they leave. You know, we will probably have to stay there for a while in order to solve it. Will you be okay with packing up the girls and living on Mary's Orchard for . . . say, a month or so?"

"I'll just let my customers know that I'll be gone for a while, and I think they'll be fine with it." Olivia grinned, "So, are you going to tell me what the mysterious happenings are, or make me guess?"

"Actually, I'm going to make you wait until we get to dad's house and let him tell you, so you hear it first hand and my preconceptions don't color your thoughts at all," Josh smiled. "It's always better to get it from 'the horse's mouth'."

"Oh dear, more waiting," Olivia laughed, sighing in pretend frustration. "You're right, though, that is probably the best way to do it. Oh, by the way, Julie was thrilled with the idea of moving in and with renting the place once we are married. She is going to start moving her stuff over right away."

"I'm so glad. I will feel much better, knowing she is staying with you, especially until we round up the Salger gang. Speaking of your safety, how are you doing with your Aikido classes? Are your wrists still getting sore, or have they strengthened up enough to handle it?"

"They are doing much better with it now, and I'm enjoying the classes tremendously, as well as learning a lot. I already feel a whole lot more confident in my ability to defend myself against an attacker, though I really don't want to have to prove it anytime soon," Olivia grimaced. "The fake attacks in class are definitely enough for now. Between that and Molly and Sheyna helping me work on my moves by tripping me, I'm getting plenty of practice, especially in falling."

Josh laughed sympathetically, "I can only imagine. I remember well enough when I first started with it, how sore I was from getting the falls wrong now and then and even from some of the falls that I got right. You can only land on the same spots so many times before they start complaining loudly."

"Well, I definitely have a couple of those, right now," Olivia laughed. "Sometimes I really wish I had a hot tub."

"Hah! Luckily my dad does, and you and I will be more than welcome to use it. You did remember to bring your swimsuit, right?"

"Barely," she smiled. "I grabbed it at the last minute and now I'm really glad I did. That hot tub will feel like a little slice of heaven on my sore places, and it'll be great to go swimming in late November without freezing. Is it indoors or outdoors?"

"It's outdoors and on the roof next to the pool actually," Josh grinned.

"So, tell me more about your dad and what he's like," Olivia leaned her head against the headrest and looked at

Josh.

"Well, people have always said I look like him, and the older I get, the more I see the resemblance. I hope I look as good as he does when I get to be his age," Josh chuckled. "He's into keeping himself fit which is one of the reasons he likes having the swimming pool, so he can swim laps every day. The other reason he has kept the big house with the pool is that he enjoys providing free housing to foreign college students who can't afford to live in dorms or apartments. He gets to learn about their culture and be around young people, which keeps him young and they get a super nice, free place to live while they're here. It's a win/win. He takes American students once in a while too."

"Wow! That's wonderful." Olivia smiled. "I spent three years of high school abroad on a foreign exchange. It was a fantastic experience for me. I think it's really great of your dad to do that."

"He enjoys them so much, I think he gets as much value from it as they do, even if his isn't monetary value. He is definitely young at heart and I honestly think being around intelligent young people keeps his mind young too."

"I'm so excited that I'm finally going to meet him," Olivia said, then sighed. "Are you sure he's going to like me? Yikes, I'm pathetic, aren't I?" She laughed at her nerves. "I'm not usually this insecure, it's just that it's so important to me that we like each other."

Josh laughed and reached over to take her hand, "You are going to love each other. I know both of you, and I promise you that. You can trust me on this."

"Whew," Olivia leaned back and raised Josh's hand to her face and kissed the palm. "Did anybody ever tell you how wonderful you are?"

"I think you might have told me that, but you're more than welcome to tell me any time you want to," Josh laughed. "You're pretty wonderful yourself Miss McKenna." He squeezed her hand again, "Have I told you lately how much I love you?"

"You can never tell me too often sweetie," she laughed, then changed the subject. "How many people does he have staying at the house right now, do you know? Are we going to be spending much time with them?"

"He has three guys that are supposed to be spending the whole year here, but one of them had to go back home for a couple of weeks, because his uncle died, so he won't be here. The other two will be sharing most of their meals with us and hanging around studying probably," Josh grinned. "Wait until you get caught in the middle of the law students and my dad debating some of the finer points of their studies. He would have been a great law professor."

"What did he do, work-wise before he retired? I never thought to ask you. I know you said that both he and your mom came from wealthy families, and that your mom was a doctor."

"Dad was a lawyer, turned real estate developer, and I guess to some extent, he is currently an investor, even though he is officially retired. He does still own a few office buildings in Boston," Josh chuckled, "Dad was a rebel in the family for going into law. His family had made their fortune in real estate investment and development and he had been expected to follow in his father's footsteps. He and his dad had a falling out and he rebelled and decided to study law instead of going into the family business. He earned his Doctor of Juridical Science degree, then started practicing business and real estate law even though he and his dad had made up fairly soon after he started law school. He and my mom got married a couple of years after he graduated and I was born a year later." Josh paused to wink at Olivia, "After his first few years practicing law, he was also gradually starting to spend more and more time working in his father's business and finally gave up his law practice. Between the investment business and his family, he simply didn't have time for it."

"Wow, he sounds fascinating," Olivia smiled. "It's funny that he rebelled by becoming a lawyer, especially by earning the highest law degree you can get. In most families, that wouldn't be considered rebellion."

Josh grinned, "You're probably right there. My dad's family was huge on tradition and he has always been a nonconformist. For them, that was enough for him to be considered a rebel. Maybe if he'd wanted to just get a law degree, that would have been okay, but he wanted to practice law instead of stepping into the place reserved for him in the company. That was unacceptable," Josh shook his head. "His old man came around pretty quickly though, when he realized that family was more important than tradition."

"Well, I am getting less nervous about meeting him after hearing all of this," Olivia took a sip of coffee from her travel mug. "Josh, on a totally different subject, have you heard anything new about Cordell Salger or James Hill? I've been happy not to have any awful things happening lately, but I'm a little afraid that no news may be bad news for James."

"Unfortunately, there haven't been any new developments and no one has reported seeing any of them. I honestly don't know if that is good or bad for James. I guess it depends on why they haven't been seen lately. Maybe they're trying to stay under our radar for a while, in which case James may be still with them and relatively okay. The other scenario is less pleasant of course. If they gave up and left town, it's likely that James wasn't around anymore to make the trip. We've got our people watching for any sign of any of them."

"Even if they are still here, I don't have a good feeling about James," Olivia spoke sadly. "I had the strangest dream last night, and even though I know if was probably only because of all the Harry Potter movies Julie and I have been watching, it worries me a little. I watched Voldemort kill James. And unfortunately, it was James Hill, not James Potter."

Josh grinned for a minute, then quickly sobered, "I'm not going to lie to you sweetheart. I've been a little surprised they've kept him alive this long, since I can't think of any reason for it now that he's apparently taken them to both of his dad's houses, as well as his sister's house."

"I know. I don't have a good feeling about it. He must have already told them everything he knows about the bank as well, so I doubt they really need him anymore," Olivia said bleakly.

"When I saw him that night, he was in pretty bad shape. I wasn't close enough to tell if he'd been shot or just beaten badly, but he definitely wasn't doing well," Josh sighed.

Olivia sighed too, as she fixed the lid on Josh's second coffee mug for him to drink from.

The miles sped by and by 11:30 they were entering the Lantern Knoll area. Olivia was amazed at the wonderful old architecture. They drove past street after street of giant row houses that had mostly been transformed from majestic homes to fancy and probably very pricey boutiques and condos. It seemed odd to her, as someone who wasn't used to row houses that the wealthy of Lantern Knoll had wanted to jam all their houses together like that when they built them. It was beautiful though.

Josh pulled up to a spot in front of a towering five-story Federal-style row house with a red brick façade, and black wrought iron railings bordering the front steps.

Olivia was charmed by the gas street lamps and brick sidewalks. Except for the cars and more modern street pavement, it was like stepping into an earlier century. She admired the pretty winter wreath adorning the elaborate wooden front door with a wrought iron and stained glass lunette above it.

Josh took Molly's lead and clipped it on her collar, while Olivia lifted Sheyna from her crate, and slipped her harness on. They gave them a quick walk to the lovely park across the street, and Olivia looked around, enjoying the walk as much as the girls. Returning to the street, she picked Sheyna back up.

She took a deep breath and Josh smiled and squeezed her hand reassuringly as they mounted the steps. Josh rang the bell and it was quickly opened by a grinning young man with an armload of books who was obviously on his way out.

"Josh, I am pleased to see you again," he said, and nodded to Olivia and bowed to Molly and Sheyna."

Josh clapped him on the back softly, "It's nice to see you Tez. This is my fiancé, Olivia."

Tez' lilting Island accent sounded musical to Olivia's

ears. She smiled and nodded back to him. "I'm happy to meet you, Tez."

"It's nice to meet you also, Olivia."

Josh held the door for him so he could manage with all his books, and he nodded again as he hurried out the door.

"I'll be back in time for dinner. See you again then." The tall, thin young man called over his shoulder, heading down the street at an easy jog.

"He seems very nice. I hope he doesn't have to jog too far," Olivia smiled. "Those books looked heavy."

Josh laughed, "He sure had enough of them, didn't he? No, he doesn't have far to run. He rides with another student in the next block who has a similar class schedule."

They stepped into the foyer and Josh looked around, then called out.

"Dad? We're here!"

Olivia looked around. Though large and elegant, the foyer did not feel uncomfortable or intimidating. *Whew,* she thought, *so far so good.*

"Josh, it's good to see you son," Josh's father hurried down the staircase to meet them. "And you must be Olivia. I'm delighted to finally meet you." He shook her hand, smiling at her warmly. "This must be Molly and Sheyna," he said, reaching to pet each of them. You girls are almost as pretty as your mother."

"I'm very glad to meet you too, sir," Olivia smiled, looking up at what seemed to be almost an older mostly silver-haired version of Josh, except with brown eyes. "I can definitely understand why Josh said people think you look alike."

His eyes twinkled, and Josh chuckled. She looked back and forth at the two of them and shook her head in amazement.

"No one will have to guess how you'll look when you grow up Josh." She teased, drawing a laugh from both men.

"I'm glad you got here early," Josh's dad remarked cheerfully, leading the way through the house. "I'll have more time to spend getting to know my future daughter, and hopefully you two will have more time to relax and unwind." He turned left into what Olivia decided was the living room. "Josh has told me a little about the case you're involved with and I'm hoping you can both have a peaceful, nice weekend away from stress and danger."

"I'm looking forward to it sir," Olivia replied.

"No sirs, please. Call me Peter," he smiled warmly. "Make yourselves at home, I'm going to fetch us something to drink and some snacks, if you're hungry. I put a bowl of fresh water over here for Molly and Sheyna, so they're all set for now. What would you like to drink?"

"I'd love a French Vanilla Cappuccino from that wonderful machine you have, if you don't mind," Josh grinned, "Livvie?"

"Oh that sounds fantastic, yes please." Olivia beamed. "I love cappuccino."

"Great, why don't you have a peek at the family pictures on the walls and the mantel while I'm making the coffee. I'm sure you'll enjoy seeing Joshua as a baby." He shot a mischievous grin at Josh as he headed from the room.

Josh chuckled, "Thanks Dad!" he called in a wry voice, gathering Olivia into his arms and hugging her. "I should have seen that coming." He unclipped Molly's and Sheyna's lead so they could check out the room.

"Oh come on, this is going to be so much fun," Olivia

teased, pulling Josh toward the mantel. "I can't wait to see you in your cute little diapers."

Josh affected a pained expression under his grin. "That's what I was afraid of. I really should have come in and hidden those first."

"Is that your mom?" Olivia asked, pointing to a large oil painting on the wall, of a lovely young woman with slightly wavy dark hair and soft blue/green eyes. "She was so beautiful. Your eyes are just like hers too, so warm and twinkly. I wish I could have known her."

"Her name was Helen. You would have loved each other Liv. In many ways, you remind me of her—gentle—kind, yet fiercely loyal and courageous."

"I will have to learn to know her through you and your dad.

"Oh, my stars, look at you!" Olivia gasped. "You were adorable. You looked just like your mom when you were little, too. Now you look just like your dad. How cool is that?"

"I know, right? It's strange how kids' looks can change like that over time," Josh smiled, as Olivia paused in front of a picture of eight-year-old Josh with both his parents.

"Except for the eyes, I don't think I'd have recognized you in this one," she laughed. "You were all skin and bones and knobby knees here. It reminds me of a couple of my younger pictures. You were so cute, Josh."

"I'm going to have to see those now, you know," Josh laughed. "I'll bet you were gorgeous right from the get-go. I just can't see you with knobby, skinned up knees."

"Trust me, I had them," Olivia's eyes twinkled. "I may have been little, but I was a definite tomboy, and pretty gangly for a short girl too at one point.

"Oh my, you were a heartthrob when you were in your teens too," she gasped. "I'm talking Teen Idol material," she gaped at a picture of Josh and his prom date, then at the one next to it showing Josh standing by the river in swim trunks and another in his high school football uniform. "I'll bet you had every girl in your school crushing on you."

Josh rolled his eyes and grimaced, "If it hadn't been for my parents, I could easily have turned into a total creep from all the attention. They sat me down and had a nice long chat with me about how much my looks really meant, especially in the long run," Josh smiled wryly. "It took a couple of talks, but after watching a few 'friends' treat people really badly, including people that had once been their friends too, I woke up and figured out exactly what my parents meant."

"Yes, it's hard not to let attention and adulation go to your head, especially when you're young," Olivia said with a slightly sad expression on her face. "My best friend's older brother was a jock, and one of the best looking, most popular guys in high school. He'd been a really nice person until he became Captain of the football team," she made a rueful face. "He definitely let it get to him and became a real jerk . . . until he was in a car wreck and ended up in a wheelchair," Olivia's eyes misted. "He found out really quickly who his real friends were, and for the most part, they were the kids he'd been snubbing ever since he became popular. A few of them, didn't want anything to do with him anymore after the way he'd treated them, but most forgave him. The other jocks and their hangers-on, stopped coming to see him after a couple of visits, and I even heard them making fun of him later. Beauty really is skin deep."

Josh hugged her and led her over to a cozy love seat. As they sat he leaned back, putting his arm around her, and she relaxed against his shoulder. They were sharing a sweet kiss when his dad returned bearing a small tray with coffee that smelled so good it made Olivia's stomach rumble.

"Oh, that smells delicious!" Olivia reached to move a delicate little trinket dish that was in the way so he could set the tray down on the coffee table.

"Wow, Dad, look at these Danish Wedding Cookies! Is that a hint or something?" Josh laughed, putting a few of the tiny sugary cookies on a plate with several tiny vegetarian sandwiches for Olivia and starting to set it in front of her. "Do you like these?" he asked, holding the plate at a hover, "or should I take them for myself."

"I like them so much," Olivia cried, laughing, "that if you take them, I'll just have to steal them back from your plate."

Josh and Peter both chuckled.

"I think I'd give them to her son," Peter laughed. "And yes, that was definitely a hint. When are your two planning to have the wedding?"

Peter handed the coffee cups around to each of them, and doled out a few sandwiches and cookies for his son and himself, adding a couple more cookies to Olivia's plate, before taking a sip of the aromatic coffee. He watched Olivia's face, as she took her first sip. Her rapturous expression said it all and he smiled at her obvious delight.

Molly and Sheyna had finished sniffing the room and had opted for lying close to the people in hopes that someone would drop something good.

"We'd been hoping to have it at Christmas time, but with all that's been going on with the case, and figuring out where to have it, it is looking like we're going back to our original plan of a spring wedding," Josh looked at Olivia.

"We'd really hoped to be able to figure out how to have it in the winter, but maybe it's for the best, as an outdoor winter wedding could be a bit uncomfortable for everyone." Olivia grinned at Peter, then turned to Josh, "Remember how cold Abby was in her dress on our double date the other night? The guests would have had to wear ski clothes."

Peter laughed, "I suppose you could have had the wedding on skis, but I think watching you try to maneuver around in a wedding dress on skis might be enough to turn it into a comedy wedding, which is probably not quite the theme you had in mind."

"That's for sure!" Olivia chuckled. "I can ski fairly well, wearing normal ski clothes, but getting around in the flats in a long flowing dress—I don't even want to picture it."

Olivia was happy at how easily she and Peter got along. She found that he was already starting to feel like an old friend or family member that she just hadn't seen for a while. *Why was I so worried?* she wondered. *Josh told me we'd like each other, and he was right. I should trust him about people he knows.*

When there was finally a slight lull in the conversation, Peter stood. "Let me show you to your rooms and help you get your things upstairs."

When they reached the foyer, he and Josh picked up the luggage and all three people headed upstairs, followed by a very inquisitive dog and cat.

Once they'd put their things away and settled in a bit, they decided to go for a swim in the heated rooftop infinity pool. They wore long bathrobes that Peter provided over their swimsuits, to keep them warm until they entered the warm water. They decided to leave Sheyna in Olivia's room, as she definitely wouldn't want to swim. Molly trotted happily into the elevator with them. Olivia's mouth dropped open when she saw how the pool appeared to flow right over the edge of the fifth story roof. Josh loved her reaction.

They swam right up to the edge, with Olivia hesitantly resting her arm on the edge, at first, then bravely peeking over. Josh showed Molly the edge of the roof, but they decided it was safer to keep her on a long lead, so she could swim and jump in and out of the pool, but couldn't accidentally jump over the edge. The warm water was very relaxing and Olivia felt like she was swimming on the top of the world. The view was awe inspiring.

They cuddled in the hot tub for a few minutes after their swim and Josh massaged Olivia's sore muscles, while the swirling hot water soaked away the bruises from her Aikido falls. She sighed in pure bliss.

"Wow, Josh, your dad's house is like a five-star resort and health spa all wrapped up in one," Olivia sighed in contentment. Molly barked happily from the pool. Olivia, holding the end of the leash, laughed at her, as she climbed out of the pool, only to race to the edge and jump back in with a loud splash.

Josh laughed, "It's pretty cool, at that. We didn't have the pool when I was growing up, and he's done quite a lot of updates gradually over the years, but overall, it's the same old home I know and love. I must say that the pool is a wicked cool improvement. He only put it in a couple of years ago. The students love it."

They dried Molly and each other off with big fluffy towels, and wrapped themselves back up in the soft bathrobes, before entering the elevator to go back to their rooms to shower and dress.

After her shower, Olivia dressed, then dried Molly off a little more with the blow drier, then brushed both her and Sheyna. Josh had assured her that the girls were welcome in the dining room for dinner, and anywhere else they wanted to go in the house, except in the students' rooms, so she wanted to make sure they didn't leave hair all over the furniture as they explored.

CHAPTER SEVENTEEN

Olivia was surprised to see Molly's and Sheyna's food bowls sitting on a small rug in the dining room, with a water bowl beside them. The bowls had been prepared just the way she fixed them at home. She grinned at Josh and shook her head in amazement. He smiled back mischievously.

As Peter came to join them in the dining room just before dinner, Olivia and Josh heard Tez heading down the stairs talking animatedly with another young sounding man.

Olivia smiled to see the contrast in the two students. Tez was tall and thin with smooth ebony toned skin over handsome, finely chiseled features, onyx eyes and a soft afro hairstyle. His companion, who Olivia decided must be the other student in residence, had short, pale blond hair above blue eyes in a very pale face, with a few old acne scars slightly blemishing his otherwise handsome appearance. He was several inches shorter than Tez. Not only was their appearance in complete contrast, but Olivia found it interesting to hear Tez's musical Island accent against the other man's harsh Germanic tone. Two pairs of startled eyes met Olivia's as the young men noticed the other people in the room and abruptly ended their chatter.

"There you are, Tez and Leon. Let me introduce you to

Josh's fiancé, Olivia McKenna. You remember Josh from last week, I'm sure, since you both had bruises from trying to get out of his hand holds," Peter laughed. "Olivia, meet Tez Alleyne, from Barbados and Leon Schmidt, from Germany. Unfortunately, our illustrious Irishman, Danny Murphy, had to go home, due to a death in the family, so you'll have to meet him next time."

Olivia smiled brightly at the two young men and shook hands with each of them.

"I'm happy to meet you Leon, and to meet you more formally, Tez." She grinned, turning to Peter, "We met Tez when we arrived and he was leaving. He opened the door for us."

Dinner was a lively, fun affair, with each of the young men trying to top the other's wildly amusing tales of their home countries. Olivia laughed until her sides hurt. After a lovely chocolate mousse for dessert, the students retired to their rooms to study for a while, leaving Josh and Olivia alone with Peter.

Olivia noticed that Peter's kitchen staff started clearing the table as soon as everyone had moved away from it. She and Josh followed Peter to the library, where a nice fire was glowing in the fireplace. Once they were all comfortably seated, a young woman in an apron brought in a tray with tea, and cups and saucers for everyone.

"You are probably wondering, Olivia, what the mystery at our vacation home in Mary's Orchard is all about," Peter began with a smile. "I asked Josh to let me explain the events to you myself, so I won't keep you in suspense any longer."

"Good idea Dad," Josh chuckled. "I felt like I was torturing her, by whetting her appetite for mystery, then refusing to elaborate on it."

Olivia playfully swatted Josh's hair, earning a quick hug. "I must say, I have been curious."

"I'm sorry to have kept you in the dark, but I wanted to meet you first," he smiled. "Josh has excellent instincts for people, but as the Bard said, 'love is blind', and this mystery is something that deeply concerns me, so I wanted to be sure you were as wonderful and trustworthy as Josh said you were. I believe you are even more so. I am going to be honored to have you as my daughter-in-law."

Olivia blushed, "The feeling is mutual, Peter. I was nervous about meeting you, as we come from rather different worlds, but you are every bit as down to earth and genuinely kind as Josh told me you were. I couldn't ask for a better father-in-law."

"See?" Josh laughed, "I get to say 'I told you so' to both of you. Now let's get on with the mystery Dad."

Peter and Olivia both laughed, breaking the slightly awkward pause that had followed the sentimental exchange.

"Right, you are Josh," Peter winked at Olivia. "I'm not sure if Josh has told you, but I've been collecting rare First Edition books for most of my adult life and have amassed quite a large and valuable collection over the years. A good portion of these books are kept in my library on the island," Peter paused, looking pained. "Over the past few months, books have been sporadically disappearing from my library on Mary's Orchard."

"Josh said you have friends vacationing there," Olivia tilted her head. "Have they seen any signs of someone breaking in? I'm assuming you trust your friends and don't suspect anything in that area."

"Yes, I do trust them, and even if I wasn't totally sure of them, the books were disappearing before they arrived. I have a staff that lives there full time, and has for the past twenty years. I trust them as much as I trust Josh or myself." He threw his arms out in frustration, "No one has seen any sign of tampering with doors, windows or anything else, except missing books. It's utterly baffling, as well as disheartening to someone who loves these old rare books as much as I do."

"I can imagine how you're feeling," Olivia said sympathetically. "There are a few of my old treasures that I would miss terribly, should they vanish like that."

"Which is exactly why I want you and Josh to investigate this, rather than involving the local police or a private investigator from the island. I know it will be something that you'll find interesting and close to your own heart," Peter smiled. "I need someone who cares about antiques or about me, and will try hard to figure it out for the sake of the books, and/or for my sake, not just because it's their job."

"Well, even if I didn't already like you, I would do it because you're Josh's dad and I love him . . . and I love books, especially old books," Olivia laughed.

"See dad, I told you she'd be even better for this than I am. So, are you still thinking of us going out to the island as soon as the Ashburn's leave?" Josh sat back on the small sofa he was sharing with Olivia. "They're leaving in about three weeks, right?"

"Actually, they asked me if they could stay on until after the holidays, and I agreed. I should have talked to you first, but I assumed that you'd rather be at home for the holidays."

"You nailed that one dad," Josh smiled, taking Olivia's hand. "In fact, we were hoping you'd come stay with us for Christmas . . . or rather with Olivia, since I'm still living in that super tiny apartment, that would see one of us sleeping on the couch."

Peter laughed, "I think I'll be bunking at Olivia's if she'll have me, then."

"Of course I will!" Olivia beamed. "As long as you don't mind staying in a house with a crazy hodge-podge of antiques and two women, a dog and a cat, you are more than welcome. We have some friends coming for Christmas dinner that I'd love to have you meet."

"It sounds like it's going to be a wonderful holiday," Peter smiled. "I'm already looking forward to it."

"That's all set then," Josh grinned, squeezing Olivia's hand and rising from the sofa. "Dad, if you don't mind, I want to try to coerce my fiancé into taking a moonlight swim with me under the stars, since it seems to have turned into a beautiful clear night."

"I think I'll hang out here with Molly and Sheyna to keep them company and let you two lovebirds enjoy the stars," Peter reached to scratch Molly behind the ears, and lifted Sheyna into his lap with the other hand. She immediately purred and nuzzled him under the chin.

"My, she's incredibly friendly and easy-going for a cat that doesn't know me. Molly doesn't surprise me at all, as most of the Goldens I've known 'have never met a stranger', but this little kitty is a very unusual girl," Peter scratched under her chin. "I'm guessing there is a story behind her."

"There sure is," Josh laughed. "We'll tell you all about it tomorrow. She's probably the most relaxed and well traveled cat you'll ever meet."

~~~

The next day flew by, as Olivia and Josh relaxed and chatted with Josh's dad and the students. Olivia felt like she'd know Peter forever by the time it came to leave.

"Peter, it was so wonderful getting to know you and I so enjoyed your amazing hospitality. I hope you really will be able to make it up for the holidays," Olivia smiled, as Josh put their bags into his car. "It's not a fancy dinner, but it's a fun time with family and friends and I think you'll enjoy it."

"I wouldn't miss it," Peter chuckled. "I must say that I'm really glad to know that my son has the same wonderful taste in women as his dad. In fact, you do remind me a little of Helen, my late wife—not in looks—more in spirit, I think. I would be honored if you thought you might get used to the idea of calling me 'dad' or 'pop' or whatever feels comfortable to you. Peter is certainly better than 'Sir', but we're going to be family pretty soon."

"I'm the one who is honored . . . dad," Olivia smiled. "I'm not sure if Josh has told you, but my parents are living in Ireland now, taking care of my mam's parents and I don't get to see them anywhere near as often as I'd like. I'm thrilled to have you as a father-in-law, and I'll feel comfortable calling you 'dad', since I've always called my parents 'mam' and 'da'."

"Well, consider yourself adopted into our family if you will have us." Peter hugged her and she hugged him back with a happy sigh.

Josh hugged his dad and they clapped each other on the back. "We'll see you soon for the holidays, dad. Thanks for the great weekend. I feel more rested than I have in
~~~

ages."

Molly barked and head butted Peter's hand, as he picked up Sheyna to say goodbye.

"Don't you worry Molly, I'm not going to miss saying goodbye to you," Peter knelt and scratched her ears with one hand while holding Sheyna with the other. "Drive safely, Josh and I'll be seeing you both soon." He transferred Sheyna to her crate and latched it while Molly jumped in and Olivia latched her crate.

"Oh Josh, your dad is every bit as wonderful as you said and then some. How did he . . . and you end up being so wonderful and so easy to love? You can't imagine how happy I am," she leaned over and kissed him on the cheek as he drove.

"I knew you'd love each other," he smiled, glancing away from the road for a second to catch her eyes. "Dad is my hero. You know how most of us guys seem to have this image we try to live up to, of who the perfect man is. I'm sure women have a perfect woman image too, which is most likely fairly similar and equally unattainable for most women." He paused for breath. "Well, anyway, I think the vast majority of guys see the perfect man as being a super dominant, aggressive sort of man, who while kind and loyal, is always strong, always in control of himself, never breaks down in front of anyone and is basically perfect in every way," Josh smiled ruefully, "How many perfect men have you met, or women either? Some men are so wrapped up in trying to be or pretending to be that impossible person that they go overboard and are control freaks who want to have complete domination of not only themselves, but of their families," Josh sighed. "Others are not as bad, but are still prone to irrational jealousy, or are so afraid of being seen as less than ultra masculine that they don't dare to show their emotions to anyone. What I'm getting at is that dad somehow managed to avoid buying into that whole perfect man image, or at least his image was not quite the same as society's. He taught me that the perfect man or woman doesn't exist. He and my mom were both pretty wise and were both non-conformists to some extent. I was taught to be kind, and allowed to show my feelings. Neither of my parents ever made me feel ashamed to cry or talk about things that bothered me and they even talked to me about how skewed society's images were. They consoled me when I forgot and showed hurt feelings or cried in front of other kids when I broke my toes and was laughed at for acting like a sissy. I wasn't a weak kid though, I was taught to stand up for myself, and for others too. I think that's one of the reasons I wanted to be a cop. Dad taught me how to box; I studied Karate and worked out with my dad. I was a strong boy. I didn't start fights . . . okay, not very often . . .that was one thing that I would get in definite trouble for at home . . . but I didn't run from them if someone picked on me. Kids stopped treating me badly once they realized that the fact that I didn't always act like a tough guy didn't mean I'd let them get away with picking on me or on anyone else." Josh chuckled wryly, "I'm not saying I'm perfect, believe me, I have my share of faults, and yes, I can get angry and be a jerk, and act a lot more macho than I should once in a while. I can and have hit first a few times when some other jerk really pushed my buttons, but at least I know better and try hard not to do those things, thanks to my dad. You have no idea how lucky I feel to have had the parents I did. If there was ever a perfect man contest, I'd vote for my dad, hands down. I think he's the closest there is to perfect."

"I think I'd vote with you on that, though you and my da might both have to tie with him in my vote," Olivia sat back with a smile. "Da and Mam are pretty special too. I can't wait for you to meet them," she took Josh's hand and hugged it to her heart for a second. "I'm grateful to your dad for raising such a wonderful man for me to fall in love with."

Josh squeezed her hand, "Your parents did an even better job than mine. We were both lucky, and I can't wait to meet your folks. It looks like we won't be able to go to Ireland until after we go to the Orchard though, since we basically promised dad that we were going to work for him after the holidays," he paused in thought. "Would your grandparents be able to fly here with your parents for the wedding?"

"I'm not sure Josh," Olivia frowned in thought. "I'll have to ask Mam. I know Pop hasn't been able to get around well because of his arthritis, and Nana with her knee replacement . . . but I'm sure they could manage with wheelchairs at the airports if they need to, so as long as nothing else is going on with their health, I'd say they should be able to, yes. When we're sure of the date, I'll ask Mam."

"We're back to thinking of a spring wedding again, right? You know, I'm starting to believe that we're being unrealistic in hoping that we can somehow manage to find James Hill, buy the Candlewick house, and be able to renovate it in time to use for the wedding, even if we're waiting until spring to get married." Josh scratched his head over the predicament. "It seems like way too much to do in too short of a time. The biggest problem, besides finding

James is that even if we already owned the house, we couldn't do much in the way of exterior work until spring thaw. What do you think?"

Olivia sighed, "Yes, you're right. I have been having similar fears over trying to start planning for a spring wedding, but hadn't mentioned it because I hate to have to postpone it. I think we will have to though. Even if we weren't trying to have it at Candlewick, we really shouldn't try to rush it so much, as it won't turn out the way we want it to and it will make us crazy trying to get it all done in time." Olivia looked glum, "I guess we need to rethink it and decide on something that makes more sense."

"Well, I think we should come up with a definite date, and work toward that. We've been leaving it up in the air because of the house, and moving it back and forth from spring to winter, to spring, and not getting anything done on it at all," Josh smiled.

Olivia grinned a little at that, "That sounds about right. Okay, so what is a realistic date? Does the middle of August sound feasible? It will be warm, but hopefully not as hot as July, and should leave us with enough time to get it all put together, if we stick to it and stop changing things around."

"I think that sounds doable and pretty perfect, sweetheart," Josh nodded. "We should have a backup location lined up in case things don't work out with Candlewick though. Have you thought about any other venues? I know dad would be happy to have it on the Orchard if we'd like that, though Candlewick is still first choice."

"Do you have any pictures of the house on Mary's Orchard, so I can see how things are laid out? It would make it easier to know if it is something that we could plan ourselves or if it would be too complicated, and we'd have to hire a planner."

"I'll dig some up from my photo albums and bring them over soon. It might be a little harder to plan than Candlewick, because you haven't seen it personally yet, but we are hopefully going there soon, so you might be able to wrap your head around it after staying there for a little while if things aren't happening with Candlewick by then. If we need to hire someone, I'm sure we can find someone who'll take us on."

"That makes sense. It sounds lovely, so I am sure we could make it work one way or another if we don't get Candlewick." She sighed again, "I really hope we can just find James, and that he'll be happy to sell us Candlewick house and will allow Sally and Jimmy to move into the other one—maybe he could even move back in with them and get some help, and everyone can live happily ever after, you know?"

"Well, that would be wonderful, but I wouldn't hold my breath on most of it," Josh said skeptically. "He doesn't have a very good track record at taking care of himself, or being remotely responsible. If he'll sell us the house and hopefully let Sally and Jimmy move into the one on the main road, I'll be ecstatic."

"Sally did think he would do that," Olivia took a sip of coffee and sat back. "He'll certainly make enough money on Candlewick to buy a small place and live comfortably for quite some time, if he is careful, especially if he settles down and gets a job."

"You're spot on, there. If he sells us Candlewick, buys a little house or moves into the house in town with his son and Sally, gets himself some help, invests some of the money from Candlewick and stays off drugs, he could be set for life."

"Wow, that really is a lot of ifs, isn't it?" Olivia shook her head, half chuckling, half grimacing. "If he is so messed up because he felt blamed for his mother's death by his own father, then maybe if we can solve it and prove that he was innocent and that someone set it up so he and his sister would look guilty, that might help him break free from his self-sabotaging life pattern."

"Sweetie, just don't get your hopes up too much," Josh said concernedly, "We haven't even found him yet, and he may never be found, or at least, not alive. I don't want to see you setting yourself up for a huge let down."

"No, I won't do that. Logically, I know the odds are not in his favor, but I will keep hoping, and I'll send up a little prayer now and then. "

Josh stroked her hand, "Your eternal optimism is one of the things I love about you. Don't let my occasional cynicism ever sway you, love. The job gets to me once in a while and makes it hard to hope for the best."

She kissed his hand, "I'm glad you're not quite as cynical as you think you are. I see how much hope and energy you put into righting the wrongs you encounter in your job . . . how you work crazy hours and hope against hope to fix things. Maybe it's good that you're getting out of it before you do succumb to the cynicism so many cops seem to have."

"Well, finding James alive would go a long way toward knocking the pessimism back a notch or two," Josh grinned. "Finding him alive and having him become a drug-free model citizen after all of this might even convert me to your special brand of optimism."

Olivia laughed and poured some more coffee into Josh's cup from the thermos of delicious French Vanilla coffee that Peter had provided.

"Oh, I forgot to tell you that I spoke with the lawyers about Jack Hill's estate again the other day and they said that if James dies before he is found, his inheritance will automatically pass to his son Jimmy, as his closest living relative, unless he has a will that can be located, specifying otherwise."

"I'm so glad of that," Olivia smiled. "As much as I'm hoping we find him in time and that things work out well, I don't have nearly as much confidence in that happening as I did when we first started looking for him, after seeing what these guys are capable of, so I'm very relieved to know that Jimmy will be taken care of financially even if we can't save James."

"Did Sally have anything else to say when you spoke to her on the phone last night?"

"Not much really, aside from how well Jimmy is doing now. He still has some pain and occasional vertigo, but seems to be healing well and is feeling a little better each day. The only other thing she said was that she is thinking of renting the spare room in her house to Dave when they move back, if he doesn't think it's too far out in the boonies for him. He mentioned how much he was enjoying her cooking and having 'roomies', and she says that he and Jimmy adore each other," Olivia wrinkled her nose, "It would certainly be a good thing for everyone, unless James actually does turn up and want to be a part of his son's life. I'm not sure how things would go then."

"I guess we'll have to wait and see what happens,"

Josh agreed. "Dave is a good guy and would be a terrific father figure for Jimmy if James isn't up for it, which personally, I have serious doubts that he ever will be, even if we find him alive."

"Yes, it would be a huge uphill battle for him to get his life on track after all this time, and he would have to want to, which according to everything we've heard about him, doesn't sound likely."

The SUV shook and was almost blown into the next lane as an eighteen-wheeler flew past them at a very high speed, a lot closer than he should have been, quickly weaving around another car ahead of them.

Olivia saw Josh's jaw tighten in anger, as his hands gripped the wheel tightly to hold the SUV in the lane.

"If I go after him in an unmarked vehicle, with you and the girls in the car, I'd be putting you all at risk, so I won't do it, but he is endangering the rest of the drivers on the road with his recklessness." He called in the license number and description on his phone. "Okay, they'll be on the lookout for him. That's the best thing for me to do here," he shook his head disgustedly. "Going a few miles per hour over the limit is one thing, but the crazy weaving and very excessive speed is another, not to mention that he's driving a huge truck, which could easily crush any car it hits. He's a disaster looking for a place to happen."

Olivia let go of the grab handle above her window and willed her heart to go back where it belonged, while glancing to make sure Molly and Sheyna were okay in their crates.

"Wow, I hope they stop him before he creams some poor little car full of people," Olivia said letting out a breath. "I thought we'd had it for a minute. Nice driving honey."

Josh was still shaking his head. "I think they'll get him. He didn't look like he was planning to settle down and play nice any time soon."

Ten minutes later, they passed the semi-truck parked on the side of the road, surrounded by three state patrol cars with their lights flashing.

Josh grinned and smacked the dash in victory, "Yes! Ha!"

Olivia laughed, "I agree. Sometimes I feel a little sorry for people when I see them pulled over like that, but for this guy, I have no sympathy. That was too scary."

Josh was still chortling, but abruptly sobered, "Even I feel sorry for people sometimes when I pull them over, but I'd feel worse if I let them get away with carelessness and later had to wipe them up off the pavement."

"There is that," Olivia agreed. "I'll remember that next time I feel badly for someone on the side of the road getting a ticket.

Dusk was settling over the town as they pulled into Olivia's driveway.

"Do you want to come in and have dinner before you go home?" Olivia asked as they got the excited animals out of the car and inside the house. Molly ran to the back door and Olivia let her out. "I can throw together something quick."

"No, thanks sweetie, but I think I'd better get home so I can get to bed early and be at work on time," he chuckled, "I'll be too tempted to stay late if I don't go home now."

Olivia was looking at a note on the kitchen table, "Julie said she went to the grocery store and will pick up dinner. She'll be back soon. I wonder what she's planning to get for dinner." She grinned. "Having a roommate is so nice sometimes."

"Julie is great and she's going to be a fantastic cop when she has a bit more experience under her belt. Tell her I said that and say hello for me too." Josh opened the back door for Molly, who scratched to be let in, then kissed Olivia and petted Molly and Sheyna goodbye. "I'll give you a call in the morning, sweetie. Have a good evening with Julie."

"Bye Josh, I love you," Olivia hugged him tightly. "I had the best weekend ever. Your dad is the bomb."

"I love you too Livvie," he kissed her again holding her close. "Let me know if Julie has any news on the Hill/Salger case."

Olivia locked the door behind him and took her overnight bags upstairs to her bedroom. Molly and Sheyna followed her and hopped onto the bed to look at her with hopeful eyes hinting that it was dinnertime.

Olivia laughed, "Okay you two, it's clear that you're about to pass out from starvation, so let's go fix your food."

They jumped up happily and led the way back to the kitchen, Molly in the lead, barking cheerfully.

Olivia had just finished washing their bowls when she heard a faint squeal of tires and Julie arrived carrying a couple of small grocery bags and a box with the fragrant aroma of spinach white pizza wafting out.

"Oh my stars, does that smell good, or what?" Olivia cried, taking the box and setting it on the table. You're the best roomie ever!"

Julie grinned, putting the groceries on the counter. "I am so happy to be living here, that I will try very hard to make sure you keep believing that. So, spill all the dirt.

How was the weekend, and what is his dad like?"

"Oh Julie, his dad is wonderful. Josh is a lot like him, and I think his mom must have been a really great person too," Olivia paused for breath. "The house is stunning! There is a full size heated infinity pool on the roof. You can swim up to the edge, hold onto the side and look over half of Boston. It's absolutely awesome in every way."

"Wow! I can't even imagine having a pool on my roof. How tall is the house that you can see so far?"

"It's a five story row house, connected to other houses on both sides. It's huge and beautiful, yet somehow still homey and comfortable, rather than austere and intimidating. It's like its owner, Peter, Josh's dad, in a way—rich as Croesus, elegant and handsome, but sweet and kind and makes you feel at home," Olivia laughed.

"I'm so glad you liked each other. I would have been scared silly, meeting someone so rich, as a future daughter-in-law. Talk about intimidating . . . whoa!" Julie laughed.

"I know, right? I was so worried, but as soon as I met him, he put me right at ease and by the time I left, I was calling him dad," she laughed in amazement. "He and Josh are so much alike, though I have a feeling Josh's mom was a super special lady, and that he got a lot of great qualities from her too. I feel so lucky."

Julie finished putting away the groceries and gave her a hug. "It's not luck, you deserve it. You're every bit as wonderful as Josh is. I think you guys are perfect for each other. Anyway, on another topic, I don't want to worry you, but I saw a suspicious looking white panel truck driving by slowly as I was starting to come in the door with the groceries, but it took off fast and was around the corner before I could have put the bags and the pizza down and run back to the car. It was too dark to see the license tag, but I have a feeling it may have been Salger from the way he acted."

"I was hoping he was going to resurface. Josh and I were discussing it and we were afraid that he might have given up, killed James and left town," Olivia said with an expression of relief on her face. "I'm hoping if that was him, that it means James is alive and we still have a chance to save him."

"You said they're hunting for an antique piggy bank. It must be worth an awful lot of money for them to go through this much trouble, not to mention murdering that poor woman in Laconia and kidnapping James," Julie remarked. "He even tried to have Jimmy kidnapped."

"If it's in good shape, it could be worth a million dollars," Olivia smiled wryly. "Even if it's in bad shape it's probably worth close to half a million."

"Yeah, I guess that's enough to do it for someone like Salger. He sounds like a real piece of work." Julie grabbed a slice of pizza as Olivia ran the wheel through the pie to loosen the gooey melted cheese between each slice.

While they ate, Olivia filled Julie in on the weekend, and told her all about the students and Peter. Molly turned on her puppy-dog eyes and focused on Julie hopefully. Pizza was her favorite people food.

"Speaking of Peter, I invited him to stay here in the guestroom for the holidays. I hope you don't mind, as I am not yet used to having a roommate and forgot to ask you. I already had a huge Christmas get together planned with friends, and I'm hoping you'll be a part of that."

"It sounds great!" Julie smiled happily. "I'm looking forward to meeting your friends, and Peter too. I've been so lonely since I started my job. You don't ever have to ask me to invite someone over, unless they're taking over my room." She giggled, "Or planning to share it with me. That would depend on how drop dead gorgeous he is."

Olivia laughed, "I'll keep that in mind . . . and thanks, but I promise I will try to remember to ask you in the future before I plan anything that will affect you, including huge dinner parties."

Once they'd cleared away all the dishes and put away the leftover pizza, Olivia found herself yawning.

"Julie, I'm sorry, but I think I'm turning into a pumpkin. I hope you don't mind if I crash out early tonight and forgo our usual movie."

"Not at all," Julie smiled. "It's been a long day for me too, and you are probably tired from the ride back. Get some sleep."

Olivia let Molly out for a few minutes in the back, then both animals followed her up to her room and jumped on the bed to keep her pillows warm.

Olivia took a quick shower, brushed her teeth and put her pajamas on, barely managing to crawl into the bed before her eyes closed. The last thing she remembered was Molly settling her furry softness against her back and Sheyna purring in her ear as she tucked herself into the spot between her shoulder and her neck.

CHAPTER EIGHTEEN

Olivia heard Julie leaving for work just before she stumbled down the stairs early the next morning in search of coffee.

She fed Molly and Sheyna, drank a protein shake then got the girls on leashes to go for a brisk walk, shaking the sleep from her head. She and Josh had walked them around Lantern Knoll quite a bit, but then they'd been cooped up in the car for the whole ride back. She enjoyed the walk up her hill and back almost as much as they did. The cold air felt good. It smelled a little like snow, which woke her up thoroughly and put an extra bit of bounce in her step.

About a block before she reached her house, she saw one of her older retired neighbors, from the side street below her, walking up the hill toward her with her blue merle Australian Shepherd on lead. Molly and Flip, the Aussie, were great friends, so both dogs were wagging all over as soon as they saw each other. Olivia knelt to pick up Sheyna, who hadn't really warmed up to Flip yet, and was showing signs of irritation at his overly exuberant approach.

"Hi Olivia, do you have guests?" her grey-haired neighbor asked, seeming a little worried. "As I was walking up past your house, I saw a strange panel truck in your driveway and three rather rough looking strange men heading toward your house."

Olivia gasped, "No, I don't have guests. Let me call the police. Thanks Margot. Don't go back the same way, in case they come out. If it's who I think it is, they're very dangerous. Hang on a second, while I call." Olivia grabbed her phone from her pocket and speed dialed Josh, quickly letting him know what was going on.

"Liv, stay away from the house until the police arrive. I'm calling it in and I'm on my way now. I just left my apartment, so I'm close. Julie is already gone?"

"Yes, she left really early, just before I came downstairs."

"Okay, just stay where they can't see you, keep walking with your friend Margot, right into her house, and if you see any signs of that truck, run and get into someone's house quickly. I'll be there in less than ten minutes."

Olivia explained the situation to Margot as the two women, hurried back up the hill and turned at the next crossroad that would take them back down toward Margot's house via an alternate route. They half jogged down the hill as quickly as they could, with Molly and Flip scampering along, excited by the fast pace Olivia was setting. Sheyna mewed her displeasure at the bumpiness of the ride in Olivia's arms.

As they climbed Margot's front steps, they heard faint shouting coming from the direction of Olivia's house, tires squealing, and then police sirens and more squealing tires. They got the animals inside and peered out the door to see if any of the action they were hearing was visible, but they couldn't see anything from there.

Just as Olivia thought her curiosity was going to cause her to do something rash, they heard a horrible crashing sound, and the sirens stopped abruptly. There was more shouting and it sounded a lot closer. Olivia shut the door and locked it, while Margot ran to check her windows and the other door.

Olivia looked out the window, trying in vain to see what was happening, but the angle was all wrong and she couldn't see anything beyond the yard except the very edge of the road. *Josh, you'd better be all right,* she thought at him worriedly. *That crash had to be Salger, not Josh. Please don't let it be Josh.* Molly nudged her, trying to comfort her, as she sensed her unease.

Several tense minutes passed before Olivia's cell phone rang, showing Josh's number on the screen. She almost wept from relief as she answered it.

"Are you okay?" she asked, without even waiting to make sure it was him.

"Yes, I'm fine, you are too?" he sounded as worried as she'd been. She could hear more sirens starting up from far away and getting closer.

"Josh, can I come out where you are? I need to see you and make sure you're okay."

"Yes, you deserve to be here, but leave the girls at your neighbor's house until everything is sorted. It's pretty chaotic around here."

Olivia asked Margot if Molly and Sheyna would be okay staying there for a while, and Margot put Sheyna in her spare bedroom, so Flip wouldn't bother her, and left the two dogs to play together.

Olivia and Margot hurried to the end of the block and turned the corner to see flashing lights from three police cars and two ambulances highlighting a smashed white panel truck with its nose half embedded in a large Hemlock tree. The side and rear doors were all wide open.

Olivia was careful to keep herself and Margot out of the way, as emergency personnel dashed by with a stretcher, stopping at the other side of the truck. She could see them carefully lifting someone onto the stretcher, while another paramedic held an IV bag suspended above the patient. Olivia strained her eyes to see who was on the stretcher. It wasn't easy to tell through the oxygen mask and the blood on his face, but finally she was able to identify James' face, as they brought the unconscious man past her toward the waiting ambulance. She let out a huge sigh of relief that he was at least still alive.

She spotted a local police officer putting a handcuffed man into one of the patrol cars, she could tell that it wasn't Cordell Salger, but not much else.

As her eyes took in more of the hectic scene, she could see another handcuffed man on the ground, with a different local police officer trying to lift him to his feet, as the man kicked out at him refusing to get up.

A noise from the side, caused her to turn in time to see Cordell Salger trying to head butt Josh as he escorted him to his patrol car. Josh dodged out of the way and held his hand at the back of Salger's neck, so that if he tried the head butting again, he would simply whip lash himself.

Josh placed Salger into the back of his car and went to assist the officer who was struggling with the kicker. Once they got the man onto his feet, they could see that he was bleeding from a head wound and was covered in glass from the wreck. Josh signaled to the paramedics to take him to the second ambulance and he sent the officer with him to ride along and arrest him on the way to the hospital.

As soon as the prisoners were secured in the patrol cars and James and the injured gang member safely were in the ambulances, Josh walked over to Olivia. He took her hands and just held them for a moment, pressing his forehead to hers.

"We've got them. You have no idea of how thankful I am that you had taken the girls for a walk when you did. I could so easily have lost you. Liv, why don't you take the girls and go home? It looks like it's finally over." He kissed her hair. "I'll come to your house as soon as I get everything processed and finish at work. I'm pretty sure we got them all, so it should be safe, but be careful just in case."

Margot watched with a smile, as Olivia squeezed Josh's hands and stood up on tiptoe to kiss him.

"You be careful with that maniac in the back of your car. He is one scary guy." She stepped back, releasing his hands reluctantly. "Please call me as soon as you are safely at headquarters and he's behind bars."

Josh smiled, "You've got it Babes." He turned and hurried back to deliver his prisoner to the jail cell he had so thoroughly earned.

"Wow, Livvie, I'd admired him from a distance when I saw him outside your house, but he's even more stunning up close", Margot chuckled, her eyes following Josh's retreating form. "So, what is the story on these guys? You seem to know all about them."

Olivia hesitated, "It's a long story and I'm not sure how much I can say right now, as it's an ongoing police investigation. All I can say for sure is that, it's a really good thing that you saw them and told me about it. You may have saved my life, as well as Molly's and Sheyna's and the man on the stretcher's life too. So, I owe you big time, and I promise to tell you all about it as soon as I can." She hugged her stunned friend.

Olivia and Margot stayed for another hour watching after a tow truck took the place of the disappearing ambulances, and Josh and two of police cars followed behind them. One police car remained, and the tow truck driver waited patiently as the cop took a few more pictures of the scene, before finally allowing him to attach a wench to the truck to pull it out of the tree and hoist it up onto the flat bed of his wrecker.

"That poor Hemlock is going to have to come down before it falls on someone driving by. It's way too damaged to stay," Margot said in an aside to Olivia, as they watched the battered truck being pulled up the ramp of the wrecker. "How did those men survive that? Wow!"

"I know, right? That was a huge bang. They must have been going pretty fast. I'm amazed they weren't all killed," Olivia sighed. "I'd better collect Molly and Sheyna and get home before Sheyna gets upset about being locked up by herself for so long," she grinned at her friend's expression. "Sorry, I didn't mean to scare you. She'd never mess up the bed or carpet or scratch things up, but she'd be really mad at me and would let me know in no uncertain terms."

Margot laughed, "They sure have a way of doing that, don't they? Flip has totally mastered the art of guilt tripping. He's even better at it than my mother, and that's saying something."

Olivia laughed, "Thanks for everything Margot. Hopefully I'll be able to fill you in soon." She picked up Sheyna and snapped the lead onto Molly's collar. Flip and

Molly looked slightly mournful, as they realized playtime was over, but Sheyna seemed to be mollified now that she'd been freed from solitary confinement and was in Olivia's arms where she belonged. She glowered at Flip, seeming to sense that he was the reason she'd been exiled to the other room.

"You know, I didn't think to ask you before Margot, but you've lived here for a long time. Do you remember hearing any gossip about Edna Hill's death thirteen years ago?" Olivia paused before she opened the door. "Any thoughts on who might have been responsible if it wasn't an accident?"

"Edna Hill, the lady from up the hill at Candlewick? Hmm, that's taking me back a ways." She frowned in thought. "I was a really sad thing, her dying like that and her poor husband finding her too. People were saying a lot of things. Everyone thought she'd been pushed down those stairs, but the police didn't have any proof of who had done it." She paused, looking unsure, "If I tell you what I remember, can it be just between us? I really don't want to get involved in something like that, and it's not something I'm sure about, just what I remember hearing."

"I can't promise that, Margot. If it's something that could help to solve the mystery of her death, I'd have to share it with Josh and the police. I won't say who told me unless it is necessary, but if it is, I would have to tell him." Olivia said honestly. "I hope you understand and will still tell me what you know or suspect. It's so important."

"Does it have something to do with those men?"

"Yes, the man on the stretcher is Edna's son James. That's all I can say right now, but for his sake, if you can tell me anything you heard about it, I'd be really grateful,"

Olivia beseeched her friend in a quiet voice.

"Oh my, that was young James?" Margot said astonishment. "He was just a boy the last time I saw him." She took a deep breath, "From what my daughter Fran and her friends were saying—they were in school with James and his older sister Jenny, in the grade between them—young James had been hanging out with some older kids, I think they were mostly Jenny's age, but one of them was a little older and a high school dropout to boot. James was still in what we called Junior High when I was in school, but they call it middle school now. Anyway, it was still a part of the same school building as the high school back then." She paused and led the way back into the living room, with Olivia and the dogs following. "It's a rather long story, so we should sit down and be comfortable. Olivia took the lead off Molly and sat Sheyna on her lap, as both women seated themselves in flowery upholstered chairs.

"Well, what the kids were saying—and I always figured they knew more than the rest of us about other kids—is that this older boy, the dropout, was flattering James and making him feel special by bringing him into the group of older kids, in order to get on his good side so James' father would hire the boy's parents to work on their estate. It evidently worked, as the Salgers did start working there even though they couldn't possibly have had good references from anyone reliable. That whole family had a bad reputation."

"The Salgers?!" Olivia exclaimed in surprise, "I should have figured."

"Everyone was surprised they'd gotten hired by the Hills, as we thought they'd have known better, but who were we to question the wealthiest people in town, even if they were pretty down to earth?" Her tone turned grave, "Several months after they started to work there, Edna died, and the rumors started flying. Most of the adults thought Frank Salger, the boy's father had done it, though some of the kids were saying the son, I forget his name, probably did it, because he was a bad seed." She sighed, "It could have even been the boy's mother, I guess. The whole family was evil. Whoever it was, everyone was pretty sure that one of the Salgers had been involved in it. Some of the other people who worked there, said they'd seen them sneaking around, searching the house when they didn't think anyone was watching."

"No one knew anything for sure?" Olivia asked. "Was there anyone else at home when Edna died?"

"Unfortunately, not that anyone knew about. If there was, they never came forward to say so, and the police didn't find out when they questioned them." She rolled her eyes slightly, "Of course the Salgers were all at home together and vouched for each other. There was absolutely no proof that they were guilty, and for that matter, they couldn't even prove Edna had been murdered, though there was little doubt in anyone's mind that she had been."

"I wish I had thought to ask you when all of this started," Olivia said in amazement. "You have practically solved the whole case for me. Now I think I know why James went off the deep end. If he knew or suspected that one of the Salgers had killed his mother, I'm sure he must have felt like the whole thing was his fault, since he'd evidently talked his parents into giving them the job. After the murder, he had to have figured out that Cordell had just been using him."

"I'm sure he must have," Margot said sadly, "Frannie said some of the boys told her that he tried to hang himself in the bathroom at school a couple of weeks after his mother died, but some kids came in and got him down before it was too late. His father must have made the school keep quiet about it, because I never heard any rumors about that, except from Fran."

"Wow, poor James. I can't imagine how he must have felt," Olivia sighed heavily. "I really appreciate you telling me all of this Margot. I will have to tell Josh about it, but I am sure he will try his best to keep your name out of it."

"Thanks Livvie," I live alone except for Flip here, and it scares me to have someone like the Salgers knowing I said anything against them." Margot stood up.

"I know how you feel, and I promise we won't put your name out there unless it is absolutely necessary and if that happens, you'll have protection, even if you and Flip have to move in with me to get it." She smiled crookedly.

"Well, for Sheyna's sake, I hope that doesn't happen," she chuckled.

Sheyna, hearing her name, jumped down from Olivia's lap, and like a streak, raced across the room, leaping over Flip to land on the piano, crashing into the keys with a thundering cacophony of bass. As the women and dogs all started in surprise, Sheyna proceeded to prance over the keyboard, producing an eerie combination of notes, that made Olivia's hair stand on end and set Molly and Flip both to howling.

"I guess she told us how she feels about Flip moving in," Olivia laughed, going to lift Sheyna from the keyboard, while Margot tried to calm the howling dogs.

Margot's shoulders shook with laughter, "She did, at

that! Sheyna is the funniest cat I've ever met."

Olivia was still chuckling as she snapped Molly's lead back on, adjusting Sheyna in the crook of her left arm and made her way to the door.

"Thanks again for everything Margot. You were my guardian angel today, and my hero for telling me the story even though you were afraid to," she gave her a quick one armed hug and walked up the driveway toward her house, lost in thought. *Boy, do I have some news for Josh,* she thought. *I need to call him the minute I get the girls home. It's high time we got to meet James. He's definitely going to need all the friends he can get.*

CHAPTER NINETEEN

It was a little after noon by the time Olivia called Josh and filled him in on everything that Margot had told her.

"The hospital is saying that James is still unconscious, and that they'll be happy to inform us as soon as he's awake and can talk to us," Josh sounded frustrated. "Cordell Salger isn't talking, neither is Ward Eakins, the other guy we brought in. I'm driving to the hospital now to try to talk to the third member of the bunch, one . . . Larry Radan. I have Fallon over there with him, but so far all he's getting from him is a lot of verbal abuse."

"I hope James is able to talk soon and can tell us everything. Is there any evidence against any of them for Jenny's death? I know we still don't have any evidence against Cordell Salger for Edna's murder, or even any proof it wasn't an accident after all," Olivia was catching Josh's frustration. "Would James' word count for anything in court, if he testified that Cordell told him he'd killed her, if he did?"

"That depends on how good Salger's attorney is, I guess. James has been on drugs and involved in who knows what for the last ten years, so it wouldn't be too hard for a good lawyer to discredit him as an unreliable witness or even to portray him as the possible murderer, and say he was accusing Salger to cover up his own crime." Josh's voice dripped with disgust. "This Salger is a pretty piece of goods, all right. If Fallon's been getting half the filth out of Radan's mouth that Salger's been spewing all over us, I can only imagine how red his face is, listening to it in front of the nurses," Josh chuckled, relieving his stress for a minute at the thought of young Fallon's embarrassment.

"Oh my, poor Michael," Olivia smiled at the image. "Hopefully, if they stay mad enough, one of them will let something slip and you'll have them."

"I hope so," Josh said fervently. "The only thing we can for sure prosecute them for right now, is smashing into your car that day. The prints from the house in town match up with these guys, but technically the house now belongs to James, so unless he is willing and able to tell us that they kidnapped him and forced him to let them in, we can't charge them for those things, and as you said, we have no evidence against them for Edna's or Jenny's deaths. The cigarette butts you got from Mr. Harkins do have DNA on them, and we are going to test it against these guys' DNA as soon as we can get it, but Salger and Eakins have refused to give it to us so far. I'm still hopeful that Fallon can get Radan to drink a soda and toss the can or something, or if not, that I can once I get there."

"Josh!" Olivia jumped up, almost dropping the phone in her excitement, "Did anyone ever dust for prints in Jenny's garage? I remember Mr. Harkins telling me that they'd searched the house, but you know they missed the cigarette butts on the back porch, and they may not have bothered dusting the garage."

"Liv, you're a genius!" Josh chortled. "I'm calling O'Brian right now and sending him to the Harkins house.

It's quite possible the local PD neglected to dust the garage, and the back porch too, for that matter, since they missed the butts." Josh's voice showed his renewed hope of solving the case soon. "I'll call you as soon as I know anything, and I'll be over when I'm done at the hospital if nothing breaks in the case by then."

"Good luck with the DNA and in getting Radan to talk. From what your guys tell me, you're the best there is at goading suspects into losing their tempers and blurting out stuff that they're trying to hide," Olivia said, in a much more cheerful mood than she'd been in earlier. "Don't forget to call me if you find out anything or if you're going to be super late, so I don't worry."

As soon as they'd hung up, Olivia ate a sandwich for her breakfast/lunch, and called Sally. She told her that James had been rescued, but that he was in bad shape and the hospital hadn't said what his prognosis was yet.

"I am so glad that he's been found alive. I'm going to keep on hoping and praying that he'll be okay and that he gets the help he needs." Sally responded.

"If there is anything I can do to help him, I'll be happy to do it. I still love him like a son. He had some really bad breaks. Regardless of what happened, he is and always will be my son-in-law and Jimmy's father. I know he loved Joanie and Jimmy, and even though he left them, I think he still loved them both, I know he still loved Joanie. I could tell by the way he looked when he heard she was sick. I think part of him died right then too. Sometimes I'm angry at him for leaving, but deep down I don't think he left to hurt them. I guess he was too broken and just wasn't capable of being what they needed anymore for some reason."

"I'm really glad to hear you say that Sally," Olivia said warmly. "I have a feeling he's going to need all the help and love he can get. I have a lot to tell you that may help to explain why he left your daughter and their son."

She told her everything that she'd discovered from Margot about how James had been used by Cordell to get his parents the job, and probably knew or suspected that they'd killed his mother, and about how he'd tried to hang himself. After they'd disconnected, Olivia wondered if she'd dumped too much information on Sally at once. *Well, obviously Sally still cares about him even after he left her daughter and stuck her with raising her grandson alone, so she deserves to know everything. Maybe it will help her deal with it better, and ultimately help the whole family to heal.*

Molly nudged her leg, asking to go out, so Olivia shook her head to clear it of all the chaos, and opened the door. Sheyna followed her and Molly into the back yard, staying close to Olivia.

Olivia smiled as she remembered when she'd first brought her home and how worried she'd been that Sheyna would run off if she ever accidentally got out. She'd finally figured out how well trained and reliable Sheyna was and stopped being afraid of allowing her to go with them into the back yard, though she still kept her eyes peeled for predators in the sky, just in case a hawk decided that Sheyna looked like an easy meal.

Olivia was running a brush through Molly's silky reddish golden hair when her cell phone rang.

"Hi Josh, is there any news?" she answered breathlessly.

"Yes, James has woken up and they are going to allow

us to have a few minutes with him. I thought you might want to come to the hospital. I can't let you go into the room when we do, but if you explain your relation to his son, they might let you speak to him after us, if he is doing well enough," Josh spoke quickly. "I'm headed to his room as soon Fallon gets back from the cafeteria to guard Radan. He missed breakfast and was starved, so I had to give him a break for food and coffee. Poor Fallon, he really shouldn't be missing meals . . . now O'Brian, on the other hand . . .." Josh chuckled. "So are you going to come down? I'll try to sweet talk one of the nurses into letting you see James if you are."

"You'd better watch how sweet that tongue of yours is getting. Joshua Abrams," Olivia laughed with a mock threat. "Yes, I'll be there in fifteen minutes. I love you Babes."

She quickly put away Molly's brush, made sure the girls had plenty of fresh water, and told them to be good.

The traffic was light and she made it in just under fifteen minutes. She hurried into the hospital, only slowing down when she was close the room Josh had told her James was in. She approached the door, managing to see Josh walking into the room before a short, thin male doctor intercepted her brusquely, practically bristling with self-importance.

"He can't have visitors right now. The police are questioning him. You shouldn't even be near the door while they're talking to him. Are you a relative?"

Olivia was startled by the doctor's rather obnoxious manner. As she was trying to figure out how to deal with him, Josh spoke from behind her. "She's with me." He escorted Olivia into the room past the blustering doctor, who instantly became obsequious in the presence of the tall detective.

Olivia smothered a giggle, at the change in the man's demeanor and Josh's lip twitched in amusement.

"Apparently, he's suffering from a Napoleon complex, but he definitely believes in sucking up to authority figures," Josh whispered in Olivia's ear as they entered the room.

Olivia stifled a gasp at the sight of James' battered face as she drew near the bed. He had numerous tiny cuts all over his face, probably from the wreck, but underlying the cuts were horribly swollen bruises, in various stages of healing, which spoke of repeated brutal beatings over a long period of time. His lips were split; he had missing teeth in the front, and his nose looked to have been badly broken, possibly more than once.

Olivia clenched Josh's hand in dismay, forcing her face not to reveal her horror and pity.

James looked at her through eyes that were almost swollen shut. She reached out and offered her hand to him.

She could see his lips tremble slightly and a tear slid down the side of his face at the unexpected tenderness. He feebly lifted his hand to hers and she saw that Cordell Salger's cruelty hadn't been restricted to James' face. His whole hand was misshapen and several fingers were discolored and swollen. *Dear God, Salger had broken every single finger!* Olivia's heart broke for him.

"Hello James, my name is Lieutenant Detective Josh Abrams and this is my fiancé, Olivia McKenna. She's a friend of Sally Tanner's, and of your son, Jimmy. We've been looking for you for quite a while," Josh spoke gently.

"Do you think you're up to telling us about Cordell

Salger and about what happened to your mother all those years ago? We have a pretty good idea, but we need to hear the whole story from you."

"It was all my fault," James said in a voice muffled by his swollen, battered mouth. He looked away in shame, "I was stupid and thought he was so cool. I asked dad to hire his parents to work for us, even though they had a bad reputation. CJ told me they'd gotten a bad rap because of one bad thing his uncle had done, but that his parents were good people." His lip quivered, "He bragged to me that I'd gotten my mom killed . . . he was right . . . I'd brought them there and he killed her, just like they killed Jenny later."

Olivia gently stroked his arm above the injured hand, "Is CJ Cordell Salger? Why didn't you go to the police?"

He drew a shuddering breath, "Yes, CJ goes by Cordell now. He said that he'd kill my sister Jenny and my dad if I said anything, and then he'd tell the police that I killed all of them, and that I'd get the death penalty for it."

"You were seen hanging around with them and getting into a lot of trouble with drugs after your mom died. Why would you stay around him if he'd killed your mother?" Josh asked carefully.

"At first he kept threatening me and making me do things, like breaking into the school and trashing stuff, then after a while, I got addicted to the drugs and then nothing mattered anymore. My dad hated me and Jenny both. CJ . . . Cordell said he told him we'd killed our mother and I guess he believed him. Dad kind of loss his mind when my mom died," he sniffled, "That's my fault too, because he'd have been okay if I hadn't gotten Mom killed by bringing Cordell's parents there."

"Do you know if it was Cordell that killed your mother, or one of his parents?" Olivia asked. "Did he ever tell you that?"

"He said she fell down the stairs, but that he made sure she was dead by breaking her neck once she hit the bottom . . .," James' voice ended in a strangled sob. "It should have been me that died, not my mom. I wanted to die every day since it happened until I met Joanie. She actually made me believe for a while that it wasn't my fault, but she was wrong."

Olivia's throat burned from holding back tears. Steadying her voice she asked, "James, do you know who cut Jenny's brake line?"

"I didn't know they were going to kill her. C-Cordell told me he was going to let me go, and that he was taking my shoes and clothes and leaving me by the road in the notch. He said I should call Jenny and tell her to come and get me, unless I wanted to freeze to death or be eaten by a bear. I was so happy he was finally going to let me go, so I called her. She said she'd be there in forty-five minutes and that I should move around to stay warm. She said she loved me." James' beaten face contorted in misery, and sobs shook his emaciated shoulders. "After I'd said goodbye to Jenny, CJ laughed and said he'd sent Ward to cut her brake lines earlier, so it was a good thing I'd said my goodbyes, since I wouldn't be seeing her again." He took a sobbing breath, "I screamed at him and tried to hit him, but he just laughed at me and Larry knocked me down. Then they tied me up again and CJ said they weren't letting me go and that they would have a surprise for me soon; they were going to bring my son for a visit. CJ said I'd enjoy watching him play with Jimmy." His hand shook violently in Olivia's.

"They didn't hurt him when they tried to grab him, did they?"

"No, Olivia was with him, and she stopped Cordell's buddy, Eddie Perkins from getting him. Jimmy just had a fun ride down the hallway. He didn't even realize it wasn't a game until the end, when Perkins threw him at Olivia and she caught him," Josh smiled, trying to ease James' obvious fear for the son everyone thought he didn't care about.

James laid back, exhausted from emotion, his hand lying limply atop Olivia's. "I left him to save him, and I still almost got him killed."

"How did your leaving, save him?" Olivia tilted her head in puzzlement. "Was Salger after you then too?"

"No, I was a jinx to everyone I loved. I always had been, I guess. I just didn't realize it until Mom died. When Jimmy went deaf, I knew that Joanie had been wrong. I was being punished for what happened with my mom, so I hoped that if I left, he and Joanie would be all right again." He rubbed his forehead with his free hand and they saw that it was as mangled as the one in Olivia's hand. "But then she died and I knew it didn't matter where I was. If I was alive, the people I loved would be in danger, so I went back to drugs hoping I'd die and Jimmy and Sally and Jenny would be okay. I went to CJ because I knew he sold drugs."

"Who actually kidnapped you?"

"Larry and Ward grabbed me as I was walking down the street and threw me into their truck where CJ was waiting. Larry drove and Ward held me while CJ hit me," he sighed. "I owed him a lot of money for the drugs. It would have been better for everyone if they'd just killed me then. At least Jenny'd still be alive. They killed her because they thought I lied about a letter they were looking for. They wanted to find an old toy bank my parents had that is worth a lot of money. There used to be an old letter in some furniture that told you all about it. CJ's mom found it once and that's what started them looking for it. That's what they were looking for when CJ killed my mother. Every time they searched somewhere and didn't find it, he'd either threaten to hurt Jenny or Jimmy. After they killed Jenny, he'd just beat me or break one of my fingers whenever he was mad."

The doctor poked his head in the door and Josh gave him a forbidding look and he scurried away quickly.

"James, from what I'm hearing you say, you're not to blame for any of the things that have happened to your family," Josh spoke firmly but gently. "You were just a child when your mother was killed. Cordell was seventeen, almost an adult. He manipulated you into a situation where he could harm your family and make you feel like it was your fault." Josh put his hand on James' shoulder. "It wasn't."

James was shaking his head, unconvinced, tears of despair leaking from his swollen eyes.

"James, Cordell Salger is exceptionally good at what he does. I think he is a true sociopath. An innocent twelve year old boy didn't stand a chance against him. We're going to get you some help and hopefully you'll finally start understanding what was done to you and be able to let go of the guilt and have some peace," Josh held his gaze. "I'm leaving an officer to make sure no one can bother you. Get some rest and I'll be back tomorrow to talk to you some more and to get your written statements about Salger,

Radan and Eakins. We're going to make sure they are locked away where they can't ever hurt anyone again."

CHAPTER TWENTY

Olivia felt numb as she and Josh walked out into the hallway. She'd known that James must have been through a lot, but what they'd just discovered was so much worse than she'd imagined. He hadn't said it outright, but from his injuries it was obvious that he'd been systematically tortured during much of the time he'd been held by Salger.

"Oh Josh, I feel so bad for him. That's more guilt and suffering than anyone should have to bear." Olivia's eyes welled up with the tears she'd held back during the interview. "Do you think we can bring Sally to talk to him tomorrow? I think it would help him to know that she still cares about him after all of this. She was like a substitute mother to him."

"I think that's a great idea, if she is willing," Josh hugged her for a moment. "I'm going to have to go back to the HQ when I get back and I don't think I'm going to make it to your house at all tonight. Why don't you go talk to Sally and see if she wants to come visit James tomorrow?"

"I had a feeling you'd end up having to go back in," Olivia smiled ruefully. "I'll give Sally a call to see if I can drop by."

"I'm going to go get Fallon and send him to guard

James just in case Salger has any other buddies working in the hospital that might try to get to him. Can you wait for me? I'll be quick."

"Sure, I'll grab a chair and sit right by the door like you cops do," she grinned, wiping her eyes. "Thanks to you, that mean doctor shouldn't try to chase me away again, especially if I look official."

Josh chuckled as he strode away to find Fallon.

Olivia decided it would be a good time to call Sally, so she walked a short distance away from James' room, so she could still keep a good eye on the door, but James wouldn't be able to hear her conversation.

"Hi Sally, How's Jimmy?"

"He's doing better every day. Have you or Josh gotten to see James yet? Do you think I can see him soon?"

"Yes, we both talked to him just a few minutes ago. Would it be okay for me to drop in on you in a couple of hours and tell you all about it? There is a lot you should know before you see him."

"We'll be here. I'll even give you dinner, since I'm already going to be cooking for us," Sally chuckled.

"You're an angel. Is it okay if I bring Molly and Sheyna? I have to run home to feed them first anyway."

"Please do!" Sally said enthusiastically. "I think Jimmy misses them a lot. See you later, and Olivia . . . thanks for everything."

Olivia went back to sit in front of James' door and Josh met her with Fallon in tow.

"Hi Michael," Olivia gave the young Trooper a little hug. "It's good to see you.

"It's good to see you too ma'am," Fallon blushed, and glanced at his boss sheepishly.

Josh laughed, “Okay Fallon, I’ll have someone relieve you at five. Just make sure no one gets to him that shouldn’t. If you don’t know the person well, even doctors and nurses, stay in the room with them at all times. If Salger still has any buddies around here, he’d be only too happy to have one of them get rid of James Hill before he can testify against him.”

Josh walked Olivia out to her car, opened the door for her and kissed her deeply, holding her tightly against his chest.

“I was so worried that they would somehow see you out there with the girls and go after you before I could get there today. Sometimes I wonder if we should rethink this PI agency thing. I’m not sure my heart can take the stress of worrying about you,” Josh shook his head and sighed. “Danger seems to seek you out every time.”

“Well Josh, think about it. That’s how I feel every day when you go to work. You could get hurt or killed any minute of the day in your job. But, you know, danger is out there all the time, just waiting for everyone. We can’t let fear keep us from doing what’s right for us.”

Josh hugged her and shook his head again, “You’re right Liv, but you’ve got to promise to keep going with your Aikido. I’m really glad Julie is living with you. We’ve arrested everyone who’s involved that we know about, but there’s always a chance that there’s someone that we haven’t heard about. Please just be careful. James isn’t the only one with loss issues.”

“Oh sweetheart, I know,” Olivia held him tighter. I promise I’ll always be careful.”

He kissed her again and stepped back, “I’d better get going if I don’t want to spend the whole night at work. Say hello to Sally and Jimmy for me and call me when you get home, okay?"

Josh shut Olivia's door once she was seated and waited until she'd started the SUV and driven off before heading to his patrol car.

When Olivia got home she took out the girls' leashes and then fed them. Realizing they were going somewhere, Molly and Sheyna gobbled their dinner and pranced around excitedly. Olivia took them out in the back for a couple of minutes to do their business before she loaded them into their crates.

Jimmy was looking much better and was thrilled to see Molly and Sheyna. Sally wiped her hand on her apron and hugged Olivia.

"Come on into the kitchen," she invited smiling. "You can make the salad while you're telling me about James."

"Perfect," Olivia agreed. "It's been an incredible day. The whole case is basically solved. Well, except for finding the antique shoe bank that caused so much death and misery."

"How is James?" Sally asked anxiously. "Is he going to be okay?"

"Physically, yes, I think so. He will never play the piano or become a surgeon, as Salger broke all ten of his fingers at least once, but they will probably heal enough for him to do most normal activity. Emotionally, he's a train wreck," Olivia's voice was sad. "He didn't leave Joanie and Jimmy because he didn't care. He left because he thought he was a jinx and that Jimmy's deafness was his fault."

"Oh no!" Sally's kind face crumpled. "I should have figured it was something like that. He always seemed to think anything that went wrong was because of him somehow."

"He confirmed that what Margot told me earlier was true," Olivia went on. "Cordell Salger got him to talk his parents into hiring the Salgers, then Cordell killed Edna when she caught him and his family snooping, looking for the shoe bank. I guess originally they'd just planned to steal whatever valuable trinkets they could while working there, but the lure of something that valuable was too big to resist."

Olivia sighed heavily as she ripped lettuce leaves, "Anyway, after he's killed Edna, Salger brags about it to James and threatens his remaining family if he talks. So, at the tender age of twelve, James feels responsible for the death of his mother and has the threat of his sister and father being murdered if he opens his mouth. He gets into drugs and runs wild, trying to self destruct for a while until he meets your daughter, Joanie. They fall in love; she's really good for him, helping him to start realizing that his mother's death wasn't his fault, and he begins to get his life together, bit by bit. Little Jimmy is born and James is happy for the first time since his mother died," Olivia paused as Sally blew her nose loudly, and wiped her streaming eyes.

"Then tragedy struck and Jimmy lost his hearing. James irrationally felt that it was because of his past actions and that he was a jinx on anyone he loved, so he divorced Joanie and ran away, hoping to take his jinx with him and spare Joanie and Jimmy any more trouble, going back to escape into drugs again," Olivia handed Sally another tissue from the box on the counter beside her.

"Then Joanie got cancer and died, and that must have

absolutely solidified James' feelings of guilt and of his loved ones being punished for his crimes. He gave you sole custody of Jimmy and gave himself over to the drugs and after a while found himself once more involved with Cordell Salger's gang, soon owing him a lot of money for drugs and being once again completely under his control, finally ending up being held prisoner while the gang searched for the bank.

Olivia paused, wincing inwardly from her own guilty memories of poor scared Jenny who she couldn't save, "He then, in a moment of weakness, after being tortured, ran them to Jenny's house, hoping she could somehow work a miracle to get him out of the mess he'd gotten himself into. They followed him and thus he ultimately caused her death."

"I should have known he'd never leave Joanie and Jimmy unless he thought it was for their own good," Sally said. "It was so obvious how much he loved them, always. I guess I was just so hurt, and angry about Jimmy's deafness, then Joanie's cancer, that I needed to have someone to be mad at."

"I'm not at all surprised that you'd have been mad. Many mothers wouldn't ever forgive what he did to your daughter, no matter the reason. It shows what a wonderful person you are that you still care about him," Olivia hugged her.

"How could I not care? He was my son, from the time he married Joanie. I knew that young man, or at least I thought I did, until he left," she smiled sadly. "I guess I did know him all along. He was just trying to spare us all. He thought he was a jinx because he felt so much guilt," She blew her nose again.

"That poor boy, he feels responsible for the death of his mother, his wife and his sister, plus the deafness of his son, and probably to a large extent, the grief, madness and untimely death of his father that resulted from it. Small wonder he's been trying so hard to self-destruct, right? I've got to make sure he gets help, so he can finally realize that none of it was his fault."

"We all want to help him," Olivia smiled. "Do you want to go with me tomorrow to talk with him? For that matter, if you'd like we can also start right away looking for a treatment place where he can get the help he needs to overcome his addition, as well as counseling to help him deal with his feelings of guilt."

"Yes, I definitely want that—all of it. Thank you, Olivia. I absolutely want to help him. I feel like I should have known all along that something wasn't right. The young man I knew wouldn't have just left like that unless something drove him to do it. I should have seen that it was his inner demons left over from childhood. Only Joanie was ever able to free him from the guilt over his mother's death. I just never knew why he blamed himself until now."

"Now, don't you start putting blame on your own shoulders," Olivia smiled, putting the salad bowls on the table. "You had more than enough on your plate."

"I guess you're right. Guilt is like a contagious disease sometimes, spreading its poison as easily as anger does." Sally washed her hands and lifted a huge steaming pan of vegetable lasagna out of the oven and placed it on a trivet in the center of the cute little kitchen table. "Why don't you serve the lasagna and I'll go get Jimmy. It was a great idea you had, to bring the girls over. "This talk would have been a lot more difficult it he was under foot," Sally smiled wryly as she went to fetch her grandson.

It was after nine o'clock by the time Olivia and the animals got home. She was bone tired and felt as emotionally wrung out as a dishrag. She called Josh quickly, letting him know the gist of her talk with Sally had to hang up a lot sooner than she would have liked, as her eyes were trying to close on their own and Josh still had a little work to do before he could go home.

What a day! She thought. *I can't believe it's all finally over. Sally will help James get through this, and I know Josh will help them find the best place and the best doctors to help him get his life together. Maybe Jimmy will finally have his dad back.* Molly curled up beside Olivia as she fell into the bed and Sheyna nudged her face with her tiny nose, tickling Olivia's chin with her whiskers. Olivia sighed contentedly and drifted to sleep wrapped in a sweet, furry animal cocoon.

~~~

It had been two weeks since James had been found and Cordell Salger and his buddies had finally been arraigned and, thanks to a smart judge who refused to allow them bail, were now safely in jail awaiting trial. Olivia was happily pulling the heavy drop cloths off of the gorgeous antique furniture in the music room off the master bedroom of Candlewick house. Molly and Sheyna were helping by chasing down all the dust bunnies that flew out of the cloth.

Josh would be coming by later, and bringing her friend Vicki, as soon as he'd finished picking up the business cards for their newly licensed private investigative agency. Olivia had told Vicki that she wanted her to see the house before they did any more work.

She'd just talked to Sally Tanner that morning and
~~~

learned that James was doing well in the private sanatorium, and had actually started showing a slight interest in possibly someday moving in with her and Jimmy and trying to be a family again. His doctors said he was making very good progress. He still had a long way to go, but things were definitely starting to look up for him.

He'd quickly agreed to give the house in town that he'd inherited to his son, and insisted that Sally and Jimmy move in right away. Olivia was thankful that he'd also been glad to agree to sell them Candlewick house. It held the happiest as well as some of the saddest memories of his life, and when Salger had taken him there to search for the antique bank, he'd felt so overwhelmed by the waves of feelings, hurling him unrelentingly through all of the emotions from his young life in that house, that he knew he'd never again want to live there.

And so, Olivia and Josh were determined to recreate the happy home that Candlewick had once been, before a sociopath named Cordell Salger came along and destroyed the lives of its occupants. James told Olivia that he was happy that the house would be lived in and loved again. It really had been a wonderful place to live and it should be again. He'd even said he would come and visit someday, if he ever managed to get his life on track.

Olivia was especially excited right now, because when she'd taken Molly and Sheyna for a walk in the woods behind the property earlier, they'd gone in a different direction from the summerhouse and after a nice little hike, had stumbled across a little playhouse, nestled deep in the woods.

She'd carefully brought back the little metal chest with the tiny lock on it that she'd found hidden against one of the walls behind some old skis and a couple of children's sleds. It was all she could manage, not to try to open it until Josh and Vicki arrived. She'd promised to let Vicki be there if when it was opened, it was ever found, and she wasn't about to go back on her word, but the suspense was killing her.

Olivia straightened, dropping the cloth she was starting to pull off of the piano. She'd heard a strange noise, and the prickling sensation on the back of her neck told her it wasn't Josh or Vicki. Using her foot, she quickly slid the little chest under the cloth covered piano and backed away from it toward the door onto the balcony, silently motioning to Molly to come with her. Sheyna was still chasing dust bunnies beside the drop cloth, hoping in vain for another mouse to chase, and so far didn't seem alarmed. Molly, on the other hand, was starting to growl softly, deep in her throat. Olivia looked around the room quickly for something she could use as a weapon, finally focusing on a large candlestick on the other side of the piano.

She picked it up just as a woman with grey hair and wild crazed eyes stepped into the room.

"Louise?" Olivia gasped, "What are you doing here?"

Louise Beck strode toward her, ignoring Molly's growl until a fierce bark erupted from her throat, getting Louise's attention.

"Where's the bank? You must have found it by now," her voice was both harsh and sing-songy, like someone in a trance.

"What are you talking about?" Olivia asked as calmly as she could, playing for time, and trying to edge her way toward the door, while holding Molly's collar. Sheyna had vanished under the drop cloth as soon as the woman had entered the room.

"Don't give me that. You know exactly what I want. I know it's here in this house. It's what I've been looking for for thirteen years." Her voice rose in volume and she took a step closer around the piano. It was then, that Olivia saw the butcher knife in her hand. Her candlestick didn't feel like quite as good of a weapon as it had a moment ago.

"Please, Louise, I don't understand. What do you have to do with this house?" Olivia's mind was racing.

Louise's voice took on a menacing sarcasm, "Maybe if you called me by my first name, Wendy, you might be able to figure it out." She took another step closer, and Olivia tightened her grip on Molly's collar as she could feel the dog's tension building.

She couldn't allow Molly to get hurt. That knife looked deadly and Wendy Louise Salger Beck, as that had to be who she was facing, had a look that was even deadlier than the sharp blade.

"Ah, so I see that you do know who I am and what I want," the deranged woman sneered. "You thought you were so clever, getting my son locked up and getting this house for yourself, so you could find my treasure and keep it. People are so stupid. I changed my hair and makeup, and got married and used my middle name when I came back here and no one had a clue that I was the trailer trash Salger woman they used to make fun of."

"I don't want the treasure Wendy, or Louise, or whoever you are. I just want to take my dog and leave. You're welcome to search the house," Olivia tried to deflect the woman's anger and appeal to her greed, anything to get her and the girls out of there alive. She didn't seem to have seen Sheyna, who was still hiding under the piano, so at least she might be able to get out alive, even if Olivia and Molly didn't make it. *Oh Josh, where are you? I promised to be careful, but I never dreamed there was any danger left here. Please forgive me if I can't stop her, I never meant to leave you alone,* Olivia thought desperately. *All I can do is my best. I can't let her hurt the girls.*

"You think you can lock up a member of my family, and keep me from what is mine and just sashay out the door with your stupid little mutt? Ha!" Wendy laughed. "I killed the other woman, Edna, the rich old hag who tried to keep me from getting the treasure. I saw her sneaking toward the basement stairs, trying to catch Frank and Cordell down there searching, so I hit her over the head and pushed her down the stairs. Cordell checked and said she wasn't breathing, but he broke her neck just to be sure."

"I thought Cordell said he killed her," Olivia said, trying to back away slowly without her noticing.

"Nah, he just made doubly sure. He always did try to take credit for other people's work." She laughed crazily, setting Olivia's teeth on edge and causing Molly to growl louder.

"Give it to me now and I might let your vicious little mutt go free."

"Let her go first," Olivia said firmly.

"Why should I do that? I've got the knife. That silly little candlestick you're trying to hide isn't going to save you."

Wendy started toward her, holding the knife in her fist, and Olivia started to turn to try to run, when a horrible crashing sound filled the air from behind them, causing Wendy to whirl around. Olivia threw herself at her, knocking the knife across the room and flattening Wendy to the floor.

The woman's insanity made her surprisingly strong, and she threw Olivia off, rising quickly and running at Olivia almost before Olivia could rise to meet her, but luckily her Aikido training paid off and she sprang to her feet, and using Wendy's momentum against her, flung her face down onto the floor, gripping her with her wrist bent back in an excruciatingly painful position, that would break it if she continued to struggle.

Molly promptly started howling and proceeded to dance around the room, as Sheyna continued prancing along the full length of the piano's keyboard, serenading them with a veritable symphony, ranging from tinny sounding treble to profoundly thunderous bass. Wendy made an interesting, though quite profane rhythm section, as she shrieked out a wide array of imaginative obscenities.

Josh and Vicki chose that moment to walk into the room and stood for a few seconds with their mouths agape. Olivia smiled and Molly wagged her tail as she pirouetted saucily in perfect time with Sheyna's beautifully auspicious, though not so beautifully off-key, concert.

CHAPTER TWENTY-ONE

The pale sunlight trying to filter its way through the light snowfall cast a spell of hope upon the neglected Candlewick estate, as Olivia and Josh walked along the old flagstone sidewalk, with Molly and Sheyna sniffing the ground as they led the way to the front door.

Olivia stood still for a moment, holding Josh's hand, entranced by the thin rays of sunlight playing off the icicles that hung from the edge of the roof, creating tiny shimmering rainbows to frame the majestic old house.

Time seemed to shift and for a moment, she could see the towns people, dressed in their finest party clothes from a decade ago, milling about, dancing and exchanging pleasantries, as a younger and obviously happy Jack and Edna Hill served food and drinks to their friends and neighbors. She could almost hear the laughter and excitement of the teenagers, young, pretty Jenny, flirting bashfully with a tall, skinny dark haired boy while a childish, carefree James played with a group of boys of his own age.

Time shifted again and Olivia caught a glimpse of an older smiling version of herself and Josh, in the place where the Hill parents had been standing, handing out plates and glasses. Across the lawn, she saw a faint image, as she were watching an old movie that wasn't completely in focus, of two children, a willowy thin young girl with wild red hair, sitting on the stone wall reading a book, and a chubby faced little boy with tousled dark curls playing ball with a dog who looked a little like Molly, but was a lighter golden color.

The images vanished, and Olivia stood blinking in wonder.

"Are you ready to go in sweetheart?" Josh's voice brought her back to herself with a joyful feeling having finally come home.

The interior of the house was starting to come along, as they'd been working steadily each day, cleaning and airing out each room, one by one, and though they wouldn't be able to get much done during the holidays, they would be able to start up again right afterward.

"Josh, how long do you think we'll be staying on Mary's Orchard? Do you think we'll still be able to get the house ready in time for the wedding, after we get back? Or should we try to find someone to work on the cleaning while we're gone? I can't believe it's only eight days until Christmas."

Josh laughed, "We are definitely not postponing the wedding again, so unless you have your heart completely set on doing it all ourselves, it might be safer to get Abby onto handling it for us. After all, she is an interior decorator, and she know your tastes. The furniture is almost all staying, as is, right? So, there is really only the cleaning, repainting and a bit of upgrading of appliances and pipes to be done."

"You're right, she'll be able to handle it and she can send us color swatches or we can go to the paint store on the island to see them there I suppose.

"I'm really glad to have seen James' lawyers sell that Old Woman in the Shoe Bank. There was so much misery and loss because of it. I can't believe this whole thing started with a nursery rhyme," Olivia sighed. "I am excited about the new mystery for your dad, though I must say, I hope it's a bit less dangerous that the last one. I'll be happier if no one is murdered."

"I'll be a lot happier with that too Liv," Josh pulled her into his arms and closed the heavy door behind them. "I'll especially be happier, if it doesn't put you in any danger," he nuzzled her neck, then kissed her. "Spending a month with you on a romantic island doesn't sound half bad either."

As she leaned against Josh's broad chest, Olivia couldn't help but wonder what new and exciting adventures might be waiting for them on the illustrious island paradise.

Made in the USA
Charleston, SC
11 March 2017